A CROWN OF ECHOES

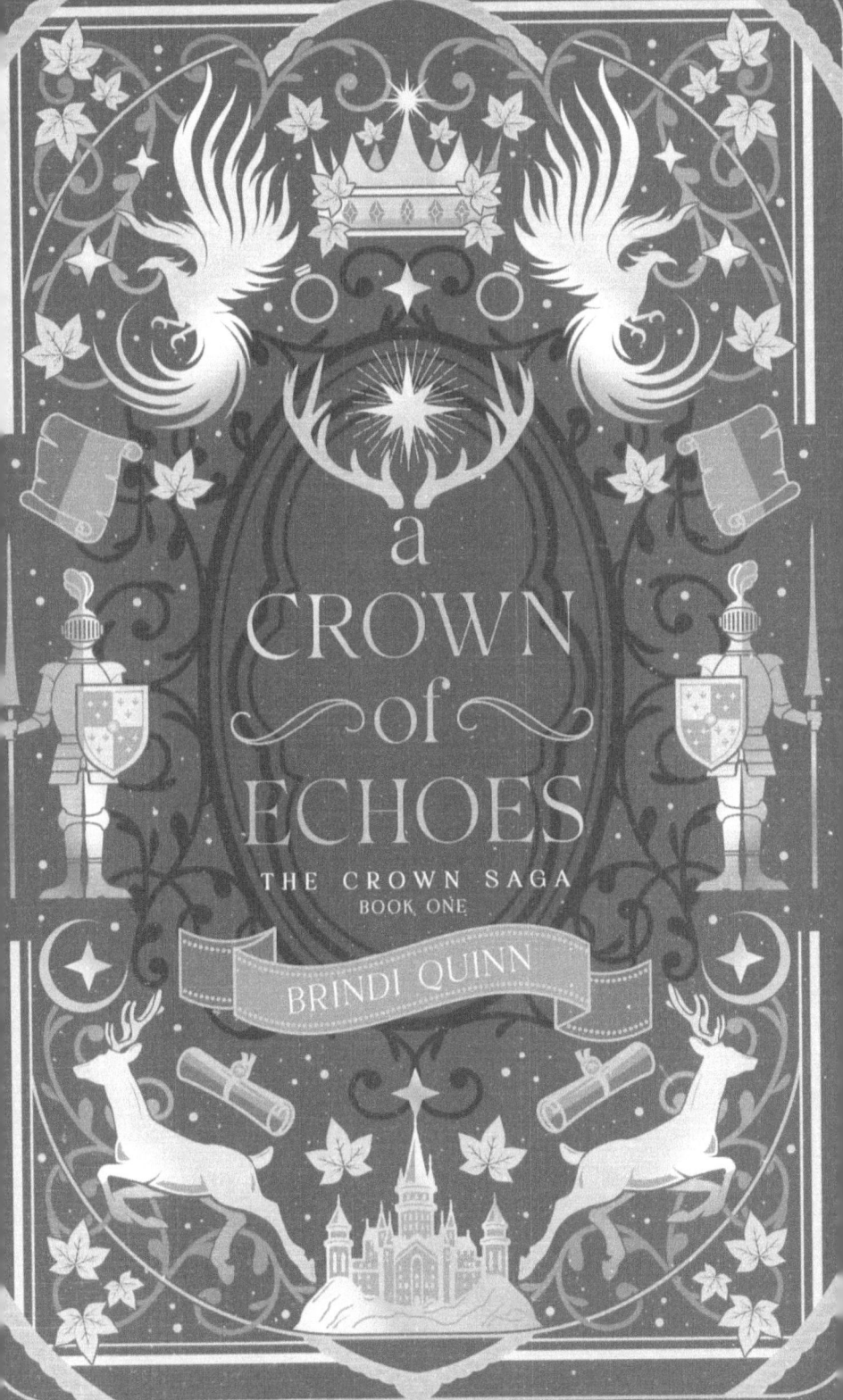

a CROWN of ECHOES

THE CROWN SAGA
BOOK ONE

BRINDI QUINN

N & E

Published by Never & Ever Publishing | @neverandeverbooks
Edited by Meg Dailey | @thedaileyeditor
Cover and title by Saint Jupiter | @saintjupit3rgr4phic
Artwork by Natascia Mora | @moranatascia
Maps by Centaur Maps | @centaurmaps
Interior by Brindi Quinn via Vellum

ISBN (Paperback): 978-1-967709-00-7

Originally published June 11, 2020.
Lovingly revised, refreshed, and re-crowned in 2025.

SERIES READING ORDER

Book One: *A Crown of Echoes*
Book Two: *A Crown of Reveries*
Book Three: *A Crown of Felling*
Book Four: *A Crown of Dawn*

For the women who dare speak loudly in rooms that demand silence.

CONTENT WARNING

The Crown Saga contains references to child abuse, child trafficking, and exploitation, which—though not depicted in graphic detail—may still be distressing for some readers. The series also features moderate to graphic violence, large-scale battles, and occasional body horror, including monstrous transformations. Romantic and sexual content ranges from mild innuendo to explicit scenes. Additional sensitive topics include coarse language, alcohol use, magical coercion, emotional manipulation, and pregnancy depicted under perilous circumstances.

DRAMATIS PERSONAE

THE QUEENS & THEIR COURTS

- **Merrin Iralore (22)** — Queen of **the Crag**. Compassionate, irreverent, occasionally reckless; commands the vine-crowned coast and an alchemist's deft touch, yet still aches for adventure.
- **Beau Lysavere (23)** — Queen of **the Clearing** and Merrin's sister-in-crown. Regal, freckled, unfailingly composed; hears the hush of roots in the Scarlet Wood.
- **Sestilia of the Cove (nearly 26)** — Tempestuous sea-queen with silver hair to the floor and a mind as volatile as the tides. Equal parts lonely and lethal; rumored to have "cleared" her own sister from the line.

KNIGHTS & ALLIES

- **Sir Windley of the South (25)** — Beau's most infamous guard and Merrin's partner-in-mischief. Hair shifts hue with whimsical magic; teasing veils his fiercely loyal depths. Chicly wields dual hatchets.

- **Sir Rafe of the North (20)** — A man of few words and colder steel; his blade exhales frost each time it clears the sheath. Loyal to Luna, goddess of tide and moonlight, and bound by quiet vows kept like snow.
- **Sir Albie (pushing 70)** — Merrin's senior knight. Weather-worn, fatherly, tougher than his twinkling eyes admit.
- **Sir Saxon (27)** — Knight of the Crag; newly posted to Merrin's private guard. Disciplined, literal, still learning that queens rarely heed protocol.
- **Mother Poppy (ancient)** — Royal tome-keeper, former regent, grandmother in all but blood.

OTHER POWERS & PRESENCES

- **The Widowbirds** — Long-tailed messengers bonded to royal blood; summoned by a filigreed whistle, each note attuned to one of the Ten Northern Queens.
- **The Echoes** — Shadow-hands that obey only the Nemophile's Crown, glimpsed behind closed eyes and heard at the mind's edge.
- **The Scarlet Wood** — Living forest of blood-red leaves; gods sleep beneath its roots and watch every queenly step.
- **The Emerald Wood** — Night-bright sister-forest to The Scarlet Wood, glowing under a hidden goddess-light.

- **The Distant Goddesses** — Principal deities of the realm, each holding her own mercies—and grudges—toward *humes*. Worship (or beware) accordingly.

Nemophilist

Noun. A wanderer drawn to the enchantment of forests; one who finds solace among trees and deep woods.

THE Queendoms

SNOWY
NORTH

QUEENDOM
OF THE
CLOUDFALL

QUEENDOM
OF THE
CANYON

QUEENDOM
OF THE
CACTI

DESERT

QUEENDOM
OF THE
CRATER

WILDERNESS

KINGDOM
OF THE
CRYSTALLINE

THE CRYSTAL
SEA

QUEENDOM
OF THE
CURRANT

QUEENDOM
OF THE
COTTONWOOD

THE SCARLET
WOOD

FOREST
FORTRESS

QUEENDOM
OF THE
CLEARING

QUEENDOM
OF THE
CRAG

INN

QUEENDOM
OF THE
COVE

THE Queenless LANDS

THE FORGOTTEN
QUEENDOM

THE
EMERALD
WOOD

D
W

WOODCU
CAB

GIANT'S
NECROPOLIS

HERMIT'S
ABODE

BEETLEWOOD
FOREST

MERAFLORA'S
COTTAGE

THE
TRADI
POS

THE
HEXED
CITY

ASCIAN'S
MANOR

THE
WILLOW
GROVE

THE GOLDEN
FIELDS

THE
EDGE OF
NOWHERE

THE BLUE
FLOWER
FIELDS

SOUTHERN
SPIRITE
CITIES

CONTENTS

I

BEAU

This story would be better if Beau were the one telling it. Beautiful, regal, freckled Beau. If Beau were narrating, you'd get something eloquent, refined—a tale worthy of songs sung for generations.

Instead you're stuck with me, offending gods and losing queens.

Brace yourselves, captive ones, for the overly candid "Merrin" version of events.

Still, everything begins with Beau.

Beau ruled the Clearing, a radiant city nestled deep within the Scarlet Wood, famed for its gilded Lunar Festival, when the moon blazed gold for three nights straight.

She was exactly the kind of queen they whispered about—the one who never let her crown slip. Strict yet fair. Sharp yet never cruel. A ruler who could read you in an instant and discern exactly what sort of person you were. Which was almost funny, considering the innocent eyes and button nose that made her look endlessly, damnably naïve.

And her domain had a sister—my Queendom of the Crag.

We weren't known for grandeur or charm, but what we lacked in elegance, we made up for in resilience. Apothecary to the realms, we crafted curatives prized across the world, remedies renowned for healing everything from headaches to fairy pox.

Just as our realms stood side by side, so did their queens—Beau and me, the Great and Mighty Merrin, queen of the people, for the people.

Or so I tried.

My realm unfurled beyond the crimson woodland, along a tempestuous coast where green veins of life—vines thick as spellwork—climbed stone towers. From those living threads we distilled medicines that kept our people nearly untouchable, and the Crag, cushioned from most worldly affairs. Resourceful, practical, proud—so were my subjects, and I was proudest to stand among them.

Beau's Clearing knew safety too, but not through potions or salves. In her land magic rose straight from the soil; she spoke to trees, quieted the forest's restless echoes, and heard the hush of roots, as her foremothers had.

But we'll come back to that.

Sister realms, sister rulers—not by blood, but by crown and necessity. Like family, only far less sticky.

On a tepid day at the edge of summer, I was riding to meet the one and only at our usual rendezvous point—a hidden fort deep in the Scarlet Wood, tucked within the tangled heart of the forest dividing our queendoms.

It was the place we retreated to discuss politics, men, and how frequently those two overlapped.

The woods were vibrant with rustling red-leafed boughs,

the air thick with chittering wildlife—a lively symphony echoing through ivory-white trunks. Only one road officially connected our lands, a narrow, heavily guarded trail suited solely for feet and hooves. But those of us on less-than-official business took an entirely different route through deeper woods.

"Albie, rein in!" I shouted to my travel detail as Ruckus— my stag and personal agent of chaos—blatantly ignored the command and plunged headfirst into a ditch.

Wind stags, symbols of our royal lineages, were supposed to be swift, elegant beasts. With coats of moonlit silk and velvet antlers spiraling skyward, they embodied grace, majesty, regality.

Usually.

Mine, naturally, was a nightmare—aptly named and forever unruly.

Then again, I'd always preferred rearing my own spirited beasts.

My detail caught up quickly, their well-mannered mounts gliding gracefully onto the path, a stark contrast to Ruckus's current mud-bath. Albie, my most senior guard, laughed openly at the sight, his booming voice rolling through the trees.

"Again, Majesty?" Saxon sighed, her tone sharp enough to chip stone.

I met her gaze, raising a brow, and she quickly found fascination in a patch of dirt at her boots.

"You'll get used to it," Rafe drawled, his voice detached and dry as kindling.

A young man of few words and even fewer emotions, Rafe's perpetually indifferent eyes hinted that little could move him. Yet on the training grounds he was lethal—lightning-swift with a sword, descendant of a rare bloodline that imbued metal with elemental magic. His ochre-brown skin, tempered by northern chill, spoke of those roots, where his affinity for frost surely began. Even now, the hilt of his blade crackled faintly with ice.

"My apologies, Saxon," I said, smoothing away my newest guard's embarrassment. "My stag has priorities. Moss-sniffing clearly outranks queenly loyalties. But Rafe's right—you'll get used to it."

"Smell a lady, does he?" Albie teased warmly from atop his mount. He alone humored Ruckus's whims—likely a habit from my childhood, when every creature had a distinct voice, vividly brought to life through his stories.

Like a father to me, Albie represented one of those cherished bonds—less sticky than blood but somehow stronger. Skin once fair as parchment, now weather-roughened and ruddy at the edges—deep creases latticed his face, lines I'd watched deepen without really seeing until lately. He'd always felt ancient to me, but only now did I wonder how many silent years had slipped onto his shoulders. His hands, worn and nicked by time, held the easy wisdom he claimed to have gathered on every road he'd ever walked.

"Come now, Ruckus. Queen Beau's waiting. There'll be plenty more does to sniff tonight," Albie coaxed with practiced ease.

With a final disgruntled snort, Ruckus bounded forward, crashing headlong into the forest underbrush. The warm, late-summer breeze tugged playfully at our cloaks, whispering mischief in its wake. Saxon and Albie surged ahead, their stags blurring into streaks of silver and cream, while Rafe lingered silently behind, dissolving into the tapestry of crimson leaves.

Our rendezvous was modest: a quaint dwelling suspended among branches, hidden from the forest floor yet commanding an unparalleled view. From the belvedere high in the canopy— if you knew just where to look—you could glimpse my vine-crowned coast to the east and Beau's disciplined woodland to the west. We'd met here since childhood, escorted by the same wardens who once guarded our mothers and, one day, would shepherd our own heirs.

Tradition ran deeper than the tree's roots. Each visit we carried a filigree widowbird whistle—an heirloom passed from queen to queen. A few sharp notes, and a long-tailed widowbird would wing its way to the other sovereign, no matter the distance. A trinket, really, but precious to us—our private signal in a world of ringing bells and royal decrees.

Beau and her company had already arrived. One of her guards waited beneath a white-barked giant, its trunk spiraling upward into the staircase that led to our hidden door.

Rafe nudged his stag aside with a low, wordless murmur, pausing only to take a brief report from another scout. Saxon dismounted to tend our mounts, leaving Albie to escort me along the winding, leaf-carpeted trail.

Patting Ruckus gently in farewell, I gathered my pack and approached the staircase coiling toward the canopy. Albie would've preferred me in full regal attire for such occasions— but clearly, he'd never attempted scaling rough tree bark in formal gowns. Some things simply weren't practical, no matter how hard he pretended otherwise.

The canopy thickened around us as we ascended, blood-hued leaves swallowing our forms, round and round, until—

"Finally here, are we?"

Beau.

She leaned casually over the fort's balcony, wrapped in regal splendor, her long, sleek ponytail slipping over the railing like a silken rope. Sunlight kissed her pale, freckled skin, lending a deceptively gentle air to the sharp wit flashing in her eyes.

"You know Ruckus," I called back lightly. "He's chaos wrapped in velvet fur."

"Only because he's spoiled," Albie grumbled from behind me, his voice rough with affection.

"And who does most of the spoiling, hmm?" I countered, tossing a grin over my shoulder as he chuckled.

"Greetings, Sir Albie," Beau called cheerily, offering a bright wave before slipping gracefully away from the railing, dark hair trailing after her like a living shadow.

"Goodness," I whispered to Albie. "At least someone's excited to see *you*."

"I assume she's giving you shite for being late."

"Hardly my fault."

The top of the staircase came into view, and a hand emerged from the shadows to help me into the foyer.

It wasn't Beau's—her hands didn't bear rings like these, and hers were certainly far too polished.

No, these hands belonged to a guard.

And that blackstone ring was a dead giveaway.

I took the offered hand—only to be yanked insistently through the doorway, like the recoil of a fishing line that had just lost its catch.

"Ah yes, our stalwart reminder that good help is hard to find these days." I swatted the hand away with mock indignation, meeting the smirking face of my favorite among Beau's guards—a son of a bitch named Windley, leaning smugly in the doorway.

Windley had shadowed Beau for the better part of a decade. And in all that time, one thing had remained constant: he was, first and foremost, a bastard.

And that was exactly what I liked best about him.

An intoxicating mix of easy menace and effortless charm, Windley had a knack for lassoing every eye the moment he entered a room.

"Nice hair, pinkie," I said.

Most days his skin lounged in a honey-amber glow, sunlight spilled over warm sand, yet it sometimes borrowed the faint tint of whatever color his mercurial magic flirted with that hour. Pointed ears slanted through strands refusing to behave: one moment storm-gray, the next sunrise-peach, and today a pink so aggressive it could frighten a stag.

"Bold words from a hedge-snarled briar-queen." He offered a wicked smile. "Splendid as ever, Majesty—mud and all—but even you can't sell bramble-tangle couture."

His voice carried none of Beau's courtly lilt—more a lazy, far-coast drawl that made even his jabs feel like inside jokes. As for his lineage, he deflected every question with a wink; mystery fit him far better than pedigree.

"Bramble-tangle is the latest style—didn't you hear? Far less garish than strawberry-sundae chic." I tipped my head. "Stay sharp, Windley. You might spot another flaw if you squint."

He clicked his tongue. "Royalty—get snagged on a thorn and insist it's embroidery."

"Care to workshop that quip?"

Bootsteps sounded behind me. He straightened at once. "May I take your cloak, Majesty?"

I swallowed a grin. "You'd better. Sir Albie will be on us in three...two..."

Favoring flair over formality, Windley performed an exaggerated bow before stepping close enough for his breath to graze my ear as he slipped the cloak effortlessly from my shoulders. He flicked a mud-speckled ringlet that had strayed across my collarbone, one brow arched in mock admiration.

"You look like a lion today, Queen Merrin," he murmured.

"A lion?" I repeated, amused. "And when exactly have *you* seen a lion?"

A feral spark lit Windley's eyes. "I've seen more things than *you* can imagine."

Before I could answer, Albie—having lingered within earshot—dumped an armful of travel packs into Windley's arms and fixed him with a knowing look. "Maybe so. But I've witnessed at least one sight you haven't, lad."

Windley raised a brow. "And that would be?"

Albie stroked his beard like a sage. "A mandolin player."

Windley scoffed. "Everyone's seen a mandolin player."

"Aye," Albie allowed, mischief curling his tone, "but not one who plays using only his—" He cut himself off, shooting a quick, protective glance at me before whispering the rest into Windley's ear.

Skepticism melted to intrigue. "You're joking. You actually saw that? When? And do you have parchment? I'll require diagrams."

"Perhaps once our queen is safely on her way," Albie said, grave as a judge.

I cleared my throat, lifting my chin. "If I'm old enough to manage a realm, Sir Albie, I'm certainly old enough to survive your scandalous stories."

"Why not?" Windley offered. "You're already excruciatingly late. What's another hour or two to Queen Beau, tapping impatiently inside?"

Damn it. He was right.

I sighed, shooting Albie a resigned look. "Sir Albie, do keep an eye on our favorite knave here while Beau and I are occupied."

"Oh, I intend to, My Queen," Albie promised.

On my way out, I caught Windley sinking into his favorite corner armchair, fingertips steepled idly beneath his chin as he prodded Albie further.

"Tell me more, Sir Albie—and please, spare no details."

Few were bold enough—or foolish enough—to pester a senior knight for sordid stories.

When he first arrived at Beau's court, I'd assumed we were the same age, but somewhere along our teenage years I realized he was slightly older—not that it changed anything. I was twenty-two now—hardly wide-eyed—but Windley still treated me like the scrappy girl he'd taunted up that spiral trunk our first summer.

He'd never shown even the slightest ambition to rise in rank...

By now, he could've easily ventured out, as most guards our age did, eager to taste freedom and see the world beyond their queen's borders. Yet Windley remained exactly where he was— willingly leashed at his queen's side, contentedly tethered to Beau, and smugly charming everyone within arm's reach.

What I wouldn't give to steal him for my own court.

The "knave" flashed me a lazy grin and a wink, the faintest glint of feline fangs catching the low light, before I retreated down the hall.

The hallway that led to the inner sanctum was a narrow passage rich with the comforting scents of musky lumber and aged fabric. Everyone had a true home, and maybe Beau and I had always felt like sisters because ours was shared. These were my favorite halls to roam, every creak in the wood and chip in the stone nicked with a myriad of memories.

The sanctum was reserved solely for rulers of our sister queendoms—a space to convene in private confidence. The one place we were ever truly alone. Within these secure walls, no guard dared intrude. Warm saffron spilled through the ajar door, illuminating walls decorated with maps of our realms, marked calendars, and sketches for the approaching Lunar Festival. Since last I'd visited, Beau had clearly been busy; countless new drawings peppered every available surface.

Now, bundles of paper and colorful fabric samples sprawled across a table that may have once held strategic war plans. Beau sat at its center, delicate hands folded in her lap, her ponytail perfectly smoothed since its earlier rebellious escape over the balcony rail. The Queen of the Clearing was thoroughly disarming, freckles lightly peppering her nose and cheeks. Her dark hair was forever sleek, nails perpetually polished, and ears often adorned with gleaming hoops of precious metal.

"Dearest Beau," I greeted her in our habitual way. "Were you waiting long?"

Habitual—considering I habitually arrived late.

Beau stared at me for an extended, unblinking moment before elegantly flicking her hand. "Only long enough to settle in."

As I may have mentioned, you could always identify someone from the Clearing by their lilting cadence—every word refined before leaving their lips.

Unlike my own manner of speaking, which outsiders often called down-to-earth, unpretentious, or direct—and even the latter, I wore with some pride.

"If you're curious," I went on, crossing the worn floorboards, "we're late because I had to deal with that roseroot mess before leaving. Remember the shipment that vanished to the west? We rushed a whole new harvest. That's life in the Crag—crisis, fix, repeat. It's exhausting, and my council can spin plates for a few days without me while we sort out festival diplomacy." Casually, I lifted Beau's notepad from the clutter. "So, how goes the festival planning?"

Her palms struck the table suddenly, scattering candlelight into frantic shapes on the walls. I set the notepad down with extra care.

"You cannot be serious, Merrin!" Beau burst out, eyes blazing with incredulity. "I thought you were jesting earlier! But you truly don't realize it, do you?"

The Queen of the Clearing was always composed. *Always* refined. The very epitome of grace and beauty, admired even among the world's fairest nobles. But I'd long since learned how to pierce through that cultivated façade. Few had ever glimpsed it slip, and even fewer could bring it out as I could.

"Your hair, Merrin! You let Windley see you like that? And the other guards?"

In a flash, Beau was on her feet, swiftly ushering me into the seat she'd just vacated.

"One of them is new yet!" she added, aghast.

She was referring, of course, to my supposed state of dishevelment. Blowing an errant curl from my cheek, I shrugged. "Blame the wind. It's unusually fierce this season. Who cares about Windley? And the others—I'm certain they've seen worse. Besides—"

"When you let it get snarled like this, it becomes impossible to fix," she lectured, gently working her fingers through the chestnut curls. "And isn't that precisely what cloaks are for? Didn't I gift you a new one last birthday exactly for this reason? Your hair is beautiful, Merrin. Honestly, it deserves better care —wait, is this a *stick?*"

She spent the next ten minutes meticulously extracting bits of the forest from my tangled mane.

"Have you considered," I teased, "that I leave my hood down purely to lure you into detangling me?"

"I wouldn't put it past you." She sighed. "Festival planning is dragging. Too many ideas, too little decisiveness. The merchants delivered everything, but now I'm drowning in options."

I pictured what she meant—food-carts perfuming the air with roasted spice, stalls glittering like moonlight on gold leaf, fallen leaves dampening the ground so it shimmered underfoot. All that potential, waiting on her word.

Perfection is a sly traitor; it froze Beau more often than any enemy could. When she asked for "help," she rarely wanted true collaboration. Banners cerulean or violet, lutes or flutes—I honestly didn't care. My real job was to give a confident yes or no so she could feel the tug of her own preference and then choose the opposite.

"Magenta garlands," I said at random, the surest way to make her heart settle on ginger—or something equally un-magenta.

Beau's eyes drifted absently toward another, as though my words had slipped past unheard. "Perhaps ginger instead..."

A heavy thud at the sanctum's door interrupted our debate.

Windley loitered in the doorway, report in hand. Arms folded, hair now a respectable espresso-brown—still daring, just less flaming—he caught my eye with a smirk that said, *I see how she tortures you.*

I *lived* for nights like these. So did Beau; her shoulders eased the moment Windley appeared. With him, Albie, and the others, it almost felt as if we were ordinary friends sharing borrowed freedom—an illusion priceless to two queens who spent most days adored, obeyed, and fundamentally alone. True friendship was rare at our altitude; even Windley obeyed a line he'd never cross.

For us, this was as real as it ever got, and I'd cross half the realms to keep it.

Beau flicked her ponytail and turned back to her sketches. "Be sure you give that one ample conversation later—he's been unbearable, waiting for you to arrive."

Windley and I traditionally shared a drink on the balcony on the first evening of every retreat.

Before that could happen, though, I'd be subjected to hours of answering frivolous questions, jotting notes, and letting Beau fuss over my hopelessly tangled hair until it resembled something presentable.

It's tragic, really—all the thoughtful planning that went into that year's Lunar Festival.

Beneath the rich soil of the Scarlet Wood, something already lay in wait. We didn't know it yet, but there would be no festival come the dawn of autumn.

By the dawn of autumn...

There would be no Beau.

2
THE FIRST SIGN

The first sign something was wrong came that night in the treetop fort.

Beau and I had retired to our separate quarters, stomachs warm with mead, but sleep refused to find me. I preferred keeping the windows open out here, listening to the murmurs of the forest and breathing in the lush petrichor—but tonight, the summer air was relentless, determined to keep me awake. The leaves swished restlessly around the windows, like the anticipation preceding a storm. Even the old halls felt unsettled, despite the reassuring presence of stationed guards nearby.

Windley was offsite at Albie's request, leaving the place oddly hollow.

I slipped down to the pantry, careful not to disturb anyone. Midnight snack runs were a balm for the soul. The guards' chambers were dark, though muffled laughter and hushed banter drifted out. Good. They deserved to unwind on nights like this. Four were still out patrolling the forest—Albie among them, judging by the distinct absence of his thunderous snores.

Twice, I opened and closed the jar of lavender marmalade, savoring the muted clink of lid against glass. After spreading it thick on a biscuit, I wandered back through the shadowed halls, soothed by the fragrant sweetness—until a wavering glow beneath Beau's chamber door caught my attention.

Apparently, I wasn't the night air's only victim.

"Beau?" I tapped lightly on her door. "Are you as drunk as I am?"

I knew she only ever got this drunk with me.

"Windley's going to be jealous he missed out. Albie has him doing rounds—on purpose, I'm certain."

I expected a giggle. Ideally, a hiccup. But nothing came. Unlike the lively guards down the hall, Beau's room remained quiet.

"Beau? You aren't sick, are you?"

More silence.

"I'm coming in," I announced softly. "Tell me your symptoms, and I'll concoct a remedy."

As expected, Beau's chambers were immaculate—possibly the neatest of any queen's. Her books sat arranged sometimes alphabetically, sometimes by color, and occasionally faced outward, pages forming shapes like diamonds or crowns. Tiny blossoms nestled among shelves, butterflies drifting lazily through open windows. Her vanity was spotless, combs and brushes aligned neatly beside imported lotions from the Crystal Sea. Even her bed was perfectly turned down, one corner invitingly folded back, awaiting her graceful return.

Admittedly, mine looked as if a small tornado had swept through, and the tornado was me.

Though Beau's bed had clearly been disturbed, she herself was nowhere to be seen. I'd already checked nearly every room in the fort. Had she ventured outside?

I checked the balconies quickly, exchanging hushed words

with the stationed guards. It felt too early to raise an alarm, but one spot remained.

The fort's belvedere—a circular dome above the treetops—offered a sweeping panorama of the night sky. To one side, my queendom's distant sea sparkled faintly; to the other, Beau's lands stretched beneath moon-cast shadows. As children, we'd often carried armfuls of blankets up here to sleep beneath the stars. The ladder was more challenging to scale now, especially in the impractical nightgown my handmaids had insisted on packing.

Not that I disliked dresses. Dresses could be lovely.

It was the layers. Layers were cumbersome, and cumbersome slowed you down.

Perched high above the forest, the belvedere remained our treasured egg. I recalled the first time my late mother had brought me here—she'd seemed an angel, showing me the heavens beyond the trees. Even now, it remained unchanged: glittering stars fought valiantly against inky darkness, cosmos brushed broadly with celestial paints.

Thank goddess, there was movement in the shadows. I wasn't alone after all.

"Beau?"

Wrong.

"Your Majesty," came the steady, unhurried reply—like the gentle first frost of autumn.

A milky glow illuminated a handsome young guard dressed in my court's colors.

"Rafe."

Though Rafe had stood beside me for three years, he remained the most enigmatic of my guardians. Solitude clung to him, a quiet detachment that made him appear more at home beneath cold moonlight than among people. Often, I'd find him in the courtyard of ivies, halfway through a book, absently twisting a lock of his wavy hair. His disinterest in palace gossip was precisely why he'd earned a place on my travel detail—I trusted his discretion implicitly.

He lowered his softly glowing sword to his side. "Queen Merrin. Why are you awake? You'd turned in by the time we made rounds."

I couldn't exactly admit I was looking for a drunken queen.

"Restless," I said. "But I should ask the same of you. Why aren't you patrolling—or sleeping?"

Rafe's amber eyes flicked toward the dark wood beyond the windows, avoiding mine. He never seemed comfortable making eye contact—at least, not with me.

"I am on patrol," he answered evenly. "Sir Albie allowed me time to charge my blade. The moon's good for it tonight."

The natural world thrummed with magic, a language people like Beau and Rafe spoke fluently—forces beyond my sight. Over time, I'd learned magical intimacy was oddly similar to dresses: intricate and threaded—some strands hidden deeper than others.

Usually, I wouldn't dare ask.

But tonight, the mead made me bold.

"Rafe, may I watch?"

Perhaps offering a demonstration was easier than enduring more questions. With a silent nod, the frost magician raised his sword toward the sky.

At first, nothing happened. Then, the blade flickered dimly, timid against the moon's brilliance. Gradually, as he held it aloft, the glow intensified, pulsing in faint, rhythmic throbs, almost like a heartbeat. Adjusting his stance, he aligned the blade's tip perfectly with the moon's center. His eyes slid shut, reopening to blaze with moonlight, casting his handsome features in spectral radiance.

I gasped quietly, and his brow twitched in subtle response. Hastily covering my mouth, I tried not to interrupt further.

Rafe's enchantments were fueled by lunar energy. Right now, he appeared infused by it, almost ethereal.

Yet unlike Beau's magic, which always seemed deeply rooted to nature itself, Rafe's felt oddly detached. Like an echo of something long lost.

Seemingly unaffected, he continued, pale light spilling from his throat as he softly incanted for another minute. When finished, he cradled the sword's spine gently, pressing a respectful kiss to the steel—mundane, yet oddly reverent— before letting his gaze drift skyward.

When he blinked again, the glow faded from his eyes, leaving him exactly as before.

Rafe's clan was among the last able to imbue metal with such magic—a rare skill that had secured his position within the Crag's ranks.

"Rafe," I breathed, genuinely moved, "that was extraordinary."

He shrugged one shoulder, rolling his neck in what might've been discomfort—or avoidance. "We can only pull so much at once. I need to rest my veins before I continue." His eyes flicked briefly toward mine. "Then I'll resume patrol."

I held my hand toward the moonlight, feeling silver brush my palm before gripping the ladder's top rung. "How spectacular, harvesting lunar energy. It must feel warm. Thank you, Rafe—I should go."

"Warm?" he murmured as I descended. "No. Luna is colder than the coldest frost."

Midnight magic had distracted me, and upon reaching the lower level, realization struck: Beau was still nowhere to be found. It was time to alert someone.

But how foolish I'd look, popping my head back into the

belvedere to admit I'd misplaced a queen. No, I'd find Windley. He was stationed out in the woods, and the bell system would suffice—I could alert the guard at the base of the steps to relay my bidding.

As I passed the hallway windows, something tugged at my vision—a strange distortion in the distance, as though the trees themselves had shuddered.

I paused, breath held.

Nothing moved.

The usual forest sounds had vanished, replaced by a heavy, unsettling quiet.

No rustling branches. No birdsong.

Only thick, unnatural silence.

I shook myself. Perhaps it had been a trick of the moonlight, or my imagination conjuring ghosts. Either way, standing frozen wouldn't solve anything. With forced determination, I moved swiftly through treehouse shadows, calling upon memories of childhood hide-and-seek to steady my nerves. Beau's gowns always gave her away, and part of me hoped to glimpse silk slipping from beneath a settee.

For the third time that night, I passed her door.

This time, the wavering glow had vanished.

I didn't bother knocking.

"Beau!"

She sat in the dark, knees drawn to her chest in a velvet chair. Raven hair spilled loose over pale shoulders, faintly perfumed as always. In the dimness, tears glistened, giving her an almost glasslike beauty.

I rushed to her, cupping her cheeks. "What happened? Are you hurt?"

Her breath trembled. "It has yet to be seen."

My pulse kicked. "What do you mean?"

"Promise you'll keep this secret."

"You know I will."

"Tell no one."

I brushed my thumbs across her cheeks. "You have my word." She nodded, bracing herself, eyes flicking to the window as if the trees might overhear.

Her next words sliced through the hush like an oar through mirror-smooth water, sending ripples far beyond herself.

"I can't hear them anymore, Merrin. The forest is terrifyingly silent."

Cold dread sluiced through me.

The admission stole my breath. Among the northern queens, only Beau served the living forest. While we bartered and patrolled borders, her realm produced nothing; tribute flowed inward. Rooted at the heart of the Scarlet Wood, the Clearing bound our lands. The forest's magic fed the Crag's soil, kept our curatives potent—but something darker pulsed beneath those roots, forces Beau likened to trying to describe a color you'd never seen before—*echoes*, she said, born of a nature that bears no love for humankind.

Since her first breath she'd been trained to weave her will through those echoes, holding calamity at bay. Royal mother to royal daughter, the charge passed unbroken; some said the north survived only because she endured.

"How will I quell them if I can't hear them? They've never been silent—not once!"

"Since when?"

"Tonight. Just after..." She broke off, lashes lowering. "If anyone finds out—and if the forest starts to change..."

Fear clawed at me, but Beau needed steadiness.

"It could be interference," I said evenly. "An odd alignment —planets, tides."

"Merrin, that's—"

"We don't know yet. We'll tell no one and figure it out together."

Relief flickered in her eyes.

My mind whirled. The echoes were balance itself; what happened when balance broke? I squeezed her shoulder.

"We'll solve it."

These were the moments that bound us. I would hold her secret, help her carry this burden—even if its weight pressed heavier than anything I'd ever borne before.

We spent the rest of the night curled together in Beau's bed, surrounded by cool sheets and freshly fluffed pillows. It had been years since we'd done this, and as we settled into the down, I felt it—that tense stillness before a storm, the kind that prickled across skin, charged with an unspoken promise to break.

I held Beau close until, eventually, her breathing steadied into sleep.

My thoughts drifted in uneasy circles—to my people back in the Crag, harvesting leaves to craft remedies; to the children, elders, and the other queens scattered across their cities—all of us intricately tethered to the forest, to the lifeblood it provided.

Sleep remained elusive, and when it finally overtook me, I thought I glimpsed something in the corner of the room.

A flash of gleaming eyes.

A wicked, devilish smile.

Surely, it was just a trick of the light.

3

A MIDNIGHT VISITOR

In my city, life went on, none knowing the secret of the Clearing's queen.

Over the coming weeks, I watched the forest for signs of betrayal, but despite Beau's confession, it behaved as forests should—standing tall, shedding leaves of scarlet and gold into the Queendom of the Crag. While the trees remained steady, the sea on the city's opposite side thrashed and crashed, sending salt-laden mist drifting through the streets. Not so unusual for this time of year.

The sea had no love for summer's end.

Ours was an empire of fury and form, a ceaseless battle between sea and stone. Waves battered the city walls, weathering edges and leaving behind a worn, rustic beauty. But farther inland, beyond the sea's reach, the stone stood untouched, and where salt thinned, ivy flourished. The densest, greenest parts were my favorite. Nothing bad ever happened in cottages swallowed by ivy.

My palace, set at the city's heart, bridged these worlds—one half cloaked in creeping vines, the other standing bare and defiant against the elements. When melancholy took hold, I gazed upon restless waves; when content, I turned toward the serene forest.

Ever since departing the fort that day, my gaze had remained fixed on the sea.

Beau's confession echoed in my thoughts as I tried to perform queenly duties without suspicion. I oversaw shipments of curatives bound for the distant Queendom of the Cacti, where plant life grew sparse. I entertained visitors from neighboring realms and mediated disputes between northern cities. Beau and I both led neutral queendoms, but tawdry political squabbles often fell to my court, hers too consumed by the demands of appeasing the forest.

I worried for my sister queen, sending coded letters by widowbird—royal messengers famed for finding bloodlines across any distance. Beau's responses came swiftly, reassuring yet hollow. Her handwriting remained charmingly precise, but her words felt empty—scribbled pleasantries intended merely to soothe my concern.

As if that ever worked.

She admitted the echoes hadn't returned—not even after two weeks. I invited her to meet again at the fort or even venture all the way to the Crag, but she declined, insisting she must remain, desperate to rekindle something from the Scarlet Wood.

I patted the head of the long-tailed widowbird that had delivered Beau's latest letter. The creature helped itself to seed and water while I unrolled the parchment. Curiously, it lacked Beau's customary scarlet seal.

Wouldn't you love to see the southern mountain someday?

An odd line. Our secret code mentioned no mountains. Did she mean this literally?

The rest of the letter contained nothing new. Beau feigned cheerfulness but reported no return of her magic. I fed the parchment to the fire beside my throne.

There was good reason the message had to be destroyed. No one could learn the truth of Beau's lost echoes.

But that didn't mean I couldn't try to help from afar.

"Saxon." I turned to the on-duty guard, who leaned casually by a window, deeply invested in conversation with one of my prettiest handmaids.

Saxon smoothed her short hair, straightening quickly. "Queen Merrin?"

"Fetch Mother Poppy, and clear the room, please."

Looking relieved to be useful, the muscular guard hastened to comply.

If Albie stored stories within his wrinkles, Mother Poppy, royal tome-keeper, carried entire archives in hers. Diminutive and ancient as time itself, she remained sprightly, perpetually hiding at least two books somewhere within her robe—concealed treasures that had tumbled from her sleeves more than once, including straight into a crock of roast beets at last winter's feast.

Fine by me—no one but the cook enjoyed root vegetables anyway.

Mother Poppy appeared even smaller beneath the throne room's vaulted ceilings, dwarfed by marble and gold, yet she moved with quiet authority, having advised queens long before my time. She tutted softly to herself, humming an old tune as she settled into the ornate chair beside mine.

Beyond the windows, the coast stormed, masking our conversation perfectly.

"I've been dying to know, Mother Poppy. Did you find anything?"

Two days prior, I'd sent the court's tome-keeper on a discreet quest through the archives.

"Afraid not, My Queen." Her eyes, storm-gray behind jeweled spectacles, met mine with measured regret. "Nothing in the annals suggests the bond between nature and oracle has ever been broken."

"Nothing?"

She shook her head. "Not in written history."

I had suspected as much but had still clung to hope—a hidden journal, perhaps, or a buried record offering guidance.

"And in unwritten history?" I pressed.

Mother Poppy understood discretion, having served enough queens to know not to ask my purpose. She leaned back in her chair, folding wizened hands thoughtfully.

"That's another matter," she mused. "There is one tale that may interest you."

Aha.

"Mind you, it was only told in the dark, when prying ears rested. A story spoken not in truth, but in fable—and by one whose reputation was less than admirable."

She was cautioning me not to raise my hopes.

"Understood."

She continued, voice hushed to a whisper:

"Before the time of the Clearing,
when the moon hung low, heavy with secrets,
and frost reigned eternal upon the land,
two crowns slipped silently from heaven,
lost among shadows of northern pines.
The forest wept, yet none listened,

ears deaf to sorrow, hearts blind to loss.
Before the time of the Clearing,
when starlight whispered gently through leaves,
and twilight lingered long over frozen lakes,
two crowns awoke, glistening with promise,
found by souls who heard the wood's quiet hymn.
The forest sang, and they listened closely,
ears open to wisdom, hearts warm with grace."

The forest wept, yet none listened...

Was this what was happening now—echoes calling to a queen who could no longer hear?

Whatever I'd promised Mother Poppy, my hopes were already rising.

"Details, please," I urged. "You're saying the bond between nature and oracle has been broken before—and repaired by someone who finally listened?"

She adjusted her glasses, her gaze sharpening. "According to mere *fable*, My Queen."

A bit specific for mere fable.

"If it's a fable, then what's the moral?" I challenged.

Her lips curled into a knowing smile, settling into the lines at the corners of her eyes. Every storyteller relished the moral.

"That one must listen not to the loudest call, but to the truest," she replied. "A controversial parable, since replaced by the tale of the otter and the crane. Best not let the commonfolk dwell too much on lost crowns and fickle forests."

Too much talk of uncertain rulers made queens uneasy.

"You've heard that one, yes?"

More times than I could count.

Make that one more—Mother Poppy retold it anyway.

The tale of lost crowns wasn't much, but it was something.

I wanted to share it with Beau in person. Perhaps her tome-keeper would know more, given the right prompting.

I asked Mother Poppy to call for me should she recall anything else. Then I summoned Rafe to assemble a guard, intending to depart for the Clearing the following morning.

Little did I know, as Rafe hurried to prepare for a departure yet to come, another guard was racing to warn us of a departure already passed.

That night, I retired hopeful, imagining Beau's face when I offered her a scrap of reassurance. A traveling pack awaited me at the foot of my bed, courtesy of Albie and my handmaids. I swapped two gowns for britches and threw in an extra wrap for my hair, lest the wilds catch me unprepared.

My quarters were decidedly less orderly than Beau's, with sashes draped carelessly over furniture and books scattered, half-read. I liked it this way—I could resume wherever I'd left off, whichever genre suited my mood. It drove Albie mad, but I insisted staff spend time on more important matters than tidying a room few visitors ever entered.

Naturally, Albie still made them clean, though incrementally, hoping I wouldn't notice—a game we'd played my entire life.

I left the windows open, savoring what few nights of the season remained. Evening carried scents of sea and greenery, city sounds waning as darkness settled. Eventually, those churning swells calmed under the moon's rise, and all fell quiet.

Nothing outside hinted at nature's impending revolt.

· · ·

I drifted into dreams where Beau and I stood deep within the Scarlet Wood, echoes vibrating through ivory trunks. Crimson leaves littered the ground, wet and sticky, clinging to Beau's gown.

How had I never realized the forest's scarlet was actual blood?

In the darkest corner, eyes gleamed—familiar, dangerous...

"My Queen?"

A voice pulled me from sleep.

Groggily, I rose, wiping hair stuck to my forehead. Sheets tangled around me, evidence of fitful tossing. The darkness signaled dead of night.

A face appeared—Chrysanthemum, the pretty handmaid Saxon had chatted up earlier, looking far more alert than I felt. She usually kept her distance.

"You have a visitor, Queen Merrin. He insisted it was urgent. Sir Rafe permitted his entry." She shifted nervously, hoping she'd acted rightly.

"Who is it?"

The visitor didn't wait for introductions.

A cloaked figure swept in, lantern high; when he lowered his hood, the light caught on pointed ears and a mouth set in an unfamiliar, too-solemn line.

"Windley!" I yanked blankets higher, hiding my *truly* disheveled self. "What on goddess's earth are you doing here?"

Chrysanthemum clutched her throat in alarm.

"It's fine," I reassured quickly. "One of Queen Beau's guards. Fetch Sir Albie."

As the handmaid fled, Windley, who'd never before entered my royal nest, came straight to my bedside, hair changed once again—this time to midnight blue.

"Windley?"

"Merrin."

He dropped the title from my name, something he'd done only once before—an act swiftly corrected by his superiors. Something in his voice prickled my skin, a tone I'd never heard from him.

He was never this serious.

He let nothing worry him.

My stomach twisted, because it knew.

My heart sank, because it knew.

But my head didn't catch up until Windley took a breath and told me:

"She's missing."

4
THE MISSING QUEEN

Beau was missing.

Beau. Missing.

Beau.

The words screamed inside my head, drowning thought and feeling alike in an indistinguishable storm. My usual crises were crop failures, unexpected castle guests—not queens stolen from their beds in the dead of night.

People look to leaders. Leaders look to council.

Words my mother had once spoken, back when I was small enough to fit on her knee.

Now wasn't the time to fall apart. Beau was missing, and I needed to handle it like any queen who'd gone missing. I was a leader. It was time I acted like one.

Cleaned up and dressed, I found Windley already debriefing Albie and Rafe in the throne room. The three guards spoke softly around the fire, as if the flames could burn their words away before prying ears could hear them.

Windley looked battered—fatigue etched into every weary movement, shallow cuts on his face where careless branches had scored him. Gone was the usual jester's grin. He looked like he wanted to summon it—one of his carefree smirks, something to ease the tension—but couldn't quite manage. Dark shadows rimmed his normally playful eyes, dull now with fatigue. He paced restlessly near the hearth, as if sitting still had become an impossibility. His voice mirrored his appearance.

"Her door was guarded dusk to dawn. Phylo was posted there—timid chap. No way he had any part in it."

Albie, clad in full knight's armor from his patrol, clinked faintly each time he shifted. "There are simpler ways to ransom a queen if it was an inside job. This feels rushed. Frantic, even."

"Smashing through a window in the dead of night, right under a sleeping court's nose?" Windley scoffed bitterly in agreement.

I hugged my robe tighter around myself, stepping into their circle. "When exactly did this happen?"

"Last night."

"But Windley, that's impossible. I received a letter from Beau just this afternoon!"

Uh-oh.

My voice rose sharply, prompting Albie to rest a reassuring hand on my elbow. "Likely delayed," he soothed. "Message birds can be unreliable. Don't fret, My Queen. We'll figure this out." He turned back to Windley. "Have you scouted the surrounding forest?"

"All day and all night."

"Wait," I interrupted. "You said window. Surely not Beau's window? Her quarters are at the castle's highest point! Who could climb that unseen?"

Panic surged again, and another comforting touch found me—this time, from the least likely among us.

Rafe.

His hand settled on my shoulder, hesitant yet steady, as though he'd touched something fragile and was reconsidering the move.

"There are ways," he murmured, withdrawing his hand as swiftly as he'd placed it.

Strange. Rafe didn't comfort. Nor had he shown much interest in Beau—or anyone else. Besides, were we expected to believe someone had scaled the entire castle, abducted Beau, then descended unnoticed with an unwilling captive?

"My Queen?" Albie prodded gently.

Apparently, one of them had asked me something, but focusing was impossible, knowing someone had taken my dearest friend in the night. Should I reveal Beau's secret? The timing of losing her echoes seemed too convenient to ignore. Yet sharing it could plunge her already vulnerable court into deeper chaos.

Three sets of eyes watched me expectantly. Albie would sense if I held back now. I had to decide.

"Queen Merrin," Windley pressed, "are you aware of any reason someone might target us? Have you heard whispers from other queens?"

"No. Our territories have always been protected. If Beau was taken, it wasn't by anyone from the civil queendoms. None would risk aggression against our courts."

My gaze drifted toward the windows, still shrouded in night. A full day since Beau vanished. We needed a plan.

"The Crag will provide the Clearing whatever resources necessary to recover Beau. We'll keep quiet until we know more. Windley, I assume Rebella has taken the throne?"

"Why do you think I'm here?" Windley said darkly.

Beau's younger cousin Rebella trained alongside her specifically for scenarios like this, always stepping in when Beau traveled.

Poor Windley. I imagined how quickly he'd fled the moment Rebella tried to restrain him. She'd carried a rather desperate affection for him since forever.

He caught my eye, searching for direction. Without Beau, he seemed unmoored—used to taking orders, now lost without his queen.

As one of Beau's closest guards, he was likely as disoriented as I felt. Her disappearance didn't seem real. Shock had me half-convinced I was still tangled in my bedsheets, trapped in an awful dream.

But reality was creeping in, slow and suffocating. With it came the dreadful understanding that nothing would snap neatly back into place.

Later, I'd recognize this feeling not as grief—but shock.

Grief would come eventually. And when it did, it would be much, much worse.

"Your Majesty."

Lost in thought, warmth from the fire soaking into bones that otherwise felt lifeless, I only now noticed how intently Rafe was watching me.

"Rafe?"

"They need leads. Think through your last interactions, correspondences—anything."

Perhaps duty compelled his investment. Perhaps Rafe was secretly honorable. Perhaps—

Wouldn't you love to see the southern mountain someday?

I shot upright. "Wait!" My voice echoed through the room. "Beau's letter! I burned it, but I remember the exact wording. It was peculiar. I think she sent it after she'd already been taken."

Windley halted his pacing. "Define peculiar."

"She referenced a southern mountain. 'Wouldn't you love to see the southern mountain someday?' We have codes, but that isn't one. Could it be literal? A clue? The timing matches."

I aimed my question at Albie, but instead, he turned cautiously toward Windley. "You'd know best," he said quietly, almost reluctantly.

Windley rubbed the back of his neck uneasily before admitting, "If it's code, then she didn't go willingly. No one would."

"You know this place?" My adrenaline surged. "How?"

He glanced again at Albie before conceding, "I'm from... somewhere in the south. There's a place people avoid. Giants once roamed there. They've long died off, but their bones remain—piled high, forming a mountain in the middle of nowhere."

I'd heard of it before, in one of Mother Poppy's darker tales. Called—

"Giant's Necropolis," Albie supplied grimly.

Windley nodded. "That's what outsiders call it. It's the only southern mountain I know."

"And why avoid it?" Albie asked.

Windley rubbed his chin thoughtfully. "Besides it being a graveyard of giants? Well, there's one skeleton larger than the rest. It's intact, and—rumor has it—moves occasionally. Inconsequential, really..."

Charming.

"Certainly not inconsequential," I muttered. "Enchanted?"

"Either that, or something else big enough to shift giant bones. Personally, I'm not eager to find out."

"Eager or not, it's your best lead," Albie said decisively.

I seized on the word *lead*. Maybe it could be more than that. I crossed the throne room, robes snapping, and stepped onto the balcony where Beau's message cage hung against the dawn haze. Albie and the others fell in behind me, boots echoing on the tiles, but kept a respectful distance while I worked.

The widowbird inside blinked its raven-gloss eyes at me. I slid my arm through the door, and it hopped onto my wrist with a questioning chirrup. From the chain at my neck I drew my filigree widowbird whistle—silver, its surface worn smooth by years of use. I blew Beau's three-note trill, then the higher answering note—a pattern only she and I ever used.

The bird ruffled, whistled back, and launched into the air. We watched in tense silence as it circled twice, found its bearing, and arrowed due south—so straight it might have been pulled by string.

"It's flying south—look!" I pointed. The black speck cut across a sunrise washed in peach and gold, unwavering on its course.

Albie murmured a low "Aye," equal parts awe and relief, his gauntlet creaking as he tightened his grip on the railing. Windley let out a shaky breath—half laugh, half prayer—while Rafe leaned forward, amber eyes tracking the dot until it vanished.

I turned, heart hammering. "That's confirmation. Beau's alive, and the captors are moving her south. If we know their direction, we can intercept."

Windley scrubbed a hand over his face, voice rough. "Nice to have known that before riding all the way here, but yes. Send word to the Clearing—tell them to dispatch our fastest riders after me."

I would—just as soon as my mind stopped reeling from the image of Beau held somewhere inside a giant's graveyard. Thank goddess the kidnappers wanted her alive; had they meant assassination, they'd have done it in her chambers. Alive meant time, and the Clearing boasted elite cavalry.

"I'll set out immediately." Windley turned, but I caught his hood before he could leave.

"No, you won't get far in your current state. Rest tonight.

Depart at dawn. I'll send word to Rebella to dispatch backup riders in the meantime."

Windley blinked, surprise flickering across his weary features as I lifted the little whistle from my robe and let it glint in the firelight.

"He shouldn't go alone," Rafe said. "I'll accompany him."

"I expect you will—Albie too. I'll need both of you with me if the trail runs long."

Albie's complexion paled. "My Queen—"

"A separate convoy buys us surprise," I said. "If the abductors spot the Clearing's forces, they won't see us."

"Yes, but surely you don't intend to ride *with* us. For what purpose? The Crag still needs its ruler."

True. The Crag did need a ruler.

But Beau wasn't merely another missing sovereign. Behind the courtly walls that kept most people at arm's length, those few souls a queen let inside became priceless. Beau was one of them; in every way that mattered, she *was* my sister.

And there was something only I could contribute to this search.

I tightened my grip on the filigree whistle. If Beau's bird called, it would find me, and my reply would guide us straight to her.

If I stayed behind, that advantage died in a throne room. I would sit idle, hoping someone else's blades moved fast enough. Better to be in the field, whistle in hand, ready the instant Beau's message reached me. That difference could mean Beau alive—or an outcome I refused to accept.

"My decision is made," I said. "I'll explain the rest en route."

I had already prepared for this contingency. "Albie, install my cousin Lekhana as figurehead—she's twenty-one and already versed in council protocol. Mother Poppy will serve as regent, exactly as she once did for me. Saxon commands the guard in your absence, and we'll divide the cavalry so neither realm stands bare."

Albie bowed, swallowing his objections. He would air them in private—I expected nothing less—yet for now he moved to carry out the order. An ambush of arguments would come before dawn, but I would meet it ready.

Windley grumbled but didn't argue, collapsing onto the nearest couch, pulling his hood over his face, already half-asleep.

Gliding past, I draped a blanket over him.

He caught my wrist. "Thanks, queenie," he murmured, voice lower and softer than usual, before releasing me.

Meanwhile, Rafe hovered at the firelight's edge, his displeasure simmering, nostrils flaring slightly as if irritated by the delay.

But rested bodies and morning daylight would serve us far better.

Little did I know just how many secrets the icy-eyed magician concealed beneath his silence.

5

FROSTED

We set off just as the morning sun painted the sky in streaks of orange and pink.

Ruckus was groggy enough from our early start that he didn't try to steer our course, though I doubted that would last long. The mischievous stag tended to grow more restless the longer the day stretched on.

Overhead, a lone widowbird crossed our path like a miniature dragon, its wings catching the dawn's first rays. Was it one of mine? Before leaving, I'd sent half a dozen into the world with coded messages for Beau. If her captors intercepted one, another would surely slip through. It might take time, but widowbirds always found their way.

Seeing another soar south felt auspicious, a sign we were heading in the right direction. I clutched the filigree whistle around my neck, silently willing it to be true.

Uncharacteristically, Rafe had taken the lead, maneuvering deftly through the forest's blazing leaves. Usually, he lingered at the back, a shadow on the outskirts. I'd always assumed the stoic magician only accepted his royal post for convenience.

Strange that he seemed invested now. Perhaps he thrived in crisis—or maybe he was simply relieved to be away from the Crag.

In his place, Albie hung back, silently critical of our mission.

As expected, the old guard had ambushed me in the pre-dawn gloom, questioning my insistence on joining. When I'd explained my reasoning with the widowbirds, he'd pressed further, suggesting we meet up with the Clearing's cavalry and travel south as a unit. An entire army, he argued, was better suited to guarding one queen and rescuing another.

I countered that the cavalry would move faster without us. If they reached Beau first, all the better. If not, we'd catch up along the way.

With great reluctance, Albie realized he wouldn't sway me. It wasn't that I was obstinate—merely steadfast in my decisions.

Alright, perhaps I was a little obstinate.

Windley rode at my side, a scarlet cloak of the Clearing thrown over his shoulders while the rest of us wore emerald. The color and the dawn's dim angle dulled his inky hair to charcoal and seemed to tight-wind his presence—compact, watchful, a spring held in check rather than its usual swagger. A faint charge sizzled around him; tension, perhaps, or something more. I'd never seen Windley so contained.

But as the sun climbed and the scarlet cloak loosened at his throat, flecks of blue began re-emerging in the dark strands—like sparks leaking through soot.

"Seems you've finally tamed that mane of yours, queen lion," he remarked after hours of silence, his voice a shadow of his usual teasing.

Surprised by his attempt at banter, I quickly realized he was trying to distract me from Beau. I'd offer him the same courtesy.

"That's queen *lion-ess*—and this mane at least sticks to one color, unlike certain traveling rainbows I could name."

The corner of his mouth twitched into a smirk, the first glimmer of life returning to his eyes.

"We'll find her alive," I assured softly. "Beau's clever and strong, and we've both trained for situations like this. She's got plenty of tricks up her sleeve."

Her laughter echoed in my memory, vivid as our last evening together.

Perhaps I was trying to reassure myself as much as Windley.

"I wouldn't worry if it were you, Merrin. You're capable in the wilds. I suspect you would *live* in the wilds if not for your born duty." He'd dropped my title again, noticing only a beat too late. "Ah, fuck," he muttered. "*Queen* Merrin."

"It's fine, Windley. You know I don't mind...so long as no one else hears it."

Truthfully, hearing him say my name without formality sent an unexpected ripple through my stomach—not unpleasant, but oddly warm. And the aura of energy around Windley seemed to flare.

"Sir Albie would have my head."

That was undoubtedly true.

The Scarlet Wood sprawled endlessly around the Clearing, offering a safer path south than the coastal route from the Crag, which was too open and heavily guarded against outsiders.

We'd fed the citizens and most palace staff a plausible story: Beau and I were off planning the Lunar Festival—no questions, please. Anyone spotting us on the main road would have grown suspicious, so our true path veered west into the Scarlet Wood before angling south, letting us surface far from curious eyes.

I hadn't had many dealings with the south. Only one

queendom lay in that direction—the Queendom of the Cove—and they mostly kept to themselves. Tasked with patrolling civilization's southernmost borders, they acted as the final line of defense against whatever lurked beyond. Albie had sent a bird ahead to request lodging, certain his friend—the Cove's captain of the guard—would accommodate us. Albie had no shortage of old friends scattered throughout the queendoms.

Beyond the Cove stretched the queenless lands: uncharted territories filled with Mother Poppy's whispered tales and nightmares. Even Albie had never ventured that far.

Luckily, we had a less-than-human companion who apparently had.

Windley's ears flicked at every forest sound, his posture as fluid as the stag beneath him. Even in repose a quicksilver spark lit his eyes—small, unmistakable tells of the otherness I still hadn't solved.

I half-expected to spot a tail beneath his cloak.

"Better keep your eyes forward," he said without looking. "I don't trust that stag of yours not to lead you straight into a tree. Like rider, like beast, I suppose." He tapped his temple. "Dull in the wits."

"How generous of you to worry about us," I shot back, "but between Ruckus's horns and your inflated ego, guess which of you is likelier to spear the bark. Try not to admire yourself in every puddle, Sir Windley."

Windley barked a laugh, finally glancing over one shoulder. "'Sir Windley,' is it? Careful—dress me up with titles and I might start acting respectable."

Good—he was slipping back into his familiar self. I felt calmer, reassured by the steady rhythm of travel. When worry about Beau surged, I focused on the path ahead.

Crisp, earthy air filled my lungs, as if nature itself urged us forward in search of its lost oracle.

By evening, we'd broken through the woodlands, emerging onto vast plains dotted with glowing firebugs and scattered farmhouses. Like tiny embers, the bugs dimmed as we passed, brightening again in our wake.

Ruckus snapped playfully at them, though he never caught even one.

Albie consulted his map by moonlight, allowing the rest of us a moment to admire the scenery. I'd always loved how night transformed landscapes into shadowy silhouettes, black forms etched against the deep twilight.

Rafe took advantage of the open sky, unsheathing his sword to recharge its magic. Against the rising moon and dark forest backdrop, he stood solitary and unmoving, his silhouette sharp as stone.

Windley folded his arms, observing beside me. "Ugh. What even is he?"

"Funny question coming from *you*," I hummed.

The moonlight reflected mischievously in Windley's dark eyes as he chuckled.

I explained, "Rafe's clan hails from the north. Once common, a plague nearly wiped them out long ago, and apparently they're terrible at repopulating."

Windley made a thoughtful noise. "A charmer like him? Shocking."

Albie still fussed with his map, muttering under his breath. Rafe, a few strides away, murmured incantations over his blade, its glow pulsing in response.

I leaned closer to Windley. "Say, has Rafe seemed peculiar to you lately?"

He shrugged. "He's not exactly one to share his secrets."

"Again, ironic coming from *you*."

He tossed me another cat-toothed grin, elbow resting casually on my shoulder. "Ah, Queen Merrin. Is this you hinting you'd like to know my secrets?"

The gesture was comfortably familiar, a small anchor in the uncertain night.

"Alright, you three," Albie interrupted gruffly. "There's a town southwest, bound to have an inn." He stepped close, carefully lifting my hood into place. "Keep this up till we're lodged. Like at the Queendom of the Canyon—never know who's watching."

Incognito.

I flashed him a thumbs-up. "Understood, Albie."

"Mind the hood, lion queen—one strong gust and it'll be riding backward like your crown at archery practice."

"This journey should give you time to sharpen your insults," I shot back, though he wasn't wrong—the breeze kept tugging my cloak and hood askew.

Too bad Beau wasn't here to help.

The thought stung.

Albie noticed, placing a reassuring hand against my cheek. "Stay strong, My Queen," he murmured, glancing discreetly toward the others. "For them, too."

He was right.

I lifted my chin, forcing steadiness into my voice. "Thank you, my knight."

The title brought a proud twinkle to his eyes.

By the time we reached the small town's cozy inn, exhaustion had settled deep into my bones. The common room hummed warmly with conversation and crackling firelight. Windley arranged food, Albie secured lodging, and I stood beside Rafe, who eyed the bar absently.

"You're welcome to drink, Rafe."

"I'm fine," he replied distantly, familiar apathy returning. Perhaps last night's quiet comfort had been an anomaly.

Vapor curled from beneath his cloak—a freshly charged blade.

"You might conceal that," I told him softly. "No telling who's familiar with your magic here."

Rafe adjusted his cloak. "Thanks, Your Maj—" He paused, realizing the title was out of place.

I chuckled at his hesitation, finding his quiet turmoil endearing.

"Look at you," Windley said, sliding a tray in front of me. "No drink? I was sure you'd order a pitcher."

Determined to keep things light, I quipped back, "And I was sure you'd be busy flirting with the locals. Did you see the chesty one at the bar?"

"I'm a royal guard," he sniffed, as if the very suggestion offended him. "I only flirt with queens."

"Shame they never flirt back."

"They don't know what they're missing."

His irrepressible grin was a welcome buffer against the anxiety crashing through me. Windley clearly worried for Beau, yet he still kept the mood afloat—if Beau's most trusted guard could treat this like any other outing, maybe I could pretend, too. Strange how the roughest edges offered the greatest comfort.

When we finally retired to our room, there were only two beds.

Albie and I took one each, while Rafe and Windley settled onto makeshift pallets on the floor. It was rare for me to share my sleeping quarters, but tonight, with Beau's absence gnawing at me, I was quietly grateful for their presence.

At least, until Albie began his concert of rumbling snores.

If Rafe minded, he gave no sign. Windley, on the other hand, made an exaggerated fuss, fluffing his pillow noisily before repositioning it dramatically over his ears.

"It'll stop once he turns to his side," I assured, recalling the familiar rumbling from childhood.

On nights when I'd been afraid to sleep alone—usually after one of Mother Poppy's particularly frightening fables—Albie would sit in the armchair by my bed, reciting poetry aloud until I drifted off.

More often than not, he'd succumb first, his snores filling the quiet.

I was never one for poetry's lofty words, but I'd come to cherish their sound.

For they reminded me of Albie.

Eventually, the snoring subsided, and my weary body surrendered to sleep.

Sometime later, the soft creak of floorboards stirred me awake.

Through the haze of sleep, I glimpsed Rafe sitting by the window, his chin resting pensively on his knuckles as he gazed into the firebug-speckled night.

There was no need for him to keep watch; we were on the second floor, with a sturdy latch securing the door.

Perhaps he simply couldn't find comfort on the floor.

Windley, at least, seemed undisturbed.

Surveying the night, Rafe didn't wear his usual expression of detached indifference. Instead, his features appeared softer, almost...forlorn.

After several quiet moments, he pressed his palm gently against the windowpane, leaving a fragile bloom of ice behind.

Through heavy, sleepy eyes, I thought I glimpsed something else:

A faint, mirrored handprint lingering on the other side of the glass, remaining long after Rafe's had melted away.

Surely, it was just a trick of the night.

6

THE COVE

I n the chill of early morning, before other tenants stirred, we set off again, passing only the most devoted workers already tending their fields. The countryside here held a charm distinct from the Clearing and the Crag—life was simpler, yet hearty, the air fragrant with fresh hay and oxen.

Windley, who once again rode beside me, didn't seem to share my enthusiasm. He slumped into his hood like a sleepy child, head resting against his stag's velvety antlers.

"Because *someone* kept me awake with their snoring," he mumbled accusingly, pretending to pin the crime on me.

"Wrong. Lions *purr*."

He gave me a sidelong glance, clearly searching for a witty comeback, but apparently too drained to bother. "You know," he remarked instead, "you're probably the only queen left who still rides in pants. Some of the others did when we were younglings, but you've stuck to it. Special tailor?"

"Can you imagine if I didn't? Poor Ruckus would be engulfed!" I affectionately patted the stag's neck.

Ruckus seemed pleased exploring fresh pastures, though

his curiosity made steering him a chore. A chipper here, a new friend there—he was far more interested in the wildlife than they were in him. Even so, our pace had improved significantly now that we'd cleared the forest.

Albie assured us we'd reach the Cove in no time if we kept up this speed.

But we didn't reach the Cove that day, nor the next.

We rode through endless miles of farmland, occasionally dotted with pockets of civilization. The initial charm soon faded into muted stretches of grass and dry earth.

Each encounter with traveling merchants or children waving enthusiastically from farmsteads momentarily lifted my spirits, but the excitement dimmed as we pressed on beside the sinking sun.

Each night brought warm lodging and hearty meals, yet each dawn summoned another weary departure.

Conversation grew sparse, stifled by a relentless wind that muffled even Windley's attempts at banter. Eventually, even Ruckus grew bored.

Finally—after a journey that felt far longer than it surely was—the wind carried a distinct change. A scent I immediately recognized.

Salt.

Salty sea air, briny and unmistakable.

The muted palette melted into vivid golds and lush emeralds as we neared the coastline—I felt it as surely as my own pulse.

"Albie!" I shouted, slowing to take in the shifting terrain of coarse brush and jagged rock. "We're closer now, aren't we?"

"To be fair, we've been getting closer all along," Windley drawled lazily.

"Yes, but now we're *close*-close. I can feel it in my bones."

Albie rode up beside me, squinting toward the horizon. "Aye, My Queen. Not far now."

Rafe, too, seemed relieved—or at least less withdrawn. Perhaps he'd enjoyed the silence more than any of us.

Reinvigorated, I nudged Ruckus into a faster pace. Sensing my eagerness, the stag bounded forward with renewed enthusiasm, leaping over rocks and skirting bristly shrubs as the salt-touched air thickened around us.

The palace appeared first, rising on the horizon like a beacon, its tallest spire shaped fittingly into a crescent moon. Next, the vibrant city emerged, clustered around a half-moon bay. Last came the tide itself, drawing back as though beckoning us closer.

I had never visited the Queendom of the Cove, yet somehow it felt like returning home.

Eager for human interaction, I urged Ruckus toward the city, drawing curious looks from those on the outskirts—until a sudden dust cloud cut me off.

"Wait, My Queen!"

Ruckus skidded to a halt beside a startled child playing near the brush, narrowly avoiding a collision with Albie and his mount.

"You aren't presentable to meet the Cove's queen," Albie cautioned like a parent. "If we enter like this, they'll mistake us for vagabonds."

Right. We weren't yet in the wilds—proper decorum was required for meeting southern royalty.

"Do we have time for this?" Rafe asked impatiently, glancing over his shoulder, clearly eager to continue.

"We must make time," Albie replied firmly. "I wish to find Queen Beau as much as anyone, but the lands beyond are dangerous and unfamiliar. You two can restock supplies while I speak with Delagos."

Captain Delagos—Albie's old friend. Curiously, Albie didn't acknowledge that someone among our party might know even more about the south.

Windley didn't speak up, instead busily inspecting his nails.

"Queen Merrin should use this opportunity to introduce herself properly," Albie added. "Diplomatic ties are vital, especially now." He bowed his head respectfully. "Does this suit you, My Queen?"

He was right, of course. Good relations would increase our chances of securing the Cove's assistance.

I glanced anxiously at the dimming sky. Still no messenger bird appeared.

"We'll do as Albie says," I decided aloud. "But we leave at first light tomorrow."

"Yes, Your Majesty," Rafe bowed.

"Yes, your exalted eminence," Windley mocked, bowing even deeper.

"Enough." Albie swatted the back of his head.

At the city's edge, we found a mercer's shop offering a changing room lined with delicate wares—handcrafted jewelry, ornate combs, mirrors, and woven shawls. Albie paid the shopkeeper to step out while Rafe and Windley guarded the entrance.

Dressing royally without my handmaids was tricky, but Albie proved skilled at their usual tasks, carefully lacing my gown and freeing my hair from its ties so it cascaded loosely down my back.

With only my mother's necklace—simple by royal standards—and an emerald ring to prove my identity, I examined myself in the mirror. Albie had done well; the dusty traveler had vanished, replaced by a proper queen.

"Thank you, Albie. Shall we?"

"One last thing, My Queen." He retrieved a delicate silver ivy crown from his pack—not my official crown, but one reserved for foreign visits. Beau had a similar one in gold. Of course, Albie had thought ahead. He gently placed it atop my hair, his expression warming. "A queen must always look the part."

Now, at least, I truly did.

I quickly dabbed winter-berry perfume at my neck, smoothed my gown, and stepped outside into the sunlight.

The shopkeeper immediately knelt.

"Oh, please don't," I urged. While I appreciated such devotion at home, here it felt undeserved.

"Really, thank you, but it isn't necessary." I turned, palm up. "Windley, my cloak?"

Nothing.

"*Windley?*" I repeated, sharper.

He just...stared. Hair bleached to startled yellow, mouth half-open, eyes fixed on me as though I'd sprouted horns.

Idiot, what now?

Rafe muttered exactly that, wrested the cloak from Windley's limp fingers, and settled it over my shoulders. The chill of his touch at my throat steadied me.

"At least someone's reliable," I huffed. "What was I saying about good help?"

Windley blinked hard, color returning to his cheeks along with a hasty cough. "Sorry—wasn't prepared."

"For what, my fashion?" I teased, suddenly unsure. Perhaps he thought primping frivolous with Beau still missing. "Look, I may be useless with swords, but presentation matters if we're to reach your queen. Sometimes decorum *is* the weapon."

A flicker—almost pain—crossed his face before he masked it. "Queen's right," he said quietly, rubbing the back of his neck. Then, louder: "Come on, Sir Albie'll have a conniption."

I watched him stride ahead, baffled. That playful spark had entirely vanished, replaced by something I didn't quite recognize.

"How would you explain that little exchange?" I murmured to Rafe, eyes still fixed on Windley's retreating figure.

Rafe, who'd obviously overheard but was suddenly fascinated by a nearby flock of gulls, shrugged. "Not really my place, Your Majesty."

Fair enough. Windley was all small talk; Rafe was none.

Yet, foolishly, I couldn't help but ask, "And are *you* all right, Rafe?"

That shadowed look from the inn lingered—easier to detect off horseback. Without looking away from the gulls, he countered softly, "Are *you*?"

I exhaled with hesitation. "Fair."

I didn't want to answer any more than he did.

The Cove bustled with vibrant life, the air rich with fish and salty sea spray, its marketplace brimming with color and chatter. Judging by the contented faces we passed, I assumed their queen to be fair and kind.

This city felt different from the Crag, yet strangely familiar —as if our queendoms were kindred spirits.

I should invite her to visit after this is all over, I thought.

Albie dropped a few familiar names with the castle guardswomen, and true to his word, they'd been expecting us. The iron gates rolled open smoothly.

I admired the craftsmanship, pressing my palm to a carved post before relinquishing my stag to a stable boy. Seashells and polished stones lined the path, glittering beneath the fading sun. The doors—intricately etched with crescent shapes, echoing the Cove's name—stood wide, beckoning us inward like a welcoming tide.

Rafe offered me his arm, escorting me up the steps with

confident ease, while Windley dallied behind, observing everything with his usual detached curiosity.

Waiting at the doors stood a jovial man who could've passed for Albie's twin—if Albie had been stouter, redder-cheeked, and infinitely louder.

"Alb, you bastard!" the man boomed, clapping Albie heartily on the back. "Welcome!"

"Delagos!" Albie returned the embrace warmly, his grin broad and genuine. "It's been far too long, old friend."

Delagos's laughter erupted in an uproar. "A quadrennial absence was bad enough—we've doubled it! That's practically criminal. Tell me you've still got the stomach for dragon-fired whiskey."

Albie shot me an apologetic glance.

I raised a brow. "Oh, please don't restrain yourself on my account."

I already knew Albie indulged in dragon-fired whiskey late at night—whenever he thought no one was watching.

Straightening with pride, Albie announced, "May I present My Queen, Merrin of the Crag."

Delagos bowed deeply. "A lovely queen for a lovely queendom—just like her mother."

"Charmed, Captain Delagos," I offered with practiced ease, my diplomatic smile firmly in place. "I wasn't aware you knew my mother. And I look forward to hearing stories of Albie's younger years."

"No, no. There'll be none of that," Albie huffed gruffly, flushing.

We'd see about that.

"These are our companions, Rafe and Windley," I introduced.

Delagos nodded politely to Rafe, but his gaze lingered on Windley, expression shifting curiously. "A Spirite lad, eh?

Haven't seen one of those in... Wait a second..." His eyes narrowed with sudden recognition. "This isn't the same one, is it?"

My turn to be surprised.

First, I'd just learned Windley's race—*Spirite*—though I'd never heard the term before.

Second, Delagos recognized him?

Windley gave the captain a curt salute before quickly turning away. "Shall we get started on that supply run?" Then, before I could utter even a single question, he grabbed Rafe's sleeve and hauled him down the steps.

That sneak!

He'd been to the Cove before and hadn't breathed a word.

I shot Albie an inquisitive glance.

"We can reminisce later, Delagos," Albie said, too carefully. His eyes flicked nervously toward me.

He was hiding something.

And clearly, it involved Windley.

I'd get to the bottom of it—eventually.

But for now, it was time to be a queen.

I folded my hands neatly, steadying myself. Meeting a new ruler felt frivolous knowing Beau was out there somewhere, still missing. But I trusted Albie to prepare us properly for the journey into the southern wilds.

Even if he was keeping secrets.

7

A SPIDER'S TEA

The interior of the Cove's castle was unlike anything
I'd anticipated.

And not in a good way.

I'd visited five other castles in my lifetime, each distinct,
each perfectly suited to the queen it housed. I'd learned quickly
that a ruler's castle revealed far more about her than words ever
could.

The Canyon's castle was rustic, favored goats roaming its
halls—Queen Ashwind always found solace in the unexpected.
The Clearing's was elegant, romantic, meticulously ordered
just like Beau herself, each tidy space imposing order on a
chaotic world. The Crystalline's? A glittering palace of excess,
its crystal-studded walls and shimmering chandeliers masking
Queen Esma's loneliness.

If castles provided windows into their queens, I was
suddenly no longer eager to meet whoever ruled here.

The warmth and charm of the bustling city vanished as
soon as we crossed the threshold, as if the very walls had stolen
the sun. A chill crept up my spine.

Bleak. Haunted. Frigid.

From the exterior, I'd expected something oceanic—sand, shells, bright reflections of Cove life. Instead, halls forged from glass and iron greeted me, their sharp edges and obsidian floors mirroring domed ceilings above, creating the illusion of an entire underworld stretched beneath us. Jagged lanterns cast a dull glow through auburn-stained glass.

Only our footsteps filled the silence.

Captain Delagos wrestled open reluctant doors to the throne room, revealing a narrow chamber beneath a rib-vaulted ceiling and frosted, arched windows. A spider's lair, I was certain.

At the far end, a fire roared, backlighting the spired throne —complete with black velvet cushions—upon which sat the spider herself.

Spider or not, she was the most striking creature I'd ever laid eyes on.

Smooth as polished onyx, her skin drank in the fire-glow and threw it back with a quiet luster, untouched by the Cove's salt-scouring winds. A waterfall of silver hair spilled past her waist like moonlight over obsidian, framing eyes the color of glacier ice—startlingly pale, unblinking, impossible to ignore. An hourglass gown of jet-black lace clung to her frame, every thread shimmer-stitched to catch the light. Even her talon-long nails—lacquered midnight and dusted with crystal flecks— matched the jeweled black of her lips. She looked hewn from dark glass, then edged in fire-light.

"I present Queen Sestilia of the Cove," Delagos bellowed, as though such an introduction was necessary.

Queen Sestilia required no fanfare; she effortlessly commanded attention. By contrast, I felt shabby.

Dirt-scrubbed or not, I felt every weary mile of our journey.

But Albie, ever proud, presented me without a hint of embarrassment over my road-worn state.

The queen rose from her velvet perch with deliberate, mesmerizing grace. "Queen Merrin, I'm thoroughly delighted to meet you," she said, excitement glinting in her pale eyes.

She defied every assumption I'd made about the Cove's ruler.

I managed a reply without openly staring. "And you as well."

"Why don't we leave the men to their diversions while you and I get acquainted?" Her teeth gleamed invitingly.

Delagos looked as if he'd awaited precisely this invitation.

"Yes, please, enjoy yourselves, Albie. We'll be just fine." The lie slipped out smooth.

Truthfully, standing beside the spider queen prickled my nerves. I had no idea how to navigate conversation with someone whose tastes so starkly clashed with my own.

"Come," she said, turning gracefully. "Let's have tea in the library. Do you like tiger spice? I'll have it prepared."

I hesitated only a fraction. "I've never had tiger spice, but I've yet to meet a tea I didn't like."

Another lie.

Several teas displeased me greatly—tomato mint, cloudberry, and whatever questionable concoction Beau had once brewed from acorns.

Sestilia's library mirrored the throne room's vampiric tendencies: vaulted ceilings, towering shelves stacked neatly with unread tomes and grimoires. Most peculiar was a large, empty portrait frame dominating the back wall.

She settled at a wrought-iron table, where a maid had arranged tea and cakes.

I lifted a delicate painted teacup, inhaling its aromatic

steam. The scent was unfamiliar, the flavor nippy yet sweet. Whatever it was—

"It's good."

This time, truthfully spoken.

"Isn't it?" Sestilia's gaze pierced mine, her pointed nails tapping delicately against porcelain. "I truly am delighted to host you, Merrin, even briefly. You're the first queen to visit since I took the throne."

"I doubt it's lack of desire," I said carefully. "Your queendom is simply quite distant. We tend to send envoys instead."

"Indeed." She sipped her tea elegantly, not disturbing the crystals decorating her lips. "Delagos says you're out shopping for festival wares?"

The cover story.

"Yes. An annual celebration—the gilded moon. My guards and I procure trinkets for the queens' tent."

"Charming that you've deigned to do so personally."

The words were sugared; the edge beneath them was steel.

"Sestilia," I changed course, "your castle's decor seems strikingly...different from the rest of the city. Any particular reason?"

"Oh, goodness, yes! Thank you for noticing." She set down her cup, pleased. "I've been diligently working to correct this wretched thing. Once finished here, I'll move on to the city."

I nearly coughed. The city wasn't what needed fixing.

She gestured grandly toward the empty frame. "I'm undoing my predecessor's poor taste."

"Your predecessor decorated with empty frames?"

She laughed, musical yet chilling. "Goodness, no! That's where her portrait hung—my sister, the trueborn heir."

"Oh." My fingers tightened around my teacup. "What happened to her?"

She traced her cup's rim absently, tilting her head. Ice-blue eyes locked onto mine, waiting for me to understand.

"She...plummeted from her bedroom window."

There it was.

"And landed on the spikes below." A too-perfect smile curled her lips as she sipped daintily. "Such a shame."

"I—I'm sorry?"

The scrape of porcelain against porcelain as she set down her teacup was louder than the words she uttered next. "Don't be. She was quite the bitch."

That goddess-damned, diamond-bright expression again.

"Oh. Well, I suppose that changes things," I muttered.

My sarcasm was entirely wasted; Sestilia's smile only deepened.

"Splendid! You understand. So few do. I feel we shall become great friends."

Goddess above, had she even heard me?

My throat tightened.

After tea, the spider queen looped her arm through mine, casually resting her head upon my shoulder as she guided me deeper into her web, offering a personal tour of the castle. She stopped frequently, pointing out portraits of other royal relatives, detailing each one's untimely or suspicious end with alarming fondness while I offered tight, sarcastic responses that only seemed to deepen her affections.

I prayed fervently for an interruption.

At last, one mercifully arrived.

One of her handmaids approached, eyes lowered respectfully, not daring to meet Sestilia's icy gaze. "I have prepared rooms for our guests, My Queen, on the fourth floor."

Sestilia clasped my hands. "Isn't it wonderful, mouse? Queen Merrin and I are already the best of friends."

Untrue. That title belonged solely to Beau.

The maid continued, "The Queen of the Crag's guards have returned and await her in the foyer."

Thank the heavens.

Back in the cavernous foyer, my footsteps echoed across the marble, and the sight of familiar guards loosened the knot in my chest. I headed straight for Windley; the faint twitch at the corner of his mouth said he was enjoying my fluster far too much.

"*Never leave my side again,*" I whispered.

I braced for a smart remark, but his hand slid to the small of my back, fingertips catching a fold of fabric and drawing me a breath closer.

Heat rose under my collar. We fenced with words; touch was never his opening move.

Before I could read the change in his eyes, Sestilia swept in, silver hair and jewel-bright smile stealing every gaze—including Windley's. His hand dropped, and the moment scattered like dust on a draft.

I had no chance to offer introductions. Sestilia clasped her hands. "You have a *Spirite*? How *delicious*! I've only met one once before—on an outing to the southern caravans. Such *captivating* creatures."

Windley's race was rare indeed.

And she spoke as if he belonged to me.

As though he'd ever allow such a thing.

Windley didn't react outright, though a muscle in his jaw tightened before he bowed politely.

Sestilia turned to me with glowing delight. "Might I borrow him tonight? To play with?"

Had I anything in my throat, I might have choked.

Windley remained silent—only his eyes slid sideways to meet mine, the barest question in their dark depths—waiting to see what I would do.

Really? No snarky response from him? Wasn't he eager to jump at the chance to *play* with someone like Queen Sestilia? Though with her, "play" likely meant pleasure, pain—or both. Perhaps he sensed danger beneath the surface.

"I'm afraid I must decline," I said. "He's sworn to another queen."

Sestilia glided closer, black lace whispering at her heels. "Then the choice is his." She tugged Windley's scarf, drawing him near, her lips inches from his—before abruptly turning to face me. "Unless *you* intend to play with him tonight?"

This time, I did choke, though there was nothing in my throat.

After, I squared my shoulders, determined to save Windley from an unknown fate. "I'm afraid I'm not fond of sharing."

A small curve tugged at her lips before widening, luminous as cut glass. "You and I are practically the same person, Merrin!"

A horrible judge of character, clearly. Yet her own ego protected her from the truth: we were, in fact, nothing alike.

"You three must be tired," Sestilia relented finally. "Go, get settled. I'll have the help fetch you for dinner."

We wasted no time departing.

As we ascended the stairs, Windley trotted beside me, roots of his hair shifting from sunny yellow to burnished copper. "It seems you've found a bigger, badder lion than yourself, Queen Merrin. Careful not to get bitten."

"Oh, I'm certain if anyone gets bitten here, it'll be you," I said, relieved that he was acting normal after all that awkwardness downstairs.

That familiar ease had returned to his stride.

Meanwhile, my pulse hadn't fully steadied from Sestilia's unsettling advances toward him, nor from the odd intensity I'd glimpsed in his eyes as his hand found my back. In all our years of casual flirtation, I couldn't recall being so distinctly aware of his closeness.

"And how was your queen time with the other queen?" he asked. "Get the *decorum* out of your system?"

Good. Expected. Totally expected behavior from him.

And good on him for seeing beyond beauty that I suspected was the very definition of skin-deep.

"Besides terrifying, and that I'm nearly certain she tossed her own sister off a balcony?" I answered, mindful of the steward ahead. Somehow, I'd earned the mad queen's favor, and I intended to stay firmly on her good side—lest I end up tossed off a balcony myself.

Rafe's curiosity was piqued. "Is that what she told you?"

"In not so many words."

Windley hummed thoughtfully. "Too bad you rescued me. It would've been either the best or worst night of my life."

"I can still arrange it, if you'd like."

He slung an elbow over my shoulder. "Thank you, no. I'm good."

This banter was a welcome distraction from the real reason we'd come. But now that we were away from the spider queen, reality felt heavier again.

Silence fell as we walked on through the hellish castle toward our rooms.

"Windley, about the widowbirds..."

"Mm?"

"The ones we sent to the Clearing for backup."

"Mm-hm."

"They would've arrived that first day, right? And the cavalry would've set off immediately. Even if we stopped here or there, they would've kept going." I hesitated. "So even if we..." I swallowed. "Even with a stop like this...others may reach Beau first."

Windley slid his arm from my shoulder, turning to face me fully. There was something knowing—something soft—in his eyes. "Yes," he said. "The others will ride through the night, searching high and low until they find the lost queen."

Exactly what I needed to hear. Because the thought of Beau—clever, strong, beautiful Beau—at the mercy of someone unknown...

Windley shook his head, voice steady and sure. "We have a reason to be here. The formalities aren't a waste, and one night in this queen's lair won't determine Queen Beau's fate. This is what it means to divide and conquer. It's standard, and we're just one envoy. Even if we fail, the others will succeed."

His assurances landed this time, unraveling the knot in my chest.

"Hear that, Rafe?" I called over my shoulder, making a conscious effort to include him.

But instead of the usual indifference, Rafe's expression appeared troubled.

"Rafe? Are you upset?"

Before Rafe could answer, the steward halted abruptly. "Here you are," he announced, gesturing to two heavy doors at the end of the fourth-floor hall.

That was when I noticed it—the knife at the steward's belt. It glowed faintly red, like the embers of a dying fire.

Another metal-enchanter, like Rafe?

As if sensing my stare, the steward hastily swished his cloak over the weapon, concealing it from view.

Rafe bowed his head almost too quickly, as though he couldn't bear the weight of whatever emotion lay behind his eyes. Before I could even get a proper read on him—he turned and disappeared into the guards' quarters.

Strange, unsettled behavior from him again.

Windley moved to follow, swinging his satchel of goods into the room behind Rafe.

Like hell I'd let him escape that easily.

"Not so fast." I grabbed him by the hood. "*You* have some explaining to do."

8
HIDDEN TALENTS

I had no intention of letting Windley evade me as easily as Rafe had.

With determination, I ushered the incorrigible guard into my chamber, which—by some small mercy—was pleasantly untouched by Sestilia's eccentricities. The room was bright and inviting, draped in tasteful fabrics, with polished mahogany furniture. A relief, considering I'd half-expected velvet-clad gloom.

Windley folded his arms and lounged casually against the wall beside the door, eyes lit with familiar mischief. "What do you want with me, lion queen?"

I weighed my angle. If I let him, he'd dance around every question; tonight I needed straight edges, not banter.

Windley was maddening, magnetic—my favorite sparring partner when Beau wasn't around—but I had never pressed him for history. For years I'd let his past remain a locked box; lately the hinges looked loose. Sestilia's hungry interest, the captain's cool reception, Windley's own stray remarks about "being from the south"...

They'd all turned a passing itch into a genuine need to know.

"I have questions," I said at last. "And for once, I'd like answers, not riddles."

He tilted his head, more intrigued than threatened.

"Firstly," I began, "Spirite. What does it mean?"

Windley sank lazily into a sitting chair, sprawling as if he had no intention of moving anytime soon. "Firstly," he mimicked, "why do you suddenly care?"

"Perhaps because I'd never *even heard* the word until today?"

He twisted the blackstone ring on his finger, eyes sliding sidelong toward me.

I perched on the edge of the bed, ignoring the unfamiliar flutter building in my chest. "Consider my curiosity piqued. You've always been something of a mystery, Windley. Now I've glimpsed a few enticing details, and I want to know more about the guard who hails from the land of giant skeletons—*something you conveniently neglected to mention* even after all this time."

"Remind me when you ever asked?"

"How would I have known to ask that?"

"Well...what if you don't like what you hear?"

"My opinion of you is already far from spotless."

He chuckled, though shadows flickered briefly behind his eyes.

"Oh, come on, Windley," I pressed. "Is there some reason you don't want me to know? Perhaps I should try *commanding* it out of you. See if that works."

He didn't respond as expected anyway. He looked away grimly, saying almost absently, "Lest we forget, I owe you no fealty, queenie..."

I sensed it—a hesitation that made me suddenly feel like a bully. Beneath his stubbornness, something else lay hidden.

Oh.

In the following silence, I eased up from the bed, pulling the ivy crown from my hair and placing it carefully on the bedside table as I closed the distance between us. Windley's eyes lifted, questioning yet guarded, as I rested my hand atop his head. His tousled hair was unexpectedly silky beneath my touch. Warmth radiated from the roots.

"We've known each other for eight years, Windley," I said, voice quiet with genuine care. "I know enough about you to trust you implicitly. Whatever your past, nothing could change that. You don't ever have to tell me what you are or where you come from, but if you decide to—just know that I'll listen without judgment."

His dark-lined eyes searched mine and—for a heartbeat—his carefully crafted bravado broke. He went perfectly still beneath my touch.

Then, without warning, he snatched my wrist with startling swiftness, holding my hand to him before I could withdraw.

His gaze locked onto mine, fierce with a rarely shown honesty. "I'll tell you, Merrin," he whispered, heat in his words sending a shiver racing over my skin. Then he blinked, as if realizing himself too late. "Fuck," he breathed, the word escaping on a shaky exhale. "Sorry. Queen Merrin."

My pulse quickened. My breath caught at the intimacy of the contact, but I didn't draw away.

"I do hail from the queenless lands, though I left them long ago," he began quietly.

"Eight years ago?" My voice emerged meeker than intended, breathless, distracted by the realization that my fingers were still threading carefully through his hair—slow, cautious strokes far too tender to be casual.

Awareness flooded me, sudden and direct. My stomach dipped, embarrassment burning through me as I jerked my hand away.

What in goddess's name had I just done? *Caressed* a guard? Caressed *Windley* of all guards?

Windley didn't react—only loosened his grip slightly, fingers shifting to cradle the back of my hand, tracing whisper-soft patterns over my skin like he'd done it to me a hundred times before.

The touch was gentle, hypnotic. Intentional.

A slow inhale stilled in my chest as warmth unfurled where our skin touched, something deep, lush, and dizzying, sinking past my skin, beneath muscle, pooling in my bones.

Like magic.

That couldn't be right.

I blinked, trying to clear my mind, but my body was already responding, leaning subtly closer to him before I realized what I was doing.

"Spirites can draw life force from others," Windley whispered, voice suddenly like a velvet caress. "Steal it, repurpose it for ourselves. Passion, of course, being the strongest conduit."

A shuddering breath escaped me as his thumb traced the sensitive skin of my palm, sending electric pulses through my limbs, awakening nerves I hadn't known existed.

"Why does it feel so...?" My voice failed, thick in my throat.

"Good?" His eyes burned into mine, mesmerizing. "To coax you deeper. The more you crave my touch, the easier it is to steal your essence." He paused, voice dropping into something darker. "Do you crave my touch?"

"Yes," I said without thinking.

"Mm. It's a lingering instinct from what we once were," he murmured, his gaze intensifying.

"And what was that?"

"*Hunters*. Long ago, before we evolved beyond base instincts, humans were our prey. Even now, a delicate balance remains. Lose control, and a Spirite like me could drain their partner in a single moment of ecstasy."

My pulse thundered. "That's—"

"A cruel irony." His gaze swept over me, dark and a little unfamiliar. "Yes, the more fondness someone has for you, the easier it becomes to steal their vitality. It doesn't even require full-blown love or desire—just enough emotion to slip past defenses."

A thrill rippled down my spine. This revelation should have alarmed me, but instead it heightened the intensity of his touch, honed every breath, every beat of my heart.

"I'll stop now," he said, almost protectively. "Brace yourself —the withdrawal can be jarring."

"Ready," I whispered, breathless.

He released me, and the room spun, and the warmth receded, leaving an instant hollow ache where his touch had been. My fingertips flexed involuntarily, craving his return before I curled them tightly into a fist.

"And that," he said softly, eyes glinting faintly, "is why the Queen of the Cove wanted to *borrow* me tonight." His voice grew hesitant, almost vulnerable. "Tell me, Merrin...does this frighten you? Now that you finally know?"

I stared at my own hands.

Surprised? Yes. Fearful of such power existing at all? Certainly. But afraid of Windley himself?

"Never," I said, threading my fingers through his. "I could never fear you." The first shock was giving way to fascination, so I turned his hands palm-up, studying them. "But you've been sitting on a gift like that? You could bend half the realm. With your ego, how have you settled for plain old 'knight'?"

Windley's smirk widened, half proud, half relieved. "I should've guessed you, of all people, would take it in stride."

"We've touched a hundred times and it never even felt remotely like *that*."

"Not...remotely?" His smirk faltered, then softened. "Tell me how it felt for you."

Heat climbed my cheeks. "Like...a gentle tug, then a rush of warmth. That instant when honesty blooms and you're ready to lean into something lush and inviting." I stopped, a new thought sparking. "Beau must use you for interrogations."

He gave a low laugh. "Did you feel ready to spill every secret, Majesty?"

More than that—I'd felt compelled to crawl into his lap, tangle my fingers in his hair, and tell him every hidden thought I'd ever had.

In truth, it felt perilously close to falling in love. But that was something I didn't yet fully recognize—nor could I afford to.

"So Beau does know?" I asked instead, shifting back to safer territory.

Seriousness briefly shadowed his eyes. "For her safety, yes," he replied. "Which is why I would also ask your discretion."

It made perfect sense why Windley kept his abilities hidden. Coercion, intoxication, truth-telling—such gifts in less honorable hands would spell catastrophe.

Thank goddess it was only Windley.

Reassured by my obvious acceptance, Windley reclined deeper into the chair, stretching lazily like a cat basking in sunlight. "I've thought for some time how that exchange might go. Perhaps your stubbornness isn't entirely insufferable, lion queen. That was surprisingly cathartic."

I grinned victoriously. "Glad you've reached that conclusion, Windley, because now I have countless more questions! Starting with—you must have exceptional control. None of it leaks out?"

"That wasn't an invitation." He sidestepped my assault, standing to roll his shoulders deliberately as he bluntly deflected my enthusiasm. "And *leak*? Not quite. What time is it, anyway? Shouldn't you be preparing for dinner?"

Indeed, the chamber had dimmed, twilight seeping serenely through the windows.

Yet how was I supposed to focus on gowns and dinner etiquette after such revelations?

"How do you expect me to think of formalities after witnessing such hidden magic?"

He moved smoothly across the room, pulling open the wardrobe with dramatic flair. "Easily enough, considering decorum is vital to our mission." Windley selected a striking sapphire gown and tossed it casually onto the bed. "There. Perfect. Now I'm leaving, so hurry and dress yourself."

I lifted a brow at his sudden rush. "You have other powers, don't you? Your changing hair—can you control that too?"

"Perhaps," he replied cryptically, retreating toward the door, radiating renewed energy now that his darkest secret was exposed. "Or perhaps my hair simply reflects my *ever-shifting moods*." His grin was utterly mischievous. "Why don't we save that line of inquiry for another evening? You have a dinner to attend, and the haunted staff here expect their royal guest suitably dressed for their she-devil's feast."

With a lazy bow, he slipped out—but just before the door fully closed, his head reappeared, hand gripping the frame in roguish fashion.

"My hair, Merrin?" His smirk turned dangerously alluring. "Of everything you've learned tonight, *that's* what claws at you?"

He held my gaze just long enough to ignite a slow-burning heat beneath my ribs, leaving behind a tantalizing ache long after he'd gone.

His power?

9

A LOVE SO DEADLY

I put considerably more effort into my appearance for Sestilia's dinner than I normally would have, knowing exactly what I was up against. I wasn't foolish enough to try outshining her—I knew that was impossible—but I wanted to hold on to at least a sliver of regality. I wouldn't have myself known in her court as the squalid queen of the north.

The guest washroom was generously stocked, the bathwater luxuriously warm. I cleaned myself properly this time—a vast improvement from the vagabond wipe-down earlier at the mercer's shop. The gown Windley had chosen was perfect: elegant, appropriate, and fitted remarkably well. After years tending to queens, most guards developed a sense for such things. Albie was proof enough of that.

Likely, the dress had once belonged to Sestilia's sister, as it certainly didn't match Sestilia's eldritch tastes. Besides, it was doubtful I would've fit into anything of hers.

The great hall was designed in much the same style as the rest of the spider queen's domain. By the time dinner was served, the sun had surrendered to darkness, leaving only robust fireplaces at either end to illuminate the room. Candle-adorned chandeliers suspended from the vaulted ceiling offered little more than decorative light.

The first half of dinner was manageable.

Sestilia, seated mercifully far at the table's opposite end, wore another lavish black gown, this one scattered with crystals that reflected the firelight like captured stars. The distance made conversation difficult—thank goddess—and allowed me to admire her beauty safely.

She was infinitely more pleasant seen than heard.

Unfortunately, my luck wouldn't hold the entire evening.

Lonely, apparently, she scooted down to my end of the table by the third course.

"I love when they leave the heads on," she purred, poking at her food.

"Certainly reminds you exactly what you're eating," I said, failing to keep the distaste from my voice.

"Precisely!" she replied, delighted.

Regrettably, there was no one around to save me.

Rafe, Windley, and a handful of castle staff were lined obediently against the wall while we ate, and the noble Sir Albie was still gallivanting elsewhere with Captain Delagos.

"I'm so melancholy you'll be leaving tomorrow, Merrin. Promise you'll visit again soon?"

The dazzling queen rested her head on my shoulder, her shimmering hair spilling opulently over both our seats.

"Just as soon as I'm able."

A loose promise—room enough for loopholes.

"I should warn you, Sestilia," I added carefully, "we'll probably leave at dawn to stay on schedule. I don't expect you to rise to see us off."

"Oh, goodness, no. My skin needs its rest," she said, patting her perfectly smooth cheeks.

The knowledge that this would likely be my final interaction with her was enough to push me through the rest of the meal.

What a shame. Judging by my bedchamber, I might have genuinely befriended her sister, the Cove's rightful heir.

Sestilia kept me long after the final course, whispering disturbing things to which I responded with sarcasm—yet somehow, infatuation deepened in her frigid gaze.

When at last I managed to peel myself away, the final thing I told her was, "My time here has been unlike anything I've ever experienced."

It was no lie.

Moving on—the crucial event of that evening wasn't dinner or even my last encounter with the Cove's queen; rather, it was what unfolded later, in the deepest hours of night.

But first—

"Your Majesty, that took forever."

Rafe voiced a rare opinion as we approached the hallway leading to our rooms, rubbing his chest in discomfort.

"I know. Trust me, it was as painful for me as it was for you."

"Of course even she liked you, Queen Merrin," Windley said, rolling his eyes as he folded his arms.

"Oh my, was that a compliment from one of the Clearing's most smug? Tell me another, would you?"

Rafe had no patience for our banter. "We set off at first light, yes?" He peered out a nearby window where the moon hung low in the sky.

"Even sooner, if possible. I've already alerted Queen Sestilia of our plans. Now it depends on Albie. Track him down and make sure he retires at a reasonable hour, would you, Rafe?"

As the tapping of Rafe's footsteps faded into the shadows at the hallway's end, I turned to bid Windley goodnight—only to find him already watching me.

It was the same look he'd given me earlier, outside the mercer's shop.

I narrowed my eyes. "I know I must look unnatural since you don't see me dressed up often, but you have to stop staring, Windley. You're unsettling my royal composure." I rested a hand on my hip. "Which, when done to a queen, is punishable by death."

It wasn't.

"That's what you think? That I find your appearance unnatural?" He released a soft chuckle, pushing open the door to his room. Before stepping inside, he tossed a prowling smirk over his shoulder. "I chose wisely with the gown."

The latch clicked shut, leaving me standing there alone.

I stared blankly at the carved wood for a moment, blinking.

Oh.

It suddenly occurred to me—perhaps he'd stared not because I looked strange.

Maybe he thought I looked...*appealing*.

Genuinely. For all his teasing.

Odd musings accompanied me as I drifted off to sleep, replaying the sensation of Windley's magic fluttering through my veins.

Sleep ambushed me swiftly this time. And just like back at the forest fort, I thought I glimpsed its gleaming eyes watching me from the corner of the room—

From the very chair Windley had occupied earlier.

I couldn't have been asleep more than a few hours before someone shook me awake, hands insistent at my shoulders.

"My Queen."

It was Albie—voice hushed, smelling only faintly of ale. Perhaps he hadn't indulged as much as I'd assumed.

The room was shadowy, lit solely by a sliver of moonlight leaking through a crack in the curtains.

"My Queen," Albie repeated, urgency honing each word. "Get up. We must leave immediately."

Rafe was already in the room, hastily gathering my belongings, with Windley beside him, both weapons drawn.

Instead of a sword, Windley favored two short hatchets— though I'd never seen him actually use them in battle before. Now, they were ready, the muscles in his shoulders coiled as if prepared to spring at any threat.

I bolted upright, heartbeat thundering, blood rushing wildly enough to drown out the room's silence.

"Are we under attack?"

"Not yet," Albie said, thrusting my riding clothes into my arms. "But we soon will be."

Legs unsteady, I took the garments around the changing divider, fumbling with ties as my hands trembled, fighting to still them. "By whom? And why?"

"It seems you made too favorable an impression on the Queen of the Cove," Windley answered, poking his head cautiously into the hall before glancing back at me. "She doesn't intend to let you leave. The steward who showed us to our rooms just warned Rafe."

I nearly dropped the ties in my hands. "What do you mean? She intends to kill me? Or imprison me?"

That would be an act of war against a protected queendom —a reckless gamble.

"Neither," Albie said grimly, gathering the last of my things before guiding me into the hall behind Windley and Rafe. "She intends to wound you severely enough to render you bedridden."

"And make it appear accidental," added Rafe, ushering me swiftly down the shadowed hall.

I dug my heels into the floor, breath coming in shallow bursts. "Is she out of her goddess-damned mind?"

Untoward of a queen to curse, perhaps, but entirely warranted. Just who did Sestilia think she was?! I'd tolerated her lunacy long enough. I wouldn't flee—I'd confront her directly.

"New plan," I said firmly. "We're not running. I intend to give that madwoman a piece of my mind!"

Albie blocked my path, expression carved from stone. The other guards hovered behind him, waiting—field protocol bound their swords first to their Knight-Captain, and only then to their crown.

"No. Your safety comes first—even if I must disobey."

"Albie!"

"Think of Queen Beau," Windley cut in, voice low, urgent. "That's our primary goal, isn't it?"

The mention of Beau snapped me back to reality.

I forced myself to refocus. "Does Captain Delagos know about this?"

"Absolutely not," Albie growled softly.

"Then why not ask him for help? She cannot run unchecked. Guards must hold their mistress accountable—I'd expect the same from any of you!"

"You're right, My Queen, and wise as ever," Albie said, hand unrelenting on my shoulder as he nudged me forward. "But Delagos is incapacitated at the moment."

Meaning he'd drunk himself into a stupor.

"The ones coming aren't royal guard," said Rafe, pulling me

down the servant's staircase, his frosted blade leaving trails of cold behind us. "She's hired assassins."

"To break you enough to keep you from walking," Windley added.

"And that's supposed to look accidental?" I demanded.

"There are elixirs for memory loss from the southern wilds," Windley said tersely. "I imagine she planned to use one."

I nearly tripped over my own feet. "How would she even obtain such a thing?"

"The Cove monitors the southern border," he explained. "Traders pass through."

A cold weight settled in my chest.

Had she known at dinner—as she rested her head on my shoulder—that she planned to *maim* me later?

The thought ignited a furious heat beneath my skin.

How ironic that the most beautiful packages often concealed the most twisted souls.

"*Hold.*" Albie hissed the command, yanking me behind a corner as Rafe and Windley fell silently into position.

Sure enough, footsteps echoed along the glassy floor. Two sets, approaching fast.

Albie tipped his head toward Rafe and Windley, who instantly understood.

The stairwell was dim, lit only by a high window, yet what I saw filled me with newfound admiration for my guards. This was the first time I'd faced true danger as a queen. The first time I'd seen them fight.

It was incredible—graceful, precise, hypnotic. Sworn to different queendoms, Rafe and Windley moved in perfect harmony, anticipating each other's actions like partners in a deadly dance.

As the hooded assassins surged forth, spears gleaming wickedly, Rafe struck first. His chilled blade sliced through darkness—but before it landed, its frozen twin struck quicker. An echo of his sword, transparent yet lethal. The assassin braced for steel but never felt it—only the freezing bite of its phantom. She gasped as the cold blade shattered against her chest like breaking ice, stumbling backward down the stairs, clutching her wound. Rafe's sword was merely a decoy for the frost enchantments within.

Meanwhile, Windley engaged the second assassin. He didn't rely on magic—only speed, precision, and an abundance of arrogance. His hatchets spun fluidly, seeming weightless above his palms. As his opponent lunged, Windley let one fly— a blur of steel—dodging smoothly past the thrust of her spear. He instantly swung upward with the other blade. She dodged— but that had never been his target. The first hatchet had already severed her weapon. The arrowed tip clattered uselessly to the floor.

Windley caught her hood, yanking her close, his voice razor-sharp. "Run now, or I won't let you."

The assassin didn't hesitate. Pivoting, she bolted, leaping over her fallen comrade and vanishing into the darkness below.

The fight ended in mere seconds. Both guards sheathed their weapons, turning expectantly toward Albie and me.

"There may be more," Rafe cautioned quietly. "Stay alert."

Never had I seen the young magician so alive with energy.

And Windley? Who knew Windley was actually *dangerous*? He wasn't merely cocky—he was ruthless, controlled. Now that I'd glimpsed his lethality, I couldn't pretend otherwise. I could never, ever let him know I thought of him that way. It would go straight to his head.

Their weapons weren't just for slashing vines or scaring off bandits. They were capable protectors of the Crown.

"Rafe, take the lead," ordered Albie. "Windley lad, cover the rear. I'll stay with the queen."

They moved as if they'd done this a thousand times.

At the bottom of the stairs, a lone assassin stood guard. Windley dispatched them with a single hatchet—not a drop of hesitation.

Then we stole through the pantry, out the servants' entrance, and into the clear night air. A chorus of crickets greeted us as we raced for the stables.

Windley's unsheathed weapon glinted in the moonlight as he moved beside me. "Are you all right, Your Majesty?"

"I'm fine," I replied, and because he seemed genuinely humble, I added, "I won't say I'm impressed by all that I've seen tonight, but...perhaps you have hidden a few talents. Maybe you're not all talk after all."

His smirk widened, teeth glinting like the edge of his ax. "You have no *idea* the things I'm capable of."

"No. Stop." Yet there was no resisting that grin. Perhaps it was the thrill of the night, but despite myself, my own smile tugged insistently at my lips, growing without permission.

In the stable, I found Ruckus unharmed and unchained, hugging him around his sturdy neck.

"Thank goddess that steward took a liking to you, chap." Windley patted Rafe's sweaty back before mounting his own stag. His ax flashed once more as he nudged his stag into motion beside me. Moonlight silvered the windswept ends of his hair, turning them nearly white. Behind us, Rafe pressed a palm to his chest, lips set but saying nothing; when our eyes met, he gave a curt nod that said *ride*.

So we did—four shadows skimming through the sleeping city, hooves muffled on sand-dusted streets, until the last lantern winked out behind us and only the pale road ahead remained.

10

EVERY COLOR

We rode through the rest of the night and into morning. Albie had obtained detailed intel from Captain Delagos, including a rudimentary map of the beyonds, and the wrinkled knight led us dutifully across uninhabited fields toward what he described as "a forest of extraordinary heights." Fitting, considering our ultimate goal was a mountain made of giants' bones.

Ruckus, clearly relieved to be uncooped, trotted obediently behind Albie's stag. He was behaving far better than before our arrival at the Cove—likely afraid mischief might see him penned again.

White-haired Windley kept pace at my side, with Rafe bringing up the rear. Though exhausted from lack of sleep, we rode with urgency, distancing ourselves from the spider's queendom and moving steadily toward a fairer, kinder queen lost in the wilds beyond.

For a long stretch, I simmered silently over Sestilia's audacity. That bitch.

How did she expect to rule with the temperament of a cornered viper?

Yet, the more I thought about her devious plot, the more I recalled how easily Rafe and Windley had bested her assassins.

It left me smug—even if I'd contributed nothing myself—and I repeatedly imagined telling her off. Over the years, I'd won countless arguments in my head that never saw daylight.

At first, we encountered towns and isolated houses scattered across the fields, thinning until they vanished altogether. The final queen-ruled settlement we passed was little more than a weary inn and a handful of lonesome farms—a sorry sight for tired travelers.

A single, solitary signpost marked the end of the civilized world, pointing back the way we'd come.

I'd expected something grander—a ravine, perhaps, or a bridge.

But the landscape continued unchanged, as if the shift from the queens' territories into the unknown was merely an illusion.

Still, I was grateful for that lone marker—especially the single scarlet ribbon tied around it—confirming the Clearing's cavalry had indeed passed through.

Windley had been right; others were out there searching for Beau. Her fate didn't rest solely upon us.

Despite the few hours of rest, we covered significant ground before finally stopping to make camp, for the first time on our journey.

Gone were the comforts of taverns or inns—instead, we chose a suitable patch of land amidst a grove of dripping willow trees—my favorite kind.

I loved how their buds gathered like raindrops, forever reaching toward their roots with longing. Near the Crag, there was one solitary willow where I'd often played as a child, forcing Albie to crouch for tea beneath its drooping branches.

Here, an entire grove wept gracefully, offering decent cover.

"Brings back memories, doesn't it, Albie?"

"Too bad we forgot the teacakes," he replied fondly.

Windley's voice rose eagerly. "I want a Baby Queen Merrin story. Tell us one, Sir Albie—something deliciously incriminating."

Albie scratched his mustache. "Let's see, now..."

"Albie," I warned.

"There was the time she snuck into the wine cellar and got drunk all alone," he mused, "or perhaps when she hid that orphan boy in her bureau like a stray kitten."

"That's enough," I said, giving Albie a pointed look. I wasn't about to hand Windley ammunition so easily.

"*Later,*" Albie mouthed—to Windley's wicked delight.

I tended the fire while the two of them began pitching our tent, and Rafe prepared dinner nearby.

"In all honesty," I called over my shoulder, noticing them unpacking a second canvas, "isn't it a waste to pitch two tents?"

Albie paused, head tilted. "A highness shouldn't share quarters with her guards, My Queen."

"We did precisely that at every tavern along the way," I argued.

Not to mention the countless times Albie had nodded off mid-storybook in my own chambers.

He exhaled heavily through his nose. "It's different here. You'd be sharing ground directly with your guard—particularly young hounds like these two." He gestured at Windley, then at Rafe.

Windley feigned offense, while Rafe ignored him, slicing carrots with healer-like precision.

"But Beau and I wouldn't choose guards we didn't trust with our lives," I insisted. "Why hassle with two tents every single night? It isn't as if anyone would know."

Albie sighed in resignation. "Your command, My Queen."

"One tent," I decreed firmly. "In the interest of saving time —and Beau. And since you're so concerned, Sir Albie, you'll sleep as the barrier between the 'hounds' and me."

With the fire properly crackling, I approached Rafe to see if he needed help with his stew.

He declined, predictably. Still, I persisted, crouching beside his lean silhouette as he tended the cooking pot.

He was quiet.

Always quiet, but tonight unusually so.

Pensive. Reserved.

"Rafe?"

His whiskey-brown eyes flicked up. "Your Majesty?"

"What's wrong, Rafe? I've noticed it—at the Cove, at the castle...even before then. Something weighs on you."

Instead of answering, he nudged a cluster of carrots around the pot with the ladle, counting them under his breath—as if their orange parade required total concentration. "Please don't worry about me, Your Majesty." He kept stirring, eyes fixed on the vegetables.

I hadn't expected a confession, but the way he marshaled every carrot into line said more than words.

I rested my hand on his shoulder as I stood. "If you ever change your mind, I'm a good keeper of secrets, Rafe. I've always cared for you, and I always will."

He'd been my guard for years yet never once opened up.

I let my hand drop.

"By the way, I was glad to finally see your powers in battle."

"Luna's powers," he corrected softly.

Luna.

He was the only one I'd ever heard use that name—the only one whose connection to the moon felt nearly prayerful.

"Luna's powers," I echoed thoughtfully.

Turning, I caught Windley watching us from afar.

I'd felt it—that overt stare of his.

He'd finished packing away the second tent and now stood just beyond the fire's glow, half-hidden beneath the veil of a nearby willow, a forgotten bundle of kindling at his feet.

When our eyes met, he parted the willow's branches like a curtain, beckoning me with a finger.

I hesitated briefly, then sighed, brushing dirt from my hands as I stepped away from Rafe.

Branches whispered against my shoulders as I approached, the fire's warmth dimming behind me as I stepped beneath the willow's shadow.

"You know you shouldn't beckon a queen willy-nilly," I quipped.

"Please, oh highest of highnesses, grace me with an audience." Then, dropping the theatrics entirely: "But not here. Come with me."

Windley tugged lightly at my elbow, guiding me through the curtain of willows and into the open expanse beyond.

The dense canopy of trees thinned behind us, opening onto land untouched by civilization—an endless expanse beneath a sky blazing with the last breath of sunset.

"You know," Windley began casually, nodding toward the horizon, where day melted slowly into dusk, "if you look closely enough, you can see every color out there."

My eyes brightened eagerly. "That's exactly what I always say!"

Oh.

He was mocking me.

Windley's brow arched, slow and deliberate. "It's not as though you've mentioned it a *thousand* times before."

I exhaled sharply through my nose. "You're such an ass."

He tilted his head. "And you're predictable."

I sighed, giving him a pointed look. "Did you actually have something important to discuss, or did you drag me out here solely to mock my appreciation of sunsets?"

Windley's amusement wavered, and the easy banter fell away. His expression cooled, shadows settling behind his eyes. "Actually," he said, the shift in his voice tightening a thin wire of unease through my chest, "yes."

"What's wrong?"

He chewed the inside of his cheek, hesitating. Then he nodded toward Rafe. "For your own sake, don't waste your time with that one." There was more conviction in his tone than necessary. "He won't confide in you easily."

"What makes you say that?"

Windley dragged the tip of his boot across the dirt, pressing his lips into a thin line. "Just trust me on this. Your efforts are wasted."

He knew something he wasn't telling me, and clearly it was at Rafe's behest—that much I could deduce easily. But what did it have to do with me?

I supposed I should've been glad the loner had confided in anyone at all.

"Well, if that isn't vague and ominous." I sighed. "But I understand if you don't want to betray his trust. I'll try to go easier on him—though you know it's hardly in my nature to keep my distance."

Windley's voice gentled. "I don't like seeing you set yourself up for disappointment."

Silence stretched between us, filled only by the distant

crackling of the fire and the whispering of willow branches in the breeze.

At last, Windley spoke again. "Now it's your turn."

I cocked my head. "For what?"

"There's something you want to ask me, isn't there? Now that we're alone? I can see it all over your face. Go ahead."

He wasn't wrong.

Damn his intuition.

Sometimes he articulated things even I wasn't fully aware of myself.

Truthfully, ever since leaving the Cove, I'd been searching for the best way to ask how he was coping with Beau's disappearance.

His queen's disappearance.

The only trouble was, I didn't know how to broach the topic without uncorking a flood of Beau-centric emotions myself.

Making matters worse, Windley wasn't technically my guard —and technically this wasn't even my mission. I was borrowing him to rescue my friend, contributing almost nothing myself.

Even the widowbirds had kept their distance—despite my occasional attempts with the whistle—and that had been my most hopeful contribution.

Windley was Beau's guard; her absence cut him as deeply as it did me.

Yet I hadn't even asked how he was dealing with the loss. With Windley I always hid behind banter; heavy truths felt safer unspoken. Still, standing next to him steadied me.

He spoke first, quiet but certain. "We'll find her, Queen Merrin." The words slipped the cork back into place. He held out his hand, an easy smile chasing the strain from his eyes. "Eyes forward—together. Deal?"

Instinct pulled my own hand toward his—until the dusk itself seemed to inhale, something unseen stirring in the warm air between us.

For a brief, vivid moment, my mind returned to the night before—when he had implied, in not so many words, that he enjoyed seeing me in that sapphire gown.

A familiar, wing-like flutter brushed the nape of my neck.

I cupped the spot with the hand I'd been about to offer Windley.

"Windley," I said quietly, "last night, when you showed me your power...do you have the ability to make a person feel that way without even touching them?"

He dropped his hand slowly, and then a new expression appeared—one I wasn't entirely sure how to interpret.

"If you feel something, queenie, it's not my magic."

"I never said you affected me," I clarified hastily. "I was only curious."

The fading light slipped across his face, briefly etching one side in shadow and making whatever he was thinking impossible to pin down.

II
THANK LUNA

We returned to the others with the last of the sun's light, ate the stew Rafe had prepared—a bit heavy on carrots—then retired for the night.

Rafe took first watch while Albie formed a barricade between Windley and me. Unsurprisingly, the wrinkled knight fell asleep first, filling the canvas tent with nasally snores that ruffled his mustache.

"Oh my goddess. Can't we stick him in his own tent?" Windley thrashed about dramatically. "You need to change your ruling, Queen Merrin. I say one tent for us, and one for Sir Albie."

His discomfort was hilarious.

"Next time, we'll make him take first watch to give us a chance to fall asleep," I said, laughter warming my voice.

"It isn't funny!" Windley turned onto his side, cramming bedding atop his exposed ear. "It's in your best interest for your escorts to be well-rested, isn't it? Stop laughing at my agony!"

Yet even he couldn't fully hide the humor lacing his words.

"Goodnight, Windley." I burrowed into my blankets, focusing on my breathing to drown out Albie's snores.

Some minutes later, the scent of charred firewood pulled me back from the edges of sleep.

"Stop it, Windley," I mumbled groggily.

"Excuse *you?*" his voice retorted sharply.

Oh.

The scent had nothing to do with Windley.

It was Rafe.

A shift in the canvas, a break in the darkness—his head poking into the tent.

"Your Majesty? Are you awake?"

I pushed up from my tangled nest of blankets, which looked as though I'd wrestled with them. Of all the things I was, a tidy sleeper wasn't one.

"I am now."

"I apologize, but I didn't think this could wait." He hesitated. "It appears you have a visitor."

For a moment, I thought he was joking—we hadn't seen another soul for miles—but Rafe wasn't one to jest.

Especially not now.

In the dead of night. On a mission to rescue a lost queen.

And was it just me, or did he sound almost...eager?

Windley, nowhere near sleep, unwound the blanket tied around his head and scurried after us, keen for an excuse to escape Albie's symphony of snores.

The scent of char intensified as we stepped into the ebony night.

When I first saw the visitor Rafe spoke of, my heart leapt. The only thing better would've been the lost queen herself. Perched atop the tent was a sleek black bird with a humorously long tail.

"A widowbird!" I gasped, immediately offering my arm as a perch. "Did Beau send you?"

The bird glided gracefully from the tent's peak to my arm, a tiny roll of parchment fastened to its leg.

"Well done!" I whispered excitedly.

"How did it find you all the way out here?" Windley asked, folding his arms skeptically as he leaned against a willow trunk. "I thought they only traveled between castles."

A common misconception.

"Widowbirds sense royal blood and are trained to track it," I explained, carefully unrolling the scroll. "Unless something stops them, they always find their mark."

"It senses your *blood*?" Windley eyed the bird warily.

"Supposedly part of some ancient pact," I said, my fingers trembling with excitement. "But who knows. People often tell stories in the absence of understanding."

Regardless—

I held up the parchment triumphantly. "This is exactly why I wanted to come along!"

Windley let out a low whistle. "Well, well."

Rafe's reaction was something else entirely.

The young guard stood nearer than usual—close enough that I caught the faintest hint of his scent. Smoke, leather, and something faintly herbal, like crushed sage lingering in the cold. He craned his neck to see the message, formality be damned.

Sure enough, the elegant script was Beau's.

The message read:

Glad to hear you're wearing in your new shoes. The southern mountain is huger than expected. Give Timber my deepest regard.

Stifling the pounding of my heart, I read it aloud.

Wearing in my new shoes?

Beau was glad we were voyaging toward her.

She seemed to acknowledge we were on track by seeking out Giant's Necropolis.

But the last part—that was puzzling.

Timber.

A codename.

For *Rafe.*

Upon hearing it, the handsome magician with bored eyes and wavy hair dropped to his knees beside the fire. His fists slammed into the earth. He let out a breath—half-gasp, half-sob, like something being ripped from him.

In that moment, I questioned my astuteness—or rather, my lack thereof.

I'd always considered myself perceptive, even clever.

But I had been blind to the obvious. Caught up in my own narrative of our journey. And here Rafe was, doubled over, hands in the dirt, trembling with emotions I hadn't recognized.

"She's alive," he panted. "Thank Luna."

"Rafe? And Beau, she…"

The words fumbled in my mouth like soup too hot to swallow.

Realization dawned slowly.

Rafe's strange behavior the night Beau disappeared.

His insistence that there were "ways" to climb to her bedchamber.

The sadness he'd desperately tried to hide.

I turned slowly toward Windley. "Are Rafe and Beau…?"

"The scamps hid it well." Windley tapped his chin. "I only found out because I caught him mourning the night I came to your castle."

Then that meant—

I sank to my knees beside the shaken guard.

"Rafe, are you Beau's *lover?*"

He didn't need to answer. The evidence piled up rapidly as I retraced memories.

He'd always avoided advances from my handmaids—sitting poetically in the courtyard, reading novels, twisting locks of his hair. Never had I imagined he was secretly meeting with my sister queen.

Goddess—how long had this been happening right under my nose?!

And Beau! That fox!

Why hadn't she told me?

Because such things were forbidden. And Rafe was my guard, not hers. She likely viewed their affair as a disrespect. Something shameful.

Queens were expected to choose mates from royal bloodlines.

"Forgive me, Your Majesty." When Rafe lifted his gaze from the dirt, his eyes were glossed—shimmering with emotions too threadbare to hide. "I've broken our royal covenant." His voice fractured. "I didn't intend to pursue her, but I couldn't help myself. I understand if you wish to banish me, but please let me help retrieve her first. *I beg it.*"

His vulnerability hit me like a gust of wind.

The gravity of his risk settled heavily between us.

Beau. My dearest friend.

His lover.

"Are you serious?" The words left my mouth untempered.

Rafe winced. "Very well. I know I'm undeserving."

Beau was perfect in every conceivable way. Many had vied for her. I'd always fretted over who might win her heart—what fool, what charmer, what prince.

But Rafe?

My guard?

"That's not what I meant." I shook my head. "Of course you don't deserve her—but only because no one does."

I studied him anew. Strong. Even-tempered. Quietly steadfast. Not the worst choice. Not even close.

So this was who Beau had chosen.

"It may not be possible for you to marry or have a conventional life, but if she loves you, I'd never jeopardize it." I gently squeezed his shoulder, grounding us both. "What I mean is, the only way you're getting banished is if you break her heart, Rafe."

Rafe furrowed his brow, searching my expression. "You'd allow me to remain in your guard, despite my transgression?"

Windley exhaled a whistle. "Told you she wouldn't care," he sing-songed.

"Of course," I said, glancing cautiously toward the tent. "But Albie can't know. He'd have you transferred to another queendom immediately."

Rafe sank into a reverent kneel, clutching his chest as though pledging fealty anew. "Thank you, Your Majesty. You're more merciful than I ever expected."

"That isn't necessary, Rafe." I motioned him up, then turned to Windley. "And you—keep your mouth shut, too."

Windley scoffed, resting a hand on his hip. "Isn't that what I've already been doing? I can keep a secret, you know."

He had a point.

"I have so many questions, Rafe," I ventured, "but I know you'd hate answering them, so I'll save them for Beau. I'm just glad we're aligned in our love for her."

I reread Beau's note.

"At least we know we're still heading the right way."

Wherever the scandalous queen was, she could at least send messages.

How quickly hope had returned.

Rafe nodded, words caught in his throat.

I patted the widowbird gratefully, but it fluttered away, landing on a branch above Windley.

Windley gave it a suspicious side-eye, clearly still wary about the blood-pact revelation. I hadn't noticed until now, but at some point during the night, his hair had shifted from moonlit white to gentle lavender.

He sidled closer to Rafe. "You've had quite the night, chap. Want me to take your watch?"

Rafe shook his head. "I wouldn't sleep anyway. Give me a bit more time. I'll wake you after midnight."

"If it's even possible to sleep with Sir Albie's racket," Windley muttered, revealing his true motive.

We left the lovesick guard beside the fire, emotions still raw.

As we ducked into the tent, we found Albie's snoring had stopped—because the old knight had rolled onto Windley's previous sleeping spot.

Windley's eyes widened. "Now what?" He looked between my nest, the tent's center, and back again. "This feels like a trap. Are you sure he's not setting me up, lion queen?"

Because our options were now waking Albie, and risking another bout of his relentless snoring, or disobeying his rule and sleeping side by side. Not that I minded—I trusted Windley as much as any handmaid.

"Just lie down," I whispered. "If Albie wakes, I'll explain. Besides, you'll switch with Rafe soon anyway." I patted the ground beside me. "Between the two of you, he's far more concerned with your mischief than Rafe's. He won't even notice."

Windley gasped in mock offense. "*Me?* I'm not the one sneaking off to devour sweet Queen Beau."

"You have that look about you. Rafe, on the other hand, seems like he's afraid to breathe too close to a maiden for fear she might shatter."

Windley considered this, grudgingly lowering himself beside me. "Fine. But if I'm whipped, it's entirely your fault." He rolled theatrically onto his side. "And Sir Albie stole my favorite blanket, the scoundrel."

"Would you rather have your blanket or silence?" I tossed him a spare.

A subtle shift filled the air between us—perhaps just the romance of the night heightened by Beau's revealed affair.

I tried to sleep, but my mind spun endlessly. Imagining Beau and Rafe, their hidden rendezvous. How had Windley managed to keep quiet? It was scandalous. And Rafe—he was younger than us all. When had it started? How had it started?

Once we found Beau, she and I would need ample wine and sweets to unpack this thoroughly. I missed her desperately.

I wanted to gossip with Windley, but knowing he had limited rest, I held my tongue. Still, it was strange, lying so close I could hear his breathing. Was mine too loud? I tried quieting it, resulting in an embarrassingly loud gasp.

Now my breathing sounded annoyingly uneven.

"Why aren't you sleeping?" Windley's voice pierced the dark, amused. "Your thoughts are deafening. Knock it off in there."

"I'm trying," I whispered back, frustrated. "It's just...a lot."

"Are you picturing them groping each other?"

"...I am now."

He snorted softly.

I couldn't make out his features, only the gleam of his dark eyes, polished coal in darkness. Waiting until they closed, I closed mine too.

Some time passed. Windley's whisper drifted across the darkness, brushing the edges of sleep.

"Still awake?" Gentler now. "I could help you sleep, you know."

A pause.

"I only need to touch you, Merrin."

My stomach fluttered at his use of my unadorned name.

Was this real?

It felt like vapor.

Tasted like moonlight.

Sleep-heavy, I extended a fingertip. Instead of merely brushing it, Windley clasped my wrist and eased me into his arms.

A dream, surely; waking-Windley would never be this bold. And because it was a dream, I offered no protest.

Like last time, his Spirite magic was intoxicating. Held in his arms, warmth cascaded through me, quickening my pulse, melting me into a hazy, blissful state.

"Ready?" he breathed at my ear. "I'm going to let it flow."

But...hadn't he already?

No.

The sensation deepened. With dream-Windley pressed close, slow tides of heat lulled me toward oblivion.

The last thing I heard was his voice, barely audible:

"It feels good to hold you at last...my queen."

12

THE EMERALD WOOD

"Time to rise, My Queen."

In the dewy dawn, Albie drew me from slumber. I opened my eyes to find I was appropriately alone at the edge of the tent, cuddled with only my blankets. Per usual, my hair billowed out in every direction, disrupted from the night. I always woke up looking much worse than when I went to sleep—even more so, apparently, when sleeping in tents.

Albie seemed chipper enough. His smile lines creased, meaning he'd seen nothing inappropriate the night before.

Because it had *been a dream.*

Of course it had. In it, Windley had called me *his* queen, something he'd never called me before, something he shouldn't be calling me now. Beau was his queen, not me. Apparently, I had projected Beau's romance onto my own situation, creating a snuggle-infused reverie featuring the pointy-eared "hound."

"Your hair really is most unruly in the morning, lion queen."

I jumped at how close his mouth was to my ear.

Windley was acting himself—not like we had done something wayward.

Because *surely* it was only a dream. The way he'd surrounded me and settled his lips near to, but not touching, my neck. The way we had breathed in unison. The waves of warmth lulling me to sleep.

I swatted him away and tended to Ruckus, who grazed a short distance away while the guard packed up camp for departure.

"Careful, he's hyper today," Rafe said as he passed.

Was that a *jab*? Of all the things Rafe was, playful was rarely one of them. Was he warming up now that his secret was out?

"I'm not *hyper*." Windley stretched. "I just happen to have an abundance of energy today."

"I'm certain that's the definition of hyper," I said.

Rafe glanced back, expression deadpan. "I was referring to the queen's *stag*."

From the grove of willows, we traveled ever southward. Rafe was right; Ruckus was unusually energetic. Windley too. Even Rafe himself seemed reinvigorated, the weight lifted from his shoulders, replaced by newfound hope that Beau was alive and we were drawing nearer to her with every gallop. The widowbird from last night soared ahead, carrying my next message to the lost queen. We wouldn't keep it in our sights for long, but it would find her—of that, I had no doubt.

According to the map from Delagos, if we kept heading this way, the plains would transition to tall-reaching trees before long.

"Marked by a field of emerald moss, I think," Windley said, rubbing his head. His memory wasn't very crisp—the reason Albie had turned to Delagos for help in the first place. I didn't press him, figuring it must've been easy to forget things from eight years ago.

Even easier when there were things worth forgetting, I would soon learn.

Windley was right, though. Like verdant tides washing ashore, emerald patches bloomed across the mismatch of grass and dirt—the earliest signs of what was to come.

The first time Ruckus stepped on some, he recoiled as if he'd stuck his hoof into mud. "Squishy, Ruck?" I patted him. "It's okay. You won't sink."

He didn't listen, instead looking to Albie's stag for guidance. Albie's beast had spent years with the knight, the most obedient of the lot. Obeying Albie's tongue-click, it took to the front of the pack, and the others followed.

"See, Ruck? Told you."

No use saying so. Ruckus wasn't one to admit when he was wrong.

Not long after the moss washed over the land, we saw the treeline rise on the horizon, and I finally understood what Albie meant by a forest of extraordinary heights.

To call the trees tall was an egregious understatement—they were colossal, towering higher than any of the six castles I'd visited, higher even than the tallest tower back home.

Even from a great distance, I could tell. The massive trunks loomed, an arboreal barricade to lands beyond. From afar, the wall of green and brown seemed impenetrable, an unbroken fortress of wood.

But up close, truth revealed itself.

The trunks stretched impossibly wide—a dozen people, hand in hand, would barely encircle one. Slivers of light slipped through the canopy, casting shifting beams upon the forest floor. Far above, unseen branches stirred against the sky, whispering secrets to the wind.

Inside the wood, the world hushed, its sound swallowed by the forest's crown.

Even standing among them, it was impossible to grasp the full scale of the trees. Yet despite their daunting height, this place wasn't dark or foreboding—it was *magical.*

Fractured light illuminated patches of vivid mushrooms sprouting from thick moss. Emerald vines draped over fallen branches, weaving through undergrowth like living thread. The air carried an earthy richness—cool and fresh—reminiscent of the Scarlet Wood.

I dismounted Ruckus, boots sinking into mossy ground. The instant my feet touched down, the soles of my boots tingled softly—like static, or stepping barefoot onto sun-warmed stone. It passed so quickly I thought I'd imagined it. No wonder the stags mistook it for mud.

"Does the forest have a name?" I asked.

"The Emerald Wood," Windley said quietly, gaze fixed on the trunks, a faraway look in his eyes—enough to prompt Albie's question:

"You okay, son?"

I stopped gawking, studying them more closely. Windley brushed Albie off, usual flippancy intact. But something about the way he lingered...

Perhaps he'd passed through here eight years ago. If so, it would've been fearsome for a young vagabond. Maybe that was why Albie seemed concerned.

We pressed deeper into the Emerald Wood, moss welcoming our footprints. The serenity, crispness—it felt strangely like home—not in appearance, but in essence.

As I drew clear, bracing air deep into my lungs, a thought surfaced—one I should've considered sooner.

If Beau had an illicit relationship with Rafe...did he also know her deepest, darkest secret?

I can't hear them anymore.

I'd pushed it from my mind, distracted. But if anyone knew more, had been trusted—it was Rafe.

He walked ahead, leading his stag.

"A moment, Rafe?"

He met my gaze, voice measured yet distant. "Your Majesty?"

When he turned, I caught stiffness, weight in his posture. His hand pressed absently to his chest, rubbing as though it ached.

Had emotional strain begun manifesting physically?

"Your chest—are you all right?"

"It's fine," he dropped his hand too quickly. His eyes skipped away. "What do you need?"

I stepped over a cluster of tangerine-colored toadstools, voice lowered. "Did Beau mention anything strange before she was taken?"

His expression tightened, guarded. "Strange?"

I hesitated, choosing words carefully. "Just...any changes or concerns?"

For a moment, I worried I'd dug wrong.

Then—a shift. Comprehension sparked his eyes.

His voice dipped. "Not now, Your Majesty." He cast a furtive glance toward Albie, studying Delagos's map. "Tonight."

So, she'd told him something. Judging by his caution, it was the same something she told me.

"Tonight, then," I nodded. For now, I'd have to wait.

But as I stepped away, Rafe exhaled tightly, rubbing his chest again, kneading something unseen.

Curious.

"Windley, a word?" I called.

The guard meandered through trunks, sharing an apple

with his stag.

"At your royal service," he quipped. "No, we aren't almost there. No, I won't carry you. No, you can't have our apple." He wrinkled his nose at his stag.

"In that case—" I feigned disinterest, turning to leave.

Windley hooked an arm around my neck, reeling me back. "Wait. I'm already bored. What is it you really want?"

"Well..." I hesitated. How to start? "This forest reminds me of the Scarlet Wood."

"Because it has trees?" Dry, painful sarcasm. "They're nothing alike."

"The air—it feels similar," I argued.

"Smells like dirt," he countered. "Two things, then. Trees and dirt."

I sighed. He was the worst—and best. But my conscience felt heavy with an uncertainty I'd been carrying too long alone. I hadn't told anyone Beau's secret, yet Windley had a way of peeling truths from me without effort.

"Windley...southerners acknowledge the oracle and echoes, yes?"

He tilted his head, thoughtful, perhaps sensing this was no casual inquiry. "They do. But they call her something else."

"Then they believe calamity follows if the oracle's whispers ever stop?"

His brow furrowed slightly, dark eyes sharpening with sudden interest. "Yes. Are you worried Beau won't be able to perform from captivity?" He leaned in subtly, voice softer, tinged with a cautious intrigue. "Is there something you haven't told me?"

My pulse quickened beneath his scrutiny. Windley was perceptive—too perceptive. Clearly, he didn't yet know Beau had lost the echoes. Still, it surprised me how far that belief in calamity reached. And yet...no immediate sign of nature's ruin. Perhaps calamity spread slower, more insidious.

When Windley's gaze remained fixed on mine, curiosity intensifying, I deflected. "What do they call her here?"

He studied me another beat before he answered, clearly unconvinced by my shift but willing, for now, to let it pass. "The Nemophilist," he said. "Means 'haunter of woods.'"

The name sent whispers down my spine.

Nemophilist. More poetic—but haunting. Like this forest. Shadows shifted; the air thickened, heavy with unseen eyes. Windley leaned closer, his voice coaxing. "You can tell me," he hummed gently. "As recent events have proven, I'm an excellent keeper of secrets."

Tempting—but not yet.

Instead, I studied him, needing to shift the subject smoothly. "Windley...has your hair been changing more rapidly than usual?"

He straightened, clearly caught off guard. "How should I know? I can't exactly see it myself."

I hadn't considered that.

"Well, it is changing." I eyed him carefully. "Yesterday it was white. Today, it's already turned a deep violet. Won't you finally explain how it works? We have the time."

"Only if you tell me how *your* hair works." He shot back. "Does it feed upon the souls of your fallen enemies?"

"Precisely," I returned. "I'm always accepting volunteers."

He feigned offense. "Surely Rafe doesn't deserve to die just because of a little *canoodling*?"

I huffed a laugh. "I meant you, of course, but interesting how your mind jumped straight to Rafe. Understandable, though, given his looks and gentlemanly ways."

"Cheeky," Windley approved with a hum. "Fine. If you must know, my hair simply does whatever it pleases." He ran a casual hand through his bangs. "I could force it into a certain color, but that requires precious energy I'd rather conserve."

"So it just shifts randomly? It's not related to your mood or surroundings?"

"I'm not some goddess-damned chameleon, Merrin." He caught himself instantly, glancing toward Albie before hastily correcting, "I mean, Your Majesty."

Last night might have been nothing more than a dream, but hearing my name without honorifics had the same undeniable effect. My stomach dipped sharply before righting itself.

"So...what's the point of it?" I asked, ignoring the fluttering sensation altogether.

He looked suddenly uncomfortable.

"Hmmm?" I prodded.

Windley sighed, relenting. "You're familiar with ignis fatuus, yes? Or as northerners like to call them—will-o'-the-wisps?"

I nodded. Beautiful spheres of colored flame, drifting through northern forests, tempting travelers astray. Legend claimed they devoured the souls of those who followed them—or at least, that was what Mother Poppy had told me as a girl.

"They're meant to be enticing, aren't they?" Windley's voice lowered with intent. "Well...it's similar. In ancient times, if I wanted to lure someone away to steal their life force, I'd simply change my hair to whatever color best enticed them."

He spoke so casually—as though stealing life had once been as easy as breathing. The way he said *lure someone away* felt suddenly intimate...and dangerous.

Because his kind were once predatory?

"You said you had extra energy today," I ventured carefully. "Will you show me how you change it intentionally?"

"If you'll help me." His brow arched subtly, fingers

extending toward me like a prince's invitation—deliberate and unhurried.

A hush settled over the forest, the immense trees standing silent, as though watching.

Windley's eyes gleamed with something wicked and effortlessly tempting. I wanted to take his hand immediately, to give him my energy freely—but something restrained me: pride, doubt, a lingering guilt. Perhaps all three.

I was a queen, a ruler responsible for many. Though I might not have appeared the type, I was good at ruling—my people were content, our alliances strong, my court relaxed. I was cherished, just as Beau was.

Was it truly acceptable to offer Windley my life force so willingly?

The first time had been an innocent demonstration.

The second, merely a dream.

But now?

Now it would be because I wanted to.

Because I couldn't resist.

Because it gave me a perfect excuse to touch him again.

"You're not using your powers on me right now, are you?" I breathed, an ache blossoming within my chest, demanding release.

His expression shifted—amusement tempered by something else, something careful. "Not the way you mean." His voice eased, faintly contrite. "I can't make you feel that way without touching you first."

That familiar, phantom flutter teased at the nape of my neck.

His fingers twitched slightly, as though tempted to reach again, but instead, he lowered his hand. The blackstone ring on his finger glinted briefly in a shaft of sunlight.

"I was afraid of this," he murmured, avoiding my gaze. "You're wary of touching me now."

Something twisted uncomfortably inside me.

He wasn't wrong.

For the last eight years, we'd flung arms around each other, tugged each other about without hesitation.

But now?

Now, I fought the urge to simply brush my skin against his.

I definitely shouldn't do that.

"I promise you," he went on, sincerity deepening his voice until he forgot formalities entirely, "My people abandoned predation long before I was even born. I would never harm you, Merrin. *Never*."

I swallowed, weighing my hesitation carefully. Windley was my friend—I'd trusted him implicitly for years. Which meant the person I truly mistrusted here wasn't him.

It was me.

"I'm sorry, Windley. It isn't that I fear you."

It's that I feared how much I might like it.

But I couldn't say that.

"It's just—I'm hesitant in front of them." A convenient scapegoat. I gestured to Albie and Rafe, loitering nearby with the stags. "Albie would collapse on the spot if he saw me getting...*affected* by you."

"Oh." Windley's shoulders loosened a little, tension easing. "Right. *Those* two. I'd nearly forgotten them." A breath. "I'll have to show you later, then. If I do it alone now, I'll need to stop and rest afterward. I'm a bit out of practice, so it takes more effort than usual."

"You mean you haven't been wooing Beau's handmaids back at the Clearing?"

"Only using my natural charm."

His usual playfulness had returned, but something stayed in his eyes—something I had put there.

Impulsively, I reached up, tugging lightly at his earlobe. "I'm not afraid of touching you, Wind. I promise."

Windley's hand lifted instinctively, fingers grazing along my knuckles before tracing a slow, deliberate path down my wrist. I shivered.

In the ensuing silence, my pulse echoed through my ears.

That should have been the moment I acknowledged my shifting thoughts and desires.

The moment I grew up, confronting what was plainly obvious to everyone else.

But that wasn't what happened.

Because before I could speak, something dark—an otherworldly force that had stalked us since before Sestilia's castle—struck without warning.

The moment it touched me, my entire body seized.

My knees buckled.

And I collapsed into the mossy earth.

13
NEMOPHILIST

I had never fainted before, but this wasn't how I'd imagined it. And no, *Windley did not make me swoon,* alright? One moment, I was standing in a beam of forest light. The next, darkness consumed me, as though someone had blown out a candle.

It wasn't thick like liquid, but it moved—otherworldly, shifting. Cool against my skin, yet heavy in my lungs, like breathing mist.

I could still sense my body—or at least the outline of it—translucent and shimmering, as if I might slip away at any moment. How long did a fainting spell usually last? Was I supposed to be conscious during one?

Something cold brushed against my leg. A hand? At first, I thought it might belong to Albie, Windley, or Rafe. But then more came.

Dozens of them.

They crawled over me like skittering spider legs, closing in on my face, stomach, chest. Finger-like threads without source, terrifyingly real and all over my body.

No, this wasn't a normal fainting spell!

I tried to move. Scream. Anything. But the darkness held me in place. The hands pressed closer, chilling and invasive, tracing every inch of my body like a sinister inspection.

And then—

The whispers.

"Merrin."

A presence—or was it a voice?—slipped through the void, wreathing around me like smoke.

"MeRRin," another echoed, distorted and unnatural, like it was struggling to mimic something human.

"mErriN."

"MErrIn."

"MERRIN."

The whispers dropped like stones into still water, rippling outward, bending my name as if testing it, stretching it. The hands, the voices—they crowded me, suffocating me, until—

Something shifted.

Not something I could put into words. Sort of like *trying to describe a color I'd never seen before.*

The voices deepened, twisting into something vast and ancient. *"We will tear it apart. All of it. We will rip it asunder. Devastate all who walk and crawl. Filth of the earth."*

A demon?

"We hate them. Let them burn. Dry them out. Kill them. Kill them. Kill them."

It certainly felt demonic!

I didn't hear the words so much as feel them—rage and chaos made flesh, aimed at everything and nothing.

A pressure gathered, thick and smothering. The air itself trembled, waiting for a final breath before it collapsed. Panic spiked. Whatever this was, it would crash over me like a tidal-wave of night.

For one terrible heartbeat, I thought it would.

I anchored myself.

Then—

"NO!"

Not a plea. Not a cry.

A command. Power in its own right. It ripped outward from my formless center, shearing the dark like a blade through silk. The hands recoiled; the whispers stuttered, their spell frozen mid-cast.

The pulse was mine...yet not mine.

It wasn't my voice. It was my *will*.

"*MeRRIN?*"

"*Merrin?*"

"*MERRIn?*"

"No," I commanded again—deliberate this time.

The darkness shivered. A current woke beneath my skin, ancient and coiled.

"*Kill them. Wrench them. Cleanse them. All who walk the—*"

"NO." The third command rang out, iron-sure. "You will not harm them."

Chaos pressed on every side, and I was the lone barricade. I'd been raised to speak for the voiceless; now the need felt absolute.

A ripple—more calculation than surrender—slid through the void.

Images slammed into me: humanity's own horrors—greed, betrayal, cruelty—each a pleading brief for annihilation. Each vision an argument for destruction.

I answered with proof of better things.

Albie's steady hands, gently wrapping a bandage around my wrist, the scent of minty salve filling the air. Beau's laughter, bright and unexpected, echoing off cliffs as she hugged me.

Windley's mischief, the cool night breeze brushing my skin as we whispered beneath the stars.

Sparks against the dark; fragile, but mine.

"They aren't all bad...but SOME are," the void suggested, like a bargain.

Sestilia's dazzling, merciless smile flared in my mind, almost tipping the scales.

"NO," I countered, firmer. "Even the worst carry a sliver of worth. Even her."

I forced the memories brighter, feeding them to the dark until it grudgingly drew back.

"Even the worst have merit," it echoed at last, ebbing to the edges. *"Let the earthly creatures live—for now..."*

The presence coiled out of sight, waiting on the promise of "for now."

"Merrin..."

"Mer-rin..."

"Merrin!"

That last voice was real. Crisp. Close.

My gasp tore through the trees as my eyes flew open.

Windley bent over me, hands cupping my face, usually sharp eyes wide and unshielded. His expression held something I wasn't used to seeing—

Fear.

"Majesty! Shit. Thank goddess. I swear, I don't know what I did!" His hands hovered uncertainly, fingers curling and unclenching, as if warring with the instinct to shake me awake.

"No," I rasped, my throat thick with residue. "That wasn't —" A cough interrupted me, remnants of the dark force still hovering in my chest.

Though it felt like minutes had passed, it seemed barely seconds for the others.

Albie and Rafe were still running toward us from a short distance away.

Albie slid to his knees, pushing Windley aside. Windley ran a hand through his hair, muttering curses beneath his breath.

"My Queen!" Albie cradled me against his weathered chest. "Are you all right?"

I wasn't sure.

The darkness had retreated, yet its shadow lingered.

The victory felt exhilarating yet terrifying, like slamming a door just before something unspeakable slipped through. Or maybe just slightly after.

The moment my eyes reopened, I sensed something had irrevocably shifted. The pressure, the sense of violation—it still clung to my skin. Convincing a force that vast and hateful to withdraw... I'd pushed it back, but had I truly won? A faint ringing remained in my ears—not quite a sound, more like a presence. It began as a whisper, light as breath, but quickly grew insistent, vibrating softly, filling hollow spaces I hadn't known were there. It crawled beneath my skin like restless bees seeking escape.

Then understanding struck, whether by instinct or from Beau's years of careful explanations.

The echoes.

I could hear them.

Which felt completely unnatural. Like a note struck out of tune on an instrument never meant to carry it. Like trespassing onto a throne that wasn't mine. I wasn't the oracle; I wasn't royalty of the Clearing.

Beau exchanged echoes with the Scarlet Wood. Had I done the same with the Emerald Wood? Had I truly pushed back the darkness? It seemed improbable—how could a mere human stand against such forces? Beau always said nature had no fondness for humanity. Was that darkness nature itself? Or something worse?

People often tell stories in the absence of understanding...

It felt as if I'd teetered precariously on the edge of something far older and more dangerous than I could understand.

Windley was still staring, expression unreadable, as if trying to solve an impossible equation. And Albie—I'd never seen his wrinkles etched so deeply. Was this very moment branding him with new ones?

I considered confiding right then, but Albie would demand we turn back. Rafe would assume the worst for Beau. I needed time—to grasp what happened before anyone else defined it.

"I should drink more water," I lied.

Rafe hurriedly fetched a canteen. "Please be careful, Your Majesty," he said when handing it to me.

Albie wasn't satisfied, hovering for the next several minutes, searching for another ailment. "This journey is longer than any you've taken, My Queen. We should stop here for today."

"I promise I'm fine, Albie. I'm not delicate. I have at least as much stamina as him," I kidded, nodding toward Windley.

Windley didn't take the bait, arms crossed, jaw set like stone.

"We really can't waste time." I placed a hand on Albie's chest. "That's a command, my knight."

He sighed through his teeth before giving in.

"See?" I hopped to my feet with exaggerated pep. "I feel great."

The distant echoes disagreed.

Albie stuck close afterward—not ideal, since I couldn't reassure Windley he hadn't caused my blackout. Though he didn't seem eager to hear it. He trailed at the group's rear—a scorned hound.

All the while, I waited for a chance to sneak away.

Eventually, we reached a spring trickling between trees, its bed dotted with glowing pebbles. We stopped to refill our canteens. When I lifted one stone, its glow faded instantly.

I returned it, watching the light restore.

A reminder some things simply belonged where they were placed.

I hopped over the thin stream and approached Windley, sulking near a patch of ferns.

"You should stay away," he muttered as I approached. "I clearly have no self-control when it comes to you."

"Shh." I grabbed his wrist; his body went rigid. "Over here."

While Rafe filled canteens and Albie fussed with the map, I led Windley out of earshot, pretending I'd spotted a turtle with a glowing shell.

He yanked his hand free. "Didn't you hear me?"

I rolled my eyes. "Knock it off, dramatic."

"How can you say that?! I promised I'd never harm you, and within a minute, I did!"

It wasn't like him to be so rattled.

Windley was the one with the quick quips and easy smirks —the fact he wasn't joking about making me swoon proved how shaken he was.

"Windley. Look at me," I directed firmly. "That wasn't you, alright? I need to tell you something, but promise you won't overreact or tell the others. I don't trust their reactions."

He folded his arms, temper still dark. "If this is your attempt to make me feel better—"

"I can hear the echoes."

His entire frame stiffened, his smirk wiped clean in an instant.

"Come again?"

"Beau's echoes. I can hear them."

He blinked, absorbing my words. "Actual voices? Of the trees?" His eyes flicked upward, as if expecting faces peering from the canopy. "From which end do they speak?"

"Windley!" I scolded. "Do I look like I'm jesting? Something happened when I fainted, and now I hear...things."

The sharpness in my tone sobered him. His cocky grin faltered, replaced by caution.

"You're serious?" For a second, I glimpsed the Windley hidden beneath all his bravado. "And? What do they whisper?"

"It's hard to describe. Imagine—"

"A color I've never seen before?" he interrupted, waving a hand.

"*Then why ask?*" I said through clenched teeth.

Windley's expression softened briefly, then shifted to concern. "You're certain?"

"As sure as my own name," I said. "It's bizarre. When I passed out, it felt longer than it truly was. I convinced the forest not to slaughter everyone—though it was especially tempting to let it kill off Queen Sestilia."

Windley stared like I'd grown another head.

"This forest?" He tapped a boot against a massive trunk.

"I'm not even sure if it was a forest. It was darkness. It wanted to destroy everything, and I had to talk it down." I rubbed my face with both hands.

Was I rambling?

Windley searched my eyes, finally convinced I wasn't playing. His voice dipped. "What does that mean for Queen Beau? Does that mean she's..." He trailed off, gaze drifting toward the glowing-shelled turtle, seeking solace in its slow, peaceful movements.

A single image flashed through my mind: Beau's perfect form, limp and vacant, echoes ripped away.

But no. There was a piece he didn't yet know.

I hesitated, pulling my cloak close, Beau's secret pressing like a stone I'd carried too long. Finally, I exhaled. "A few weeks before Beau vanished, she...admitted to me she'd lost her echoes."

Windley blinked three times, slowly.

Then his voice cut through the stillness. "And you're only mentioning this now?!"

That part was harder to defend.

But speaking it aloud had felt like betrayal!

"I think Rafe already knows. He intends to tell me tonight."

For a moment, we sat with the weight of it—the echoes, the secrets, the darkness nearly consuming me.

Then, as only Windley could, he shook off seriousness with a forced breath. "Good goddess, lion queen. What a mess." He rubbed his jaw. "And here I thought I'd merely swept you off your feet."

There it was.

14

LUSTFUL

Windley's gaze sliced through the flames, piercing and intense. I had ordered him not to tell Albie about the echoes, knowing my knight would make us abandon our quest the instant he learned of them. As for telling Rafe, I was still uncertain. First, I needed to know exactly what he knew, and that required getting him alone.

I bided my time, picking slowly at the roast fish Rafe had prepared. The wayward magician had finished his meal long ago and was now stretching his neck upward, inspecting those bits of night sky persistent enough to shine through the dense canopy.

"Something wrong, my boy?" Albie asked.

"Luna," Rafe murmured. "She's hard to see from here."

"Aye, but Delagos said this wood is mostly peaceful," Albie reassured him. "You shouldn't need another charge until we're out in the open."

"Only mostly peaceful?" I asked, glancing anxiously toward the resting stags.

"You aren't afraid, are you, Majesty?" Firelight flickered

across Windley's features, casting teasing shadows. "It's unlike you to be afraid."

I was afraid—but not of anything that Rafe's enchanted steel or Windley's spinning hatchets could fend off.

It was the mass of hands writhing from the darkness. How did Beau always remain so calm, knowing such a force was lurking at the edges of perception? I'd never seen my sister queen succumb as I had. She was deliberate in her meetings with the forest, often donning scarlet to match the wood. Nature had never forced itself upon her like it had on me. Was it because I was unpracticed?

I had no idea how to prepare for the next encounter.

Windley watched me intently, his posture taut, as though ready to spring to my side if I showed the slightest sign of fainting again.

Albie cleared his throat, oblivious to our silent tension, as he studied the sky. "Speaking of the moon—she'll reach peak soon. We should turn in, My Queen. Easy to lose track of time here."

Finally.

I bade the others a faux goodnight and followed Albie into the tent. The moment the first snore escaped him, I slipped out quietly, just as I'd done countless times as a child sneaking through the castle at night. Castles were always more enchanting after dark.

"Miss us already?" Windley purred. "I do understand why. Have you seen the pair of us?"

"Windley, stay put. Rafe, come with me."

Windley soured at having his flirting denied, so I gave him a pandering wave as I led Rafe away.

"Your Majesty?" Rafe's discomfort was palpable.

"I need to know what Beau said to you before she disappeared. Earlier, you indicated there was something—" I stopped short, distracted.

Apparently, castles weren't the only places more enchanting after dark.

Beyond the campfire's influence, the forest had transformed, and the farther we ventured, the more it revealed itself.

"Rafe, what is this?" I released his arm, struck with awe.

"Old magic," he answered with serene energy. "It's in the soil."

In the deep of night, the forest's effulgence had heightened, revealing another world—alien, colorful, illuminated by flares of distant light. Toadstools scattered across moss glowed iridescently. Ferns lit their leaves from beneath, spores pulsing from dim to bright. Through towering trunks, wisps of shimmering particles drifted lazily in the air.

The allure of nocturnal magic surrounded us. And there was something else. With each step, we left trails of glowing footprints that followed briefly before vanishing into the night.

"Rafe, our footprints are glowing!" I pressed my foot deeply into the lush ground, creating a bright imprint that soon faded.

"Only yours, Your Majesty." Rafe stepped carefully to demonstrate. He was right; only my prints glowed. "It must be your royal blood."

Or perhaps it was because I could now hear the forest's vehement whispers. But I wasn't ready to share that yet—and Rafe was in no condition to hear it.

With a sharp grunt, his hand shot to his chest, features pinched in pain.

"Rafe!" My stomach knotted as his shoulders curled inward. I scanned for danger but saw only a many-legged insect crawling over my fading footprint. "Rafe, what is it?"

"Nothing," he huffed, hand still pressed over his heart.

Liar. I'd seen him rubbing his chest earlier too.

"Tell me, Rafe. Is it heartache? Are you sick with worry over Beau?"

He shook his head, jaw ground. "It's not worthy of your concern." But even as he spoke, he grimaced again, knees buckling beneath him.

I gripped his arms, steadying him as he swayed. "As your queen, I command you to tell me what ails you, Rafe!"

His breathing came unevenly. "My chest," he admitted through gritted teeth. "It tightens at times. I don't know the cause. It will pass." His fingers dug into my thigh, icy and trembling.

Cold extremities. A tight chest. It could've been heart fever, devil's croup, winter sickness—all curable.

"In three years, I've never seen you like this," I pressed. "Why now?"

After several heavy breaths, he finally spoke. "*Beau.*"

The way he said her name—strained, aching—sent a lancing pang through me.

"You're saying...Beau caused this?"

He shook his head, managing to lift his gaze. "Not the cause," he rasped. "She's the cure."

The words took me by surprise. "The cure?"

He clenched his hand against the ground. I stayed quiet as he worked through the pain. Gradually, his breathing evened, tension loosening from his frame. When he seemed stable enough, I pressed again.

"You said she's the cure, Rafe? A gift as maiden of the wood?"

"I believe so, yes. I've had this for years. Until recently, the queen eased it with heat from her body."

Her body's *heat?* My mind ran wild.

I should've known—they were lovers, after all.

He avoided me, focusing instead on a cluster of glowing

mushrooms. "It's not what you're thinking." He stalled, then exhaled reluctantly. "It was her hands. When she placed a hand on my chest, her warmth delayed the episodes. That's... how we first came together."

Ah.

I hadn't expected that.

Perhaps sensing my reserve, Rafe continued, filling the silence. "The last time we visited the treetop bastion," he said, "after you and I spoke in the belvedere, I...went to her room." He swallowed visibly.

A slow realization crawled up my spine.

I'd been sleeping beside her that night!

"I'm sorry, Your Majesty. This is difficult to admit."

"Proceed," I said, keeping my expression neutral.

He nodded, fingers pressing again to his chest. "I felt an episode coming on, so I sought her out. You were asleep. She was upset but wouldn't tell me why." His voice lowered, gaze distant. "When she tried to heal me, it didn't work. That upset her even more. The episodes have grown worse since."

Since Beau lost her echoes.

I took a careful breath. "Did she know why?"

"No." He rubbed at his ribs with a slow, absent motion. "But it grieved her deeply."

He didn't know about the echoes. This was the change he'd mentioned. Beau had confided only in me.

But the lost heat and echoes had to be connected. If I'd gained one of Beau's powers...perhaps I'd gained the other, too?

"Does your chest ache now?" I asked.

He hesitated, then nodded. "But it's manageable."

"Let me try something," I said, extending my hand.

He stiffened. "What are you doing?"

"I want to see if Beau's royal blood healed you," I covered smoothly. "If so, perhaps I can too."

His eyes darted between my hand and face. "Your Majesty, that isn't—"

I reached again.

Again, he dodged.

My patience thinned. "You've suffered without her. Why won't you let me help, Rafe?"

His posture clammed up. "*Because*," he said. "This isn't your burden."

I scoffed. "You're my guard. That makes you my burden."

Fine.

I dropped my hand, resisting further pressure. "Beau wouldn't want you suffering in her absence."

His breath hitched, and after a tense pause, he released it again.

"...Make it quick."

Finally.

He complied reluctantly, modesty endearing him to me. Good for Beau—she could wrap anyone around her finger.

I placed my hand on his chest through his shirt, startled by the chill.

"You're freezing!" I exclaimed. "What is this?"

"I don't know," he admitted quietly.

I waited, half-expecting to faint again.

"It must touch the skin," he confessed awkwardly.

"I'm not undressing you," I said.

He flushed. "Of course not." With the brisk efficiency of a patient before a medic, he lifted his shirt. "Go ahead."

I braced my fingertips against his sternum, careful not to brush the plane of his abdomen.

Oh.

He was firm beneath my palm, steady—and for one quick, visceral breath I understood why Beau found comfort here.

The awareness flickered, primal, and I shoved it aside. Rafe was still in pain, and the forest whispers throbbed along the treeline.

"Feel anything?" I asked.

He pressed my hand flatter against his chest. "There," he breathed, eyes widening. "It's faint, but it's there. So it truly is a royal gift?"

"Apparently," I lied, knowing the warmth wasn't royal at all but the oracle's grace stirring in me. "I just don't know how to deepen it. Did Beau ever explain?"

"No—she'd simply tweak it, the smallest nudge, and watch me lose my composure."

I let the implication pass. "Alright—let's see what I can manage."

With my palm still resting against Rafe's skin, I drew in the cool night air, rich with damp earth and ancient timber. Eyes closed, I could almost put myself back in the Scarlet Wood—walking beside Beau, listening to the hush of leaves.

But the echoes waited.

All evening they had skimmed the edges of my mind, brushing my thoughts like fingertips on glass. I'd resisted—until now.

I let the barrier slip, just a fraction, as though tilting a vial drop by drop.

The echoes flooded in.

"There!" Rafe's fingers tightened around mine. "Whatever you did—it worked."

He was right. My palm felt changed—not hearth-warm, but charged, like the moment just before lightning cracks the sky. The heat didn't grow in temperature but in intensity, my skin thrumming with hidden energy.

I let the echoes seep farther in, rising like an unseen tide.

That's when things went...sideways.

While I focused on the currents in his chest, Rafe inched

me closer. His hand covered mine, pressing it flat against his heartbeat. A dark heat stole into his gaze; he bit his lip, head tipping back with a low groan—throat exposed, vulnerable. His fingers laced through mine, grip tightening by degrees.

This was a Rafe I'd never met.

He was usually quiet, reserved—better known for sword-work and stew pots.

But this was *wanting*.

I'd meant only to help him, yet the moment had tipped before I noticed. A pang of guilt coiled in my stomach—something I'd never want Beau to see.

Rafe sagged forward, forehead resting against my shoulder, his breath ragged with relief. "That feels...so much better. Thank you, My Queen."

It might've been the first time he'd called me such—though it was entirely proper for him to do so.

Before letting go, he guided my hand up his chest to his throat, as if savoring the last flicker of relief.

Realizing the intimacy, he recoiled and dropped to one knee, head bowed. "Forgive me, Your Majesty." His voice trembled. "You shouldn't have seen me like that."

I stared at my hand; the heat was fading, though a ghost of the moment lingered.

He was right—seeing him that way felt perilous. Rafe had always been handsome in the detached way one admires fine art, nothing more. That brief closeness blurred the line, and I disliked it.

I cleared my throat. "That was...unexpected."

"I shouldn't have let it happen." He scrubbed both hands over his face. "I didn't think it would go that far. I wasn't even sure it would work."

"It was my idea," I said, softening my tone. "I wouldn't have tried if I didn't want to help. But...is it always like that?"

Silence pooled between us, thick with unspoken things.

Finally, he admitted, "Evidently."

Another heartbeat passed.

"Yes," he added, almost to himself. "But I never imagined it could feel that way with anyone else."

Problematic.

"How often do these episodes strike?"

"Every few days. Some are milder, easier to hide." He grit his teeth. "But we shouldn't do this again. I can endure the pain."

A noble answer. The right answer. For Beau's sake.

But I had other considerations.

"Truthfully, your pain is secondary to me. With such a small guard, I can't afford you weakened during danger. Any way I look at it, we'll probably have to repeat this before we find Beau." I folded my arms. "Next time, we'll have a third party present."

"Who?" Rafe's brows knitted.

"Namely, Windley."

His expression turned almost comical. "I mean no disrespect, but how is that better, Your Majesty?"

"We can't do it alone, and we certainly can't do it in front of Albie."

And, for whatever pointless reason, it felt better than doing it behind Windley's back.

Rafe frowned, weighing my words. "I suppose," he relented, reluctance clear. "But I'm not thrilled about him seeing me...exposed."

I didn't blame him. Windley wouldn't let that pass quietly.

I cinched my cloak around me. "Let's return. Windley's probably fuming. You know how he gets when he's not the center of attention."

Rafe released a sigh, expression gray, though a hint of grudging agreement softened his features.

Then, just before I turned—

"One moment, Your Majesty." He stopped me. "Did Queen Beau mention anything else to you?" His tone became careful, deliberate. "Do you think this might have something to do with why she was taken?"

"You don't need to call her that around me," I said, stalling. "I'm sure it's unnatural for you."

I'd already decided. I wouldn't tell him about Beau's lost echoes. It would only cause him greater distress.

"I'm sure Beau's gift isn't gone forever," I answered cautiously. "She was likely overwhelmed by the Lunar Festival. You know how she gets—always overthinking."

"I do."

His eyes lifted toward the canopy once more.

And sorrow bared itself openly across his face.

15

A WOLF'S STARE

Back at camp, Windley lounged by the fire, elbow propped casually on his knee as he poked idly at the flames with a long stick, sending sparks scattering into the night.

Rafe strode past without a word, his posture rigid, like a man marching toward inevitable doom.

"Goodnight to you too, chap," Windley muttered. He turned to me, his expression melding between curiosity and carefully restrained amusement. "Good goddess, I was beginning to wonder if you two had run off together."

Grateful for any distraction from my churning thoughts, I pounced on the banter. "Rafe just showed me his *pleasure face*."

Windley froze mid-step. His smile thinned to something too bright. "Come again?"

I rolled my eyes. "Calm down, drama king—*not* literally."

The forced grin didn't ease; curiosity now edged with unease. "Enlighten me, my sweet, *proper* lion queen—how does a young woman of your pure and noble standing recognize a 'pleasure face'?"

"I have eyes, Windley," I scoffed, folding my arms. "And while I'm no scholar of seduction, Beau's taught me a trick or two."

"That," he murmured, the tension sliding back into mischief, "I believe."

Keeping my voice low, I recounted what Rafe had told me and described, briefly, the events that followed.

Windley listened, raising a skeptical eyebrow. "How positively *erotic* of you," he drawled, though playfulness had returned to his voice. "Yet you're not exactly reveling in it."

He read the unease in my gut too clearly.

"No, I'm not *reveling*. Can you blame me? It felt like crossing some invisible line with Beau's beloved. She'll understand, won't she?"

He shrugged. "How should I know? Queens are complicated."

"Not helping," I sighed, poking at the dirt with my boot. "Have you ever heard of a condition causing someone's chest to freeze from within?"

"No, but I don't exactly know much about his kind. For all we know, it's common among northern sorcerers."

"Perhaps." I sank down beside him, watching the firelight dance between us. "I'm in an uncomfortable position. Healing him felt...wrong. But with our guard so small, I can't afford any of you falling ill."

Windley's expression turned suspicious. "Why are you looking at me like that?"

"Well," I began, testing the words, "I was hoping you'd be there next time."

"What, just to kill the mood?" Windley snorted. "Actually, I wouldn't mind. The poor chap was probably petrified."

I huffed a laugh. "Please—I'm only frightening if you've done something worth dreading."

His mouth quirked. "Lucky for me, then." He reclined, lacing his fingers behind his head—pure mischief simmering in his eyes.

He was baiting me. When I refused to bite, he continued anyway.

"You're his queen," he said, more seriously now, "and he respects you—but Rafe's always been wary of you, Majesty. He once told me that when you look at someone, it's like a wolf sizing up prey."

I narrowed my eyes, testing whether he was baiting me again. "You're serious? What does that even mean? If anyone's the wolf here, Windley, it's the one baring fangs at every joke."

He lifted one shoulder, unruffled. "Others see it, too—your stocky new guard, for one. Honestly, I agree. That stare isn't just regal; it's piercing, like you're reading people's seams."

His words hung in the hush between us.

"Well, great," I muttered. "Now I'll wonder whether I'm terrorizing everyone with my...what, predatory glare?"

"It rattles Rafe—poor chap's heart is promised elsewhere. But anyone who wilts under it doesn't deserve it." Windley nudged my elbow, eyes sly. "It's a gift, Merr. Wield it."

My stomach fluttered—no one, not even Beau, had ever used my name so freely.

Windley immediately backtracked, face flushing slightly. "Queen Merrin. *Shit*. Sorry, Your Majesty." He pressed a hand to his forehead. "With you, I forget."

The quiet between us thickened, broken only by the soft pop-and-hiss of the fire. I hesitated, torn between scolding him and brushing it off.

I didn't want to undermine myself, yet hearing him say my name so casually was far more appealing than I cared to admit.

Windley traced a slow, deliberate line through the ashes. His voice became casual but measured. "And you?"

I frowned. "And me what?"

"You haven't mentioned the echoes," he clarified. "I expected you'd be shaken—or are you merely waiting for the perfect moment to panic?"

I tensed. I didn't want to think about it. Not now. Not after everything else tonight. "I just...need time," I told him simply.

He studied me for a beat, unreadable. Then, seemingly satisfied, he let out a slow breath and relaxed, slipping easily back into himself. "Fair then. I'm all for ignoring problems and enjoying the scenery."

At his mention of the scenery, I sprang up. "I—I almost forgot!" I seized the first distraction that came whirling at us. "Come away from the fire, Windley. I want to show you something."

Before he could protest, I grabbed his hand and pulled him into the night.

Rocks glowed faintly; leaves pulsed with vespertine radiance. I led him past the slumbering stags and into the forest's enchantment.

"Look, Windley—my feet are *magical*." As we moved, the air shimmered softly. Each step left glowing emerald footprints in the moss.

"Yes," he mused dryly. "Like glowing markers that say, *Come see the Nemophilist*."

I paused mid-step. I hadn't thought of that.

Turning quickly, I caught the pleased look on his face. He folded his arms. "Too easy. This wood is *mostly* peaceful, remember?"

Good. We were back to normal.

"I figured it was because of the echoes," I speculated aloud, now dancing patterns into the glowing ground. "Rafe thinks it's my royal blood. He mentioned the soil here holds old magic. Is there something special about the Emerald Wood?"

"Why assume I'd know?" Windley feigned haughtiness.

"Oh, pardon me. Perhaps because you're from 'somewhere in the south,' and conveniently knew about the emerald moss?"

Windley's playful demeanor faltered. He opened his mouth as if to retort, then seemed to reconsider. After a moment, he glanced away, his expression sobering.

My dancing slowed, curiosity mounting. "Windley?"

He drew a breath, visibly weighing something. When his gaze returned to mine, the usual gleam had vanished. "Might as well share it so you'll stop questioning why I'm being so *withholding*. Do you remember I told you about memory-loss elixirs made in the southern wilds?"

How could I forget? Our favorite spider queen had intended to use one on me.

"Well," he continued cautiously, "I took one once. A strong one."

"Willingly? Why?"

He shrugged, though the gesture felt strained. "Hell if I know. It took much of my past. Bits and pieces remain, but major events are blank. The Emerald Wood, for example. I know I've been here, but I couldn't tell you how many times, or with whom, or why."

He spoke calmly enough, but something in the way he avoided my eyes twisted my stomach. "Goddess, that must be frightening." I placed a comforting hand on his shoulder, suddenly understanding Albie's earlier concern. "Are you okay?"

"If I weren't, I wouldn't remember it anyway, right?"

Typical Windley to brush it off.

I searched his face for a tell—some flicker of feeling—but found only blank quiet, and my pulse skipped. The longer we stood there, the harder breathing became. And I couldn't think of a single thing to say.

Was this the old magic, or something else?

Meanwhile, Windley appeared utterly unbothered, his breathing steady as ever.

When I let my hand slip from his shoulder, he caught my wrist, drawing me deftly closer. "Still want that demonstration?" His voice dropped—mischievous, but edged with something darker. "Or have you had enough eroticism for one night?"

I should have scoffed, should have pushed him away.

Instead, I met his gaze, something warm and traitorous stirring inside me.

"Show me." The words were out before I could think better of them. Earlier, I'd hesitated to let him steal my energy for parlor tricks, but now, the thought of resisting felt pointless.

It felt like the only way to erase what had happened with Rafe.

A slow, satisfied smile curled his lips. His black eyes gleamed in the forest's glow, *wolfish* and knowing.

Hands less steady than usual, Windley drew me toward him, placing my palm against his shoulder. "Keep it here," he ordered.

I complied, and his fingers settled over mine, holding me strictly in place.

The wood drew tight around us, fox-fire seams sewing the dark together like curious sprites. Without the warmth of the camp-flame behind me, night's cool breath grazed my skin, and something deep beneath my ribs answered—a slow, tidal pull.

Windley's thumb skimmed the inside of my wrist, and the sound that left me wasn't quite a gasp, but close.

"I should be able to manage the hair by touch alone," he

murmured, eyes intent, "but I may need more from you if you'd like something better."

Then, artfully, intentionally, his thumb stroked up my arm from wrist to elbow.

I didn't know what better meant, but I didn't care. With each careful caress, warmth spiraled beneath my skin, unraveling my composure.

"Are you taking energy from me now?" I breathed.

His jaw flexed subtly. "Only a little." Another slow stroke of his thumb. "Priming you."

Priming me.

A thrill shivered down my spine.

I imagined how it might have been in olden days—Windley tempting a maiden into the woods, coaxing her to surrender life itself.

I knew he would never harm me. But perhaps that was precisely how he was built—to be disarming. The realization didn't frighten me; instead, it ignited a yearning that surprised me. As though I longed to be chosen. As though surrendering wouldn't be so bad.

The boundary between his influence and my own blurred. If he were a predator, he was a masterful one.

"Is everything happening inside me your doing?" I asked.

"Some of it," he confessed, eyes darkly amused. "Is my hair still violet?"

I nodded, words trapped in my throat.

"What color would you prefer?" he asked curiously.

"Scarlet?" I whispered.

"Like the wood?" He chuckled kindly. "Predictable."

I might have retorted if I could think beyond the stirring in my chest, the hush in my mind, the creeping warmth settling through my limbs. My breath slipped through me like wind rustling leaves, my body suspended in the moment.

My knees began to weaken.

Windley froze instantly, thumb pausing mid-stroke. "Is it too much?"

"Don't stop."

His gaze locked on mine—a bare flash of something raw before it shuttered again. Almost without thought, my free hand slid to the warm column of his neck, fingers threading into his hair. Heat pulsed there, echoing the current unraveling inside me. I drew him nearer, head tilting, breath skimming shallow between us.

This was like before, when I hadn't been able to resist running my hands through his hair.

Except this time, Windley reacted.

With a sudden inhale, he jerked back, breaking our connection.

The warmth, the serenity, the bliss—snatched away instantly, leaving only abrupt emptiness behind.

My pulse stuttered, and I swayed, disoriented. "What—"

"You startled me," he said tightly. "Are you all right?"

No. The sudden withdrawal of his magic left me reeling.

"I feel empty," I whispered, this new hollow world stark and unsettling.

He swore under his breath, then exhaled sharply. "My fault." His hands settled carefully on my arms, touch sinuous but sure. "Let me fix it."

I hadn't realized how desperately I needed him to fix it until the warmth began returning with each careful stroke of his fingers.

"Tell me if you want to stop," he said like a gentleman.

"Don't."

His expression darkened. His throat worked tightly with restraint. "This might be too much for me, lion queen."

His eyes tracked me like a hunter weighing the distance to

its prey—shoulders tight, breath clipped, desire barely leashed. Yet his touch never stilled: slow circuits over my skin, drawing off power in steady sips while I, just as hungry, skimmed my fingers through the hair at his nape and coaxed him closer.

"I'm going to alter my hair now," he said, forcing composure. "You might feel a brief dulling."

I wasn't sure what he meant until his next touch rendered my skin numb in its wake.

"Did it work?" He glanced upward at his own head.

In that brief moment, his hair had changed from dark violet to a rich, vivid scarlet.

It suited him so perfectly I couldn't find words.

"I'll take that expression as a yes," he said, quietly pleased.

Something about the scarlet stirred me deeply. I'd thought my choice random, but now I wasn't so sure. Perhaps his powers had guided me all along. Perhaps this was how he lured his prey.

His voice leveled out, smooth and inviting. "I'd like to show you something else. Can you manage? You're not feeling weak, are you?"

Weak was the furthest thing from what I felt.

"Show me."

"I can't do this with touch alone," he explained, just above a whisper. "I'll need a more direct line. You may find it...inappropriate." He leaned in, lips grazing the shell of my ear. "Tell me to stop if you do. Nod to show you understand."

Heart hammering, breath shallow, I managed that nod.

Satisfied, Windley sank into a knight's kneel, pulling my wrist down with him.

For a long, suspended moment, everything else faded. A thrill of something raw and possessive surged deep within. Windley had never knelt before me. It was wrong in so many ways.

He glanced toward the tent, ensuring we remained unseen. Then, slowly, deliberately, he brought my fingertips to his lips, so close his breath warmed my skin.

And with that single breath, the world fell away.

A fierce shiver burst through me—beginning at my chest, fracturing outward, spiraling down my spine as, one by one, Windley kissed my fingertips, leaving each cold as he stole life from them.

He'd been right.

It was inappropriate.

Yet there wasn't a single part of me, noble or otherwise, that wanted him to stop.

"Everyone has a color, Merrin," he murmured, lips brushing lightly over my nails. "One that traps them completely. Tell me yours."

"Scarlet?" I breathed, voice barely audible.

"Wrong."

He blinked. When his eyes reopened, they were no longer black.

They were vivid green—deep, endless, glittering like polished emeralds.

I was helpless beneath his gaze, breath shallow, body rooted in place. Windley's eyes had never changed before.

"I dull them," he murmured, pressing another kiss to my fingertips, "to keep from enticing everyone I meet. Otherwise, they'd follow me everywhere."

By the enchanted glow of the forest, Windley was the most captivating thing I had ever seen.

"You may be tired tomorrow," he continued softly, lips trailing my fingers. "I took more than I meant to." His voice dropped further, this time a definite whisper. "I got carried away."

His stare pinned me, merciless and bold.

And then, he said it:

"I've wondered how you'd taste for so damn long."

The magic of the wood danced quietly around us.

"You taste better than I ever imagined...my queen."

He shouldn't be calling me that.

Beau was his queen.

And I had a serious problem.

I wasn't supposed to feel this way.

16

THE DREADFUL WITHER

Under the aurora of morning, I kept close to Ruckus as we navigated the remainder of the Emerald Wood. Windley had been wrong—I didn't feel tired at all. I did feel something, though.

My queen.

My. Queeeen.

I was stuck in my own head, replaying the way Windley had whispered those words—not like a title, but as if they were an indulgence. The memory of his lips numbing my fingertips. His emerald eyes, bright with desire. The warmth of his breath trailing across my skin.

Afterward, I'd been unable to walk on my own, still caught in the aftermath of his power. He'd brought me safely back to bed, standing watch outside as I drifted off—every bit the loyal guard I knew him to be, secret predator or not.

The many sides of him were at war. So were mine.

Part of me wanted to walk beside him, trading easy banter as if nothing had changed. Another part wanted to remind him of my station, that I was a queen, not a prize to be devoured. And still, a dangerous part of me wished to return to last night and let him finish the job.

It was becoming impossible to deny that the night beneath the willow—the night he'd first murmured those words—had not been a dream at all.

It feels good to hold you at last...my queen.

Windley's eyes had reverted to their usual black, but twice now, I'd made the mistake of catching them, only to glance quickly away, uncertain of what I'd see if I looked too long.

I couldn't speak for Ruckus, but I was content to let the stag shield me, staying toward the rear of our small party. Rafe walked at a distance, withdrawn after what had transpired between us. But compared to Windley's intensity, Rafe's incident felt inconsequential—like comparing a spark to an inferno.

"You're quiet today, My Queen. Did something happen?"

Leave it to Albie to notice my inner turmoil. He added, with mischief glinting in his eyes, "The hounds haven't been misbehaving, have they?"

Both Rafe and Windley stiffened noticeably.

"Just thinking about Beau," I deflected—though it wasn't entirely a lie. She was certainly part of my thoughts. "It'd be comforting to receive another message from her, so we'd have a better sense of how far she is."

"Don't fret, My Queen," Albie reassured. "By now, the Clearing's cavalry must be scouting the wilds beyond. With any luck, we'll encounter them soon enough."

True. The cavalry was out there, steadfast and determined, drawing nearer to Beau with each passing sunrise. That was where my thoughts should stay.

On Beau.

Beau would know what to do. Beau had navigated these

dark waters before. I needed her—I ached for her—as though she'd taken part of my heart with her.

We traveled on through dense greenery, the forest growing thicker around us, passing streams, rocks, and tangling brambles. While the others enjoyed the silence, to me, silence had ceased to exist. Instead, a distant, unsettling rumble reminded me constantly of the shadowy forces lingering just beyond sight.

It was thoughts like these that made me long to run straight into Windley's protective embrace.

A chill settled in the air, alive with gusts of wind. Windley's newly scarlet hair stirred around his pointed ears and teased at his neck. Rafe left behind a faint, frosty trail, and Ruckus shook his shaggy head whenever the breeze disrupted his pelt.

Albie had instructed us to listen for waterfalls. Delagos's map had promised that the southern reaches held pristine pools ideal for camping or bathing.

But though I strained to hear the soothing rush of water, all that filled my ears was the murmuring of something older, darker, and far more insistent.

Eventually, the stags alerted, noses lifting in unison toward the east, tails pricked and ears swiveling attentively.

"What is it, Ruck?" I asked, tightening my grip on his reins as he shifted, restless to pursue whatever he sensed. "A chipper?"

"They want to head that way," Windley said, wrestling to keep his own stag in check. "What lies eastward?"

"According to the map, nothing," Albie replied. Even his well-trained stag stomped impatiently. "We should investigate. They might smell water."

We followed their instincts through swelling greenery,

foliage rising up to our waists. Once more, I was grateful for extra britches; a gown would have never survived this trek. I busied myself murmuring calming words to Ruckus, aware of Windley's presence beside me. Was he watching me? It certainly felt like he was.

Or perhaps it was merely remnants of his power.

We emerged into a glade—a perfect, unnatural circle carved from the forest, barren despite full sunlight.

The atmosphere changed instantly. The fresh scent of earth and pine vanished, replaced by something stale and acrid, like ashes left too long in the damp. A weight pressed down on my chest, thick and oppressive, as though the glade itself were holding its breath.

Inside, the underbrush was blackened, decaying—a grave-yard of twisted roots and brittle stems. Dead trees protruded at grotesque angles, stripped of bark, limbs frozen in clawing postures. Beneath our feet, the soil was cracked, charred, stub-bornly resisting any attempts at life.

"Don't enter, Ruck," I warned, tugging him back by the reins as he shifted nervously. "Looks cursed enough to me."

I half-joked, the way I always did when something felt off— strange blooms, unnatural reflections, trees split too neatly.

Albie chuckled softly. "Unlikely, My Queen. Lightning must have struck here."

Whatever had happened, it didn't belong within the rest of the Emerald Wood's vibrant life.

"Not lightning." Rafe knelt, running gloved fingers through darkened soil. "The earth itself feels wrong here."

"See?" I said again. "Cursed."

I glanced to Windley, expecting a jest, but his expression was serious, nearly severe. He studied the scarred landscape carefully, chin resting in his hand, the usual mischief absent from his face.

Did he recognize this place?

A chill traced my spine.

When he noticed me watching, he masked his discomfort quickly, lips curling into a faint, teasing smile.

I began to smile back, welcoming the chance to reclaim our easy dynamic, when Ruckus had other plans.

"Ruckus? Whoa! Ruck—!"

My unruly stag chose that exact moment to wrench free, plunging hooves-first into the cursed clearing.

"Ruckus, NO!" My heart surged, but he was already tearing ahead.

Damned stag.

Albie was right—he was spoiled.

I lunged after him, my foot striking down into the blackened soil the same instant Windley's desperate shout pierced the air:

"Merrin, DON'T—!"

Too late.

The instant my foot met the earth, a frigid pulse shot up my leg, cold tendrils clawing through my veins. The dead soil clung to me, creeping up my ankle in a slow, sickly spread—like rot sinking its teeth into fresh flesh.

At the same time, one of the dead trees lurched.

Not a tree—an *antler*.

The ground shuddered beneath me as the beast rose over me—massive, hulking, pulling itself from the decay where it had been waiting, watching.

It looked like a wind stag. Only wrong. Its body was too large; its massive antlers gnarled and reaching, matted pelt as black as a moonless sky. And its eyes—goddess, its *eyes*—a violent, glowing red, watching me with a keenness far too intelligent for something so monstrous.

Ruckus skidded to a halt, nostrils flaring. He veered

sharply, hooves kicking up dead soil, fleeing out of the circle, away from me.

But I couldn't move.

My foot was stuck.

Dark muck clung like tar, dragging me down.

"Shit." Behind me, Rafe swore, the cold hiss of his sword slicing the air as he unsheathed it. But I barely registered the sound.

The stag advanced toward me. Its breath rumbled—a deep, guttural exhale, smoke rolling from the maw of something ancient.

Time slowed as I stared death in the face.

Then the creature charged, hooves eerily silent against the cursed earth.

Time snapped back, and strong arms encircled my waist, wrenching me violently backward.

"It's a fucking blood stag!" Windley shouted, voice ragged with distress. "RUN!"

He heaved me into the lush green, away from the circle of decay, shoving my shoulders forward and forcing me into motion.

"That's a blood stag?!" Albie roared. He drew Faylebane—his legendary blade, rarely unsheathed—gleaming menacingly in his grasp. "Goddess above, it's even uglier than the tales!"

Mother Poppy had woven nightmares of these creatures—hell-born beasts, feeding on the blood of virgins to fuel their crimson eyes.

"I thought they weren't real!" I cried.

Apparently, the part about virgins was bogus; the blood stag barreled directly toward Rafe.

Rafe spun neatly, sword slicing air—but his blade met no resistance, passing through the beast like smoke. His footing faltered. "It isn't solid—"

"Don't lower your guard!" Windley's voice cracked through the chaos.

Good advice—but too late.

The stag flickered back into flesh. This time, its impact sent Rafe flying. He crashed into a gnarled tree, breath punched from his lungs.

"Get the queen out of here!" Windley shoved me toward Albie. "These things are hard as shit to kill!"

Albie seized my wrist, yanking me after him—but not before I saw Windley fling himself forward, hatchets whirling.

"Albie! Windley's playing bait!"

"As he damn well should!" Albie's grip tightened, dragging me through waist-high brush. I twisted, desperate to witness the fight behind us.

Windley slashed fiercely with one hatchet, forcing the stag to dissipate briefly. The instant it solidified again, he struck with the other.

"He hit it!" I planted my feet, resisting Albie.

But the triumph was fleeting.

A rattling hiss filled the glade.

Horror surged as another antler tore free from the dead soil, black and twisted. The earth shuddered violently as a second stag clawed upward, shaking off rot as it joined its companion.

"No!" I cried. "Another monster?!"

Windley's attack had barely slowed the first!

Rafe was already back on his feet, sword blazing with ice enchantments—blows landing even when the stags phased to shadow. With both beasts distracted, Windley circled for openings, a defiant, reckless smirk on his lips. Rafe's eyes burned fierce and otherworldly, ablaze with Luna's glow.

"My Queen, come!" Albie barked urgently.

"They need to run!" I shouted back.

Albie's jaw hardened, gaze shadowed by grim resignation.

"They won't flee. These fiends crave blood—once awoken, they'll hunt us endlessly. It's kill or be killed."

Realization plunged into my chest like a blade.

Albie didn't expect Windley and Rafe to survive.

He was ready to sacrifice them for my escape!

"No, Albie." My voice turned steel. "There has to be another way."

"Aye, but I won't let you risk it." Before I could protest, he hoisted me roughly over his shoulder. "Rulers lead, Merrin. They don't fight."

His words sliced deep, igniting fury in my chest.

Rulers don't fight?

Rulers don't FUCKING FIGHT?

"If I weren't willing to fight," I snarled, "what kind of ruler would I be?"

I struggled, but Albie's hold was iron.

"Enough, My Queen! You've no plan—and an entire queendom to think of!"

But a true queen didn't abandon her people.

A true queen fought—even when victory seemed impossible.

I stopped struggling and turned inward.

Until this point, I'd feared the darkness, resisted it. Now, I opened myself fully, inviting it to take hold.

"Merrin?"

Eyes closed, I sank into the void. Albie's grip became distant, Windley and Rafe's battle fading to silence.

"MeRRin."

"mErriN."

"MERRIN!"

"I need your help." I whispered into the blackness, and it surged forth—

Hands. Hundreds of them. Swirling, repeating my own words back to me:

"They aren't so bad. Let them live. We'll let them live for now."

"No!" My will cut through harshly. "Some deserve punishment!"

The darkness shuddered violently, eager and ravenous.

"All are bad!" it raged back. *"We'll rip them apart! Destroy them all!"*

Too far.

"Not all," I commanded, will ringing with authority. "Only these."

With all my strength, I convinced the darkness some beings must be destroyed. That some would kill unless killed first.

"The red-eyed beasts!" My intention sharpened like a blade. "They have no merit!"

The void quaked.

"Yes!" I cried, feeding the darkness my certainty. "They must die!"

Power roared within me, and I ripped free of Albie's hold, racing toward the cursed glade. His shouts, panicked, faded behind me.

Ahead, Rafe fought desperately, sword raised, chest heaving. Windley lay bloodied on the ground, narrowly dodging the second stag's charge.

"They have no merit!" the echoes shrieked, wild and ecstatic. *"Unleash our wrath!"*

"End them!" My voice thundered through both worlds.

A force erupted—not wind, but darkness made manifest. Echoes surged through my veins, molten and searing, erupting through my fingertips in a torrent of shadow and fury.

The darkness struck true.

Both stags stilled instantly, monstrous bodies collapsing, crimson eyes fading to empty white.

Windley and Rafe stood frozen in place, breathless, stunned at the devastation I'd just unleashed.

I didn't pause.

Sprinting forward, my boots skidded on soil already reclaiming life from decay. I reached Windley first, gripping his shoulders firmly. "Are you all right?"

Blood streaked his cheek, shirt torn, skin scraped raw. He stared at me, throat working before finally giving a tight nod. "Yes." His voice was a rough whisper. "How did you...?"

I turned quickly to Rafe. "Rafe?"

He stared blankly. "...I'm fine?" His tone questioned reality itself.

Albie charged up behind us, halting abruptly as his eyes scanned the glade, gasping in disbelief. "You've bested them!" He released a labored breath. "Well done, lad!"

Lad?

Relief flooded Albie's face. "Didn't know your moon-power could do that!"

He hadn't seen the shadows—only their devastation. He thought it was Rafe.

"No—" Rafe started.

"Seems the chap's been holding out on us," Windley interrupted smoothly, his gaze briefly flicking to mine.

Rafe hesitated, confused. I subtly shook my head.

"...I can't use it often," he finished quietly, uncertainly.

"I should think not," Albie muttered, still shaken. "Never seen a spell like it."

Windley's eyes lingered meaningfully on mine, unreadable yet incisive. "Certainly was impressive."

Slowly, the echoes withdrew, phantom touches whispering

farewell against my skin. Yet even as they receded, I felt them clearly:

Their hunger.

Their pleasure.

And in that moment, I finally understood the echoes' urge to destroy.

Because destruction felt *good*.

17
FEEDING THE MONSTER

"Come. Hither."

Speaking of wolves, the deepest, most dangerous stare had found me.

I'd been dreading this—the moment Albie left me alone with the hounds, forcing me to explain myself, both to them and to my own conscience.

We'd settled by two glistening forest pools, one spilling into the other via miniature falls that sang a gentle lullaby. The clear, shallow water sparkled with luminous rocks. Fragrant blooms dotted the shore—an apothecary's dream.

Windley and Rafe tended their wounds near the fire, while Albie had gone scouting for our missing stags. We assumed they weren't far. Ruck was a shameless coward; he'd wander back eventually, and the others would do so out of loyalty.

"You dare summon a queen so casually?" I said imperiously.

"Don't give me that," Windley muttered through the torn cloth clenched between his teeth. His hair appeared darker—

the scarlet deepening to maroon, shadowy roots peeking through. "What in goddess's name was that back there?"

"One thing's for certain." Rafe folded his arms. "It wasn't me."

Both stared expectantly, judgment practically rolling off them in waves.

"Did you tell him about the echoes yet?" I asked Windley.

"What sort of secret-keeper would I be if I had?" he retorted.

Rafe sighed impatiently. "I covered for you. You owe me an explanation."

He was right.

"I'm sorry, Rafe. I didn't tell you because I didn't want you to worry."

In one breathless ramble, I confessed everything—Beau losing her echoes, my fainting in the forest, my experience in the other world—the voices, the grasping darkness.

When I finished, Rafe pressed a thoughtful hand to his jaw. "That's why she couldn't heal me, but you could," he murmured, piecing it together. He was surprisingly calm. At least he hadn't thrown himself on the ground again. "Then maybe Beau was taken because she lost her abilities."

"I've considered that," I said slowly.

"Or perhaps someone stripped her of them deliberately—to make her easier to abduct."

That possibility hadn't even crossed my mind.

Windley exhaled dramatically, his voice dripping sweetness. "If it's not too much trouble, *Your Majesty*—what in the *absolute hell* was that earlier? Please, enlighten us."

I matched his charm with a wicked smile. "Only because you groveled." I pressed on, "You know how Beau injects her intentions into the forest's will, calming nature's fury?"

They nodded cautiously.

"Well, I did the opposite. I convinced the forest those blood stags deserved to die."

Silence.

Windley's brittle grin barely held. "So, you can talk nature into killing anyone you want?"

"Perhaps. Though I've only tried it the once."

Windley flicked an ember from his sleeve. "Well, if that doesn't curdle the blood."

"I didn't even know it was possible," Rafe admitted. "Beau never mentioned such power."

"Not to me either," I agreed. "I see why she kept it secret. A queen who keeps nature peaceful is a treasure. One who can bend it to her will is a threat."

Even now, the echoes whispered restlessly at the edges of my mind, stirred up after tasting blood. I'd have to soothe them later.

The realization struck me—

I was starting to think of them as beings to appease or care for. Was that really wise?

"No one in my clan wields power that potent," Rafe warned. "Magic can be fickle, Your Majesty. Please, exercise caution."

"I will. And thank you, Rafe—for your discretion. Albie doesn't need to know yet." I fixed him with the look of a queen who'd made devils kneel.

Rafe swiftly dropped his gaze, bowing. "Understood, Your Majesty."

Amused by his predictable aversion, I rose to my feet. "I'll make some salve for your wounds. There's tweedberry nearby —it'll heal you quickly."

Before I could take another step, a deft hand caught my shoulder, gently drawing me back. My breath faltered as

Windley carefully lifted my hair, leaning in close to whisper, "You and I still need to talk."

Then, smoothly looping his arm through mine, he raised his voice to a casual drawl. "Mind if I accompany you, Queen Merrin?"

The earlier battle had provided distraction, but as the chameleon-haired guard guided me away from camp, his body brushing mine, last night's reveries rushed back, stirring something deep within.

His eyes.

His breath.

His lips.

I've wondered how you'd taste for so damn long.

We'd linked arms countless times, yet never had my pulse raced like this.

He guided me uphill to the smaller pond that overlooked camp and stopped among the wildflowers.

"Vera-weed grows here," he noted, releasing my arm. "You'll want it for your salve."

He remembered. I hadn't mentioned vera-weed since last spring.

"Indeed." I bent to the thick leaves, the medicinal gel already slick between my fingers. "It'll numb the sting."

While I worked, Windley loitered near the water's edge, his voice low and oddly earnest.

"You were remarkable today, queenie. I thought we were finished—then you came in like a storm tide. Beautiful...and terrifying."

Heat crept up my neck.

"What sparked that?" he asked, humming the words. "You couldn't know it would work, yet you charged back in—risking yourself for a bunch of guards. Hardly textbook 'queenly' behavior."

"Who decides what's queenly?" I snapped off a leaf, still refusing to meet his eyes. "If I ask you to fight, I'll fight beside you. Anything less is unworthy of loyalty."

"Shame you're royalty," he said, a rough amusement in his tone. "You'd make a deadly guard."

"It felt good," I admitted, finally looking up. "I feared the echoes, but now...I want to wield them again." A grin tugged at my mouth. "Care for a spar?"

"I don't step into matches I'm bound to lose." He flashed a half-smile.

For a moment the grin lived between us—easy, natural.

Then he drew a long breath; the humor drained away.

"Alright—let's settle something."

His roguish spark vanished, replaced by sober regret. The air tightened.

"What happened last night went too far."

Oh no.

My pulse hitched.

"It's...too easy to forget there's a crown between us," he said, voice low. "I let want outrun sense—acted like a fool." He glanced once at Rafe before meeting my eyes again. "I'm meant to guard you, not behave like some tavern rake."

My stomach knotted.

He straightened—every inch the court knight now, though the ache lingered in his gaze.

"I crossed that line, Merrin, and that's on me. It won't happen again. You have my oath."

Crossed that line. The phrase felt wrong in his mouth, like he was trying to fence in something that had never wanted walls. And in that instant, I knew—desperately—exactly which version of myself I intended to embrace.

Crown or no crown, we'd raised a hungry thing—fed on every quip, every lingering glance, every brush of skin. It prowled under our ribs, ravenous, and I had no wish to let it starve.

I liked playing with him. I always had.

"Stop," I said—clean, commanding.

Windley blinked, as if the word had slapped him; a heartbeat of stunned silence passed before color drained from his smirk.

"The reason I keep you close is *because* you forget I'm a queen, you knave. Rafe, Saxon—they're with me because they don't grovel. If you start bowing now...I'll have no one real left."

"You were distant—I thought—"

"What did you expect? Your magic is pure temptation. I just needed a moment to...re-orient."

Half-true, yet the admission eased the rigid line of his posture.

"Thank goddess." He dragged a hand down his face, voice muffled. "I thought I'd broken you."

Something inside me cinched—dangerously close to snapping. I knelt in the grass.

Only then did he let out a long breath, shoulders loosening.

"If you haven't broken me yet, Windley, you won't." I lifted the vera pulp. "Hold still."

My fingers skimmed the cut along his cheek and lingered, tracing the drying edge of blood.

Windley's chest went still; the muscle beneath my touch flexed, then settled—coiled, waiting.

His heartbeat thudded against my palm, perfectly in time with the flutter in my throat.

Slowly, his fingers rose—warm, steady—and closed over mine.

"Merr," he murmured, eyes catching mine. "One of these nights, you and I need a proper conversation."

Silence pulled tight between us—

"My Queen?"

Albie's voice floated up from camp. Windley hissed a muted curse. I rose, and his fingertips slid from mine like a kite string slipping free.

The monster we'd raised together purred.

I was treading dangerously.

"No Ruck yet?" I asked, patting Albie's stag as the other two drank from the watering hole. Daylight deepened into evening, staining the sky with vivid hues. After hours beneath dense canopy, the open heavens felt reassuring.

Albie unloaded his pack, shaking his head. "Your coward stag will sniff us out eventually, My Queen." He paused, giving me a pointed glance. "There are many more suitable mounts out there. I don't know why you insist on him."

He meant Ruckus, but for one brief moment, my thoughts drifted elsewhere:

You taste better than I ever imagined.

"Ruckus is simply my favorite," I replied. "I admire his will and defiance."

Albie chuckled knowingly. "If you say so, My Queen."

Rafe looked up from the fire. "Do we need to worry about more blood stags, Sir Albie?"

"I didn't find any other nests nearby." Albie gestured at the open sky, tinged by sunset. "This spot will give you a clear view of the moon," he said. "Get a full charge, just in case."

Rafe's eyes connected with mine. "Understood," he said begrudgingly, not keen to claim credit for the earlier spell.

Windley rejoined us, descending the hill with tweedberries in hand. I busied myself with preparing the curative, pressing a chunk of vera into one of Rafe's serving bowls and beginning to crush it. All I needed now were the berries—which Windley silently dropped into my palm—and a dash of lavender extract from my pack.

I'd always liked the gritty sound of a pestle grinding against mortar. It ranked second only to the rough, familiar rasp of Albie's aged voice.

As a child, I'd often played on the throne-room rug while Albie briefed the guards, droning about matters beyond my young understanding. His gravelly words had blended into a comforting backdrop of scribbled notes, rustling parchment, and popping firewood, sending me drifting into sleep.

But when that same roughened voice spoke now, it carried no comfort at all.

"My Queen—a word?"

Dread settled heavy in my gut—not the pleasant fluttering I'd felt earlier, but a leaden weight of apprehension. That tone was one I'd heard often as a child, whenever I'd gotten caught doing something naughty I thought he'd never discover.

He always discovered.

I placed the pestle down and quietly followed him beyond earshot of the others.

Albie's voice was level but carried expectation. "I'll ask you again: why did you insist on accompanying us to retrieve Queen Beau?"

"For the widowbirds," I answered evenly, eyes narrowing just enough to offer a challenge.

Though my words held truth, Albie's suspicion only deepened the lines around his eyes. "Is that all?" When I didn't waver, his voice softened, as if cushioning a blow. "You know queens cannot afford...attachments, Queen Merrin."

As anticipated, the conversation quickly turned mortifying. Windley and I had been careless among the flowers, and of all the topics I didn't wish to discuss with my ever-watchful chaperone, this ranked near the very top. I merely nodded, hoping to avoid a detailed reply.

Albie pressed on, fixing me with an unwavering stare, his resolve evident. "Queens may only court from the other bloodlines. Even now, there are arrangements underway for you to meet with the kin of the Cacti. You're aware of this, My Queen."

I drew my cloak tighter around myself. "What exactly are you implying, Albie?"

The knight shook his head slowly. "You're grown now and free to make your own decisions. But I would be remiss if I didn't warn you—" He hesitated, his frown deepening. "Tread carefully. That boy has quietly loved you, I'd wager, from the first day you met."

18

FORGOTTEN SCARS

After Albie issued his warning, I waved him off with a laugh and returned to the others.

Deflection was a skill I'd honed well. If you dismissed someone's concerns with enough confidence, they'd start questioning whether they ever had reason to worry in the first place.

Wicked of me, maybe—but also necessary. Because if I let myself dwell on it too long, I'd start questioning things I didn't want answers to.

Windley? In *love* with me? It was absurd.

There were countless reasons to dismiss the idea—reasons I could list in careful order, like a queen preparing a defense before her court. First, Windley wasn't the type to surrender himself to something as consuming as love. Second, if there had been signs, surely I would've noticed them by now.

I did a good job with the dress.

I've wondered how you'd taste for so damn long.

Beautiful...and terrifying.

It feels good to hold you at last...my queen.

My stomach twisted.

Albie had gotten into my head.

I finished preparing the salve and set it aside with freshly cut bandages for Rafe and Windley. Dirtied from days of camp and travel, we would bathe in the forest pools before retiring for the night.

Of all nights, it was imperative we sleep well tonight, as tomorrow we would likely reach the far edge of the Emerald Wood, and Delagos offered little guidance for what lay beyond.

As I soaked in the privacy of the upper pool, shrouded in fragrant wildflowers and cattails, I blew dutifully on the widowbird whistle, hoping that if any were near, they would come to me. I also hoped Ruckus, stubborn as he was, might hear it and wander back to us.

Below, the guards bathed and laughed over things Albie wouldn't discuss in front of me for fear of tainting my queenly sensibilities. More stories about men playing mandolins with their nether-parts? No, thanks.

The solitude gave me a chance to calm the maelstrom of voices raging in the distance.

I tipped my head back into the pool, submerging my lion's mane, and closed my eyes.

The moment I let go, they came. A mantle of hands swarmed around me, squeezing, probing.

I didn't fight them—not this time.

They had come through for me. For Windley. For Rafe. They'd saved us in our darkest moments. Perhaps they weren't purely malevolent after all. Perhaps they were a resource.

As my physical body floated in the chilled water, my spiritual self drifted into the shadows, willingly now. I let it in. Drew its weight into my lungs, felt it press into my ribs.

"*MErrIn.*"

"*MeRRIN!*"

I sighed tiredly, allowing their presence. "Hello, you troublesome things."

"We killed them! Both of them! They had no merit. We will kill more. All of them. Tear the world apart! Purify the earth!"

They were still drunk on death.

"No," I said decisively, sending calm into their frenzy. "We expelled only those without merit. The others can live."

"MErrin."

"MeRRin."

"Next time, I'll tell you if there are others deserving of death," I offered carefully. "We can work together again, if needed."

"Let them live for now," the echoes conceded hungrily. *"Soon, we will kill again."*

Not exactly my point, but it would have to suffice.

Yet just as relief began to blossom, something shifted—

A voice sliced cleanly through the whispers, clear, distinct, sinister. *"You enjoyed it, Merrin. Such consumption. Such destruction. Admit it. Together, we'll purge everything."*

Neither male nor female, the voice stood entirely apart. At the same instant, a single hand—colder, more solid than the rest, horribly deliberate—slid up my chest and closed tightly around my throat.

The moment its grip constricted, icy panic surged, instinct striking like lightning, wrenching me from the darkness and throwing me violently back into the waking world.

I bolted upright, bursting through the water's surface, hair streaming as I desperately grasped the rocky edge of the pool, gasping raggedly.

What the hell was that?

Had I somehow summoned that darkness myself, encouraged its hunger for blood? Or was this force something deeper —ancient, powerful, and utterly beyond my control?

I strained to listen, heart pounding.

Despite the chilling encounter, the echoes had receded into muted whispers of *let them live*. Yet, deep down, I understood one bitter truth—I'd have no choice but to return eventually.

But not now. Not tonight.

The forest was darkening swiftly, shadows stretching long across the clearing. Shivering, I finished my bath quickly and dressed.

"I'm coming down!" I called. "Cover whatever needs covering."

From below came a splash, the thunk of boots against stone, Rafe's muttered curse, and finally Windley's easy laugh.

I gave them a slow count of ten—long enough for belts to buckle and modesty to be restored—then started along the narrow path that zig-zagged to camp.

Halfway down the last switch-back I paused, scanning for Ruckus. My gaze drifted to the fire—and snagged on Windley at the edge of its glow just as he tugged his shirt over his head.

Broad shoulders, lean waist, skin sheened bronze in the flames. An unwanted, molten warmth danced low in my stomach.

Goddess, Merrin. Look away.

But the light shifted, revealing something I hadn't meant to see: three raised, parallel scars slashed down his back—old, deliberate, too cruel to be from the blood-stag battle. A history lost to him yet etched forever in his flesh.

My fists clenched before I could stop them.

Windley's head turned, as if he felt the weight of my stare.

Luckily the fire lay between us; to him I was only a back-lit silhouette.

I picked my way the rest of the way down, bare feet sinking into damp emerald peat, already hunting a moss-less patch before the rising moon could betray my glowing tracks to Albie.

"Did you two bandage up properly? Even coat of salve?"

"Yes, *mother*..." Windley's drawl died the instant he faced me.

His posture hitched, hair flashing to a warm honey-auburn, as though steeped in tea.

One sharp sweep of his gaze—shoulders, still-wet hair— then the usual grin re-latched. The color in his locks ebbed, darkening by degrees until they were safely inscrutable.

"Well. Look at you..."

Albie's warning cough snapped him upright. Windley dipped his head in exaggerated reverence. "Forgive me, Majesty. Your mane's asleep—I wasn't prepared."

I raked the damp strands back. Straight, they spilled past my waist—sleek, heavy, nothing like the riot of curls camp life usually conjured.

Funny how a curtain of water can make me look like someone else entirely.

"Tamed, not shorn," I said.

"Wouldn't dare doubt it." The amusement returned—but his eyes kept flicking, quick and involuntary, to the sheen of my straightened hair, as though trying to pin down a thought that kept slipping away.

"I'll brush it, My Queen," Albie offered, and I sank at his boots while Windley kept watching, eyes reflecting every stroke.

Beau had always been the best at brushing hair—better than Chrysanthemum or any handmaid—but really, I wasn't picky. Albie's wrinkled hands were overly careful, a little clumsy, handling the strands like delicate silk when in reality they were thick and coarse.

But I loved him for his tenderness. He'd been doing it this way forever.

As the fire crackled and my hair dried, I tried to push Albie's earlier words from my mind.

Flirting was one thing, but Windley wasn't the sort to fall in love, and surely he wouldn't be foolish enough to fall in love with me.

...*Would he?*

The more I intended not to think about it, the more I did.

And all the while, the silver-tongued guard kept watching Albie brush out my hair, making small talk with Rafe but catching my eye.

Every time he pursed his lips, I remembered them brushing my fingertips.

The higher the milky moon rose, the more beguiling the details from the previous night felt.

I needed to tame this monster before it slipped its leash.

When the watchful moon reached its peak, Rafe stood at the edge of the tranquil pond to charge his blade. Paying no mind to his silent audience, he lifted the shimmering steel against the ink-black sky and closed his eyes, drawing moon-glow into its surface. Pale light pooled at his throat before spilling into whispered incantations—the same unenthused string of words he'd uttered at the tree fortress.

Above, the moon shone impossibly bright, silvering the surface of the pond. The rippling water mirrored its shape—but for a fleeting moment, the reflection wasn't quite right.

I blinked.

And saw a shadow beneath the moon's glow—a vague impression, almost human, as if the moon had a face.

I blinked again.

The illusion was gone.

Weary eyes playing tricks.

I shifted my focus back to Rafe, who lowered his blade, sealing the spell with a sorcerer's kiss.

As if on cue, a sudden rustling in the nearby trees set us all on edge.

Rafe and his newly enchanted weapon were already poised for a fight, Windley close behind, hatchets glinting, eager for blood.

"Stay sharp." Albie's command carried just above a whisper.

"MerrIN?"

The echoes stirred, sensing danger. I held them at bay, uncertain whether to suppress or summon, aware that to summon meant confronting that sinister hand around my throat again.

Windley grabbed a stick from the fire, lighting its tip before easing toward the trees, pointed ears alert for any movement.

"Oh," he said dully.

"What is it?" Rafe asked, still gripping his sword.

Windley stepped aside and lifted the torch, illuminating the antlered creature meandering toward our camp.

"Look who's finally graced us with an appearance."

If stags could look ashamed, mine certainly did.

Relief flooded me. "Ruckus!" I resisted the urge to run to him, mindful of Albie and my enchanted footsteps. Instead, Windley corralled the wayward animal in my direction, and the moment Ruck was close enough, I threw my arms around his neck. "Did you have an adventure?"

The stag responded with a gentle nuzzle. Whatever he'd been up to, it had worn him out. He took a long drink from the pool—now tainted with the flavors of Windley, Rafe, and Albie —before collapsing beside his brethren with a weary sigh.

"Get some rest, you birdbrain," Albie grumbled. "We've got a long ride ahead of us."

"Albie!" I feigned offense. "That's a *noble* steed you're talking about. He isn't a *birdbrain*."

"Like rider, like stag, I always say," Windley crooned.

To his delight, it was Albie's turn to take first watch, meaning we'd fall asleep without the usual snorts and grunts interrupting the night. I turned in first, Windley close behind, with Rafe shortly after—though not before Albie pulled the magician aside to issue some kind of order.

"What was that about?" Windley asked when Rafe returned.

"You must have done something," Rafe muttered. "Sir Albie told me to keep an eye on you."

"*On* me?" Windley clutched his chest, feigning scandal. The performance might have worked better if his hair weren't now pitch-black, making him look even more rakish.

"Both of you," Rafe corrected, lowering his voice. "Used the word *bounder*. Now move. I'm sleeping in the middle till my patrol."

"Dear goddess, the man thinks me a miscreant," Windley huffed. "I meant to take the side anyway."

So he said, but it wasn't long before he was pestering Rafe again.

"*Psst.* Switch places with me. Just for a while. I need to talk to the queen."

I could hear their whispered exchange, but barely—my heart was beating too fast, and the more I tried to quiet it, the louder it became. Surely they could hear it, too.

Eventually, Windley convinced Rafe by promising something in exchange. There was a rustle, followed by the distinct sound of a predator crawling closer.

I squeezed my eyes shut, feigning sleep—poorly.

"Tch. You're not asleep. Stop faking."

Exposed.

I rolled to face him, finding him crouched beside me, eyes sharp with amusement.

"Well, I was nearly asleep, thank you. And what are you doing over here, anyway?" I narrowed my eyes, though my pulse betrayed my boldness. "Didn't you claim you're no bounder?"

"Oh? Is that what you want?" he quipped, voice steeped in mischief.

That was starting to affect me more than it used to.

"Is that what *you* want?" I countered.

Apparently, it affected him more now, too. His smirk wavered briefly, throat bobbing, but the longer we stared at each other in the dimness, the more that smirk reasserted itself.

"W-who ever thought it was a good idea to make you a guard?" I muttered.

Annoyed, Rafe groaned and yanked a pillow over his head.

"Sorry, Rafe," I whispered, then turned back to Windley. "What do you really want?"

He shook his head and mouthed, *Wait*—implying he didn't want Rafe to hear. Then he slid into a lying position beside me, propping his cheek up on his knuckle. We stayed that way several more minutes, facing each other in silence, until Rafe's breathing turned heavy.

Windley checked over his shoulder at the sleeping magician, then at Albie's silhouette beyond the tent's canvas, firelight dancing behind him.

Then he scooted closer.

I stiffened, hyperaware of how loudly I was breathing, how quickly, how deeply.

"I've been thinking..."

His voice slipped across the darkness between our bedrolls, pitched so low I had to lean in to catch it. "What if the echoes left Queen Beau of their own volition?"

I tensed. "What do you mean?" I matched his whisper.

The faint scrape of linen sounded as he shifted, weighing

his reply. "She's never done anything like what you did," he murmured. "It isn't in her nature. What if the echoes left to find someone who could put them to better use—a more worthy host?"

A shocking assertion.

I didn't know how to respond, so I took the diplomatic route. "Beau is your queen, Windley, and the echoes are her ancestral right. You can't say things like that."

His voice remained quiet, almost conspiratorial. "It's just that the south's version of the Nemophilist is different from the north's," he mused. "She's supposed to be a fucking badass. An ender of wars. A wielder of tremendous power. That's not Queen Beau. That's you."

Flattering. And blasphemous.

Again, I didn't know how to respond. This time, he offered me an out.

"I know you can't condone it," he said. "But now you know my thoughts on the matter."

That was dangerous.

He was dangerous. The way I felt wielding the echoes was dangerous. It was as though I was being tested on all fronts.

"So, what's your plan here?" I asked, changing the subject. "You're going to wake poor Rafe to make him switch places with you now?"

"Psh, no," he said lazily. "I'll just cuddle up next to him. Sir Albie won't worry if he comes in to see two guards spooning. Might even lay his fears to rest for the remainder of the trip."

I snorted—loud enough to risk waking Rafe. My hand flew to my mouth, but Windley was faster, covering it first.

He jerked back just as quickly, mumbling an apology, while I wrestled the sudden urge to bite his fingers. Lion instincts, apparently.

Our shared monster slammed against my ribs, hungry. The prudent choice would have been to roll over and sleep.

"Windley?" I heard myself ask instead, voice careful. "If it isn't too insensitive...what happened to your back?"

The deep lacerations, carved into his skin as though he'd been whipped or clawed at for years.

He arched one brow. "Shocking. Was Her Virtuous Majesty spying on her guards while we bathed?"

"Please. That would mean I saw Albie, too."

"Fair." He rolled onto his back with a sigh. "Thought I felt eyes. Hideous, isn't it? Don't fret, lion queen. The memories are foggy, and I've no wish to dredge them up."

"Understood." I pulled my covers higher. "And I don't find it grotesque. I was just wondering."

Wondering who—or what—could have done that to him. *They had no merit.*

Windley was quiet for a moment before muttering, "About last night—"

My heart stopped.

It seemed we kept finding ourselves in these compromising positions. Here we were again, in the dark, bodies closer than they should be, the air alive with unspoken words.

See? I should've rolled over when I had the chance.

"I almost showed you when we were young—the first time we met, actually—to impress you, but Sir Albie said you'd be afraid. For a while today, I thought he was right. I'm glad you recovered."

Had I really *recovered*? That flutter still threaded through me, settling in all the vulnerable places—neck, spine, ribs, belly.

"Maybe that's why Albie marched you back to the Clearing instead of the Crag," I murmured. "He decided *I* was the greater risk. If he hadn't, you'd be my guard now, not Beau's. Imagine it—forced obedience."

A beat of charged silence.

"You'd have tired of me quickly," Windley said at last. "By every account I was an insufferable brat."

"Hardly. You said the things I only *wanted* to say. I probably learned half my mischief from you."

He huffed a quiet laugh. "My legacy—corrupting a queen." Rolling onto his side, he met my eyes. "Don't kid yourself, Merrin. You were born a troublemaker. Sir Albie's wrinkles are your doing, not mine."

Smirking, he studied my eyes, but then his gaze dropped lower—to my lips. The lion in me bit them.

Windley noticed.

His jaw tensed. Rafe made a noise in his sleep. Outside, the fire cracked.

"Can I ask you something unusual?" I whispered.

"You outrank unusual—you're a royal, aren't you?"

Unusual was a fig leaf; *indulgent* was the truth. I didn't care about the answer—only about where the question might lead.

"Do people...taste different to you? When you do your... thing?"

His smile re-formed—slow, knowing. "They do."

"And what do I taste like?"

Blackstone ring turning beneath his thumb, his gaze slid over me—dark, unreadable. "Is that an invitation?"

"I—"

"Say no, and I stop," he murmured, Spirite voice a velvet threat.

I couldn't. The monster inside my ribs wouldn't rest until it was fed. My pulse—traitorous—answered for me.

"Go ahead."

The smile didn't deepen; it honed. Playfulness peeled

away, leaving intent. He took my hand, folded down every finger but the pointer, and drew it to his mouth.

"Yes, sensations vary." Eyes locked on mine, he brushed parted lips along the side of my finger. Numbness bloomed, a bright shock that shot all the way to my shoulder.

"You taste like..." He hesitated, tasting the word first. "Try imagining a color you've never seen."

"Cute," I managed.

"It isn't flavor, it's feeling. You're the top of a summer knoll—warm wind, wildflowers, endless sky. Bright, clean, freeing." He kissed the web between thumb and pointer, eyelids fluttering shut. "And now that I've had it once, I'll never escape it."

"Is that how it works?" Elation rippled through me.

"Oh, no," he sighed. "Plenty of flavors fade. Maybe it's because you're royal—or maybe it's *you*."

Was it his power making me want to fold into him?

"Do I feel different now that I have the echoes?" I asked— the memory of that milky other-world still thick in my mind. "I don't feel...shadowed?"

"Not a flicker," he promised against my palm.

His lips wandered to my wrist, heat sliding into my veins. By the time I drifted toward sleep, our fingers were woven— though I couldn't have sworn whose idea it was.

19

THE OTHER SIDE
OF THE WOOD

"Come along, cuddle buns."

Thank goddess Albie was talking about Rafe and Windley and not Windley and me. The plan had worked a little too well, leaving Albie with ample teasing fodder and Rafe in the foulest mood I had ever seen him.

Last night had been another lapse in judgment on my part, and to be completely honest, I didn't care. It felt both right and wrong, good and evil, forbidden and inevitable. I had never done anything like this for myself, and this felt *so* for myself. It felt deserved.

Windley and I rode side by side, back to our old antics, bantering as we journeyed through the remainder of the Emerald Wood.

By mid-morning, the terrain began to change, moss and mammoth trees thinning until we reached a single signpost in a language none of us could read, marking the end of the forest.

Tied to the post, flapping in the wind, was one scarlet strip of hope.

Albie had been right in his calculations; the Clearing's cavalry had already passed through here, leaving behind their signature ribbon. Below it, he tied an emerald one—a symbol of our unity.

We weren't alone. Beau would be rescued.

It was possible she had been already.

Beyond the signpost stretched an expanse of plains and rock formations as far as the eye could see. Tall golden grass swayed in the wind, dotted with boulders, caves, and rocky rubble. In the distance, large animals roamed while smaller ones grazed.

"Wallops," Windley said, rubbing his temple. "And gazelles." He concentrated harder. "There are cities to the south," he said, pointing. "The sea's to the east. Giant's Necropolis should be west...I think."

"What does your map show, Albie?" I asked.

"Not anything worth a lick." He held it up, revealing a few random Xs and circles scrawled in messy handwriting. "The Cove's royal guard hasn't come down this far, so their intel is based on travelers' tales. However"—he crouched to the ground —"the cavalry did travel west. See how the grass is pushed in? Looks like they came through here from the east, but appears they stopped to place markers on every signpost they passed."

"That means they took a different path through the forest," said Rafe. "They must have exited from the far coast and followed the forest's border."

It made sense. Mother Poppy knew of Giant's Necropolis, but her story only said it was beyond a thick forest. The Clearing likely had similar records. What better way to find it than to search the entire stretch of the forest's threshold?

Rafe yearned toward the west, clearly wondering, as I was, whether Beau had already been found.

"It's lonely out here," I said, tucking myself away from the chill of the wind sweeping across the golden prairie. "I expected more."

"More? Just as your world has an end, so does this one," Windley said. "There's no need for people from the south to come up this far."

Albie patted the Spirite's back. "Let me know if you need a break, lad. Can't imagine it's easy being back down here."

The south. Where Windley had gotten those scars.

"Are there whole cities of your kind down here, Windley?"

"There are whole cities of many kinds down here, *Queen Merrin*."

"Will we be out of place if we encounter others?" Rafe pressed.

"Your accents might be an issue, but humans are relatively common," said Windley. "Though I can't speak for whatever you are, chap."

Rafe shot Windley a perturbed glare, still irked over being cuddled against his will. In the aftermath, I noticed him rubbing at his chest.

I wasn't ready for that to happen again.

We followed the cavalry's trail west in the direction of Giant's Necropolis, keeping our eyes and ears open for any scarlet-cloaked scouts roaming the lonely landscape. Ruckus snapped at grasshoppers hiding in the tall grass as they fled from his path. He thought himself a ferocious beast.

From atop his back, I blew into the royal whistle with more urgency than ever before, willing a messenger of Beau's to find me. Other birds passed—long-necked, bright-feathered—but none were the one I wanted.

Then, a lone cabin appeared in the distance, its timber walls framed by a fence in what was otherwise the middle of nowhere. It looked to have once belonged to a woodcutter. The lot was abandoned, but a scarlet ribbon tied to the fence confirmed the cavalry had passed through.

We urged our stags onward, beasts tearing across the wild-lands with the fury of a storm, hooves pounding the earth like resonant thunder. Our cloaks billowed out behind us, snapping in the wind.

This felt right.

Surely, the scouts had found Giant's Necropolis and led Beau's cavalry west.

Surely, we were racing toward her rescue.

Or perhaps—she'd already been rescued.

Either way, I'd be reunited with Beau before nightfall.

I was certain of it.

Until—

"Whoa!"

Albie's sudden shout halted his stag abruptly, forcing the rest of us to follow suit. He was slightly ahead, perched at the edge of a small valley, and whatever lay beyond caused his voice to fracture with panic.

"Rafe, shield the queen! Don't let her see!"

His distress sliced across the gilded grasslands.

Obediently, Rafe leapt from his steed, seizing Ruckus by the reins and turning him around. As if that could stop me—I still had a working neck, after all. Hoisting myself higher on Ruckus's back, I twisted to glimpse what had frozen Albie and Windley in place.

The valley below wasn't golden—it was scarlet.

A basin drenched in blood, grotesque and deliberate, as though painted by some unholy hand.

But it wasn't paint.

Scattered across the crimson-stained grass lay three dozen stags. And three dozen riders.

Beau's cavalry had been massacred.

There are moments—captive ones—that burrow so deep they stain the pale edges of memory. I would earn two on this journey.

This was the first.

My heart seized. Clicking my tongue sharply, I urged Ruckus forward, bolting around Rafe and Albie toward the carnage, ignoring their desperate shouts, ignoring the frantic hands grasping after me.

Stopping wasn't an option.

I had to know.

Was Beau among them?

I'd never imagined a massacre clearly, but if I had, it wouldn't have looked like this.

Bodies hadn't simply been cut down—they'd been obliterated.

Smeared across yellow grass in sickening streaks, as though the earth itself had tried to erase them.

My vision blurred as I searched for Beau.

Her raven hair. That princess-like frame. Those delicate fingers.

I examined every face.

Grieved for each soul lost.

And when at last I realized Beau wasn't among them—

My strength vanished. Sliding from Ruckus, my knees struck sticky, blood-soaked grass, anguish breaking through in raw, choking sobs.

Across the field, Rafe mirrored my reaction.

Bittersweet relief—Beau wasn't here.

Yet devastating grief for those who were.

I hadn't known them, but each had been treasured by someone.

Each soul had merit.

Each deserved delicious foods, beautiful music, warmth.

None deserved this end.

"They all had merit," whispered a voice from the void. *"They deserved to live."*

Before I could respond, familiar, weathered hands lifted me carefully from the bloodied earth.

"Come along, My Queen. This is no place for you."

I curled into Albie, just as I had countless times as a child, letting him carry me. My arms encircled his neck; his wiry mustache brushed my forehead as he pressed a gentle kiss there.

"It's awful, Albie," I sobbed. "So senseless."

"Hush now, Queen Merrin. I'm here."

He carried me away from the field painted with death, setting me down beside his stag and shielding me with his cloak.

Through my haze, I heard him speaking quietly to someone.

"Can you ride, lad? Take the queen back to the woodcutter's cabin. Rafe and I will give them a proper burial."

Oh.

Windley.

Albie was talking to *Windley*.

My heart jolted, clarity breaking through the fog. Windley!

How had I not considered him? These weren't just Beau's subjects—they were Windley's comrades. People he'd trained beside, sparred with, fought shoulder-to-shoulder with. Even those he hadn't known well, or particularly liked, had still been part of his life.

And if I knew him at all, he wouldn't show his grief.

He'd bottle it until it consumed him whole.

I rose shakily, steadied myself against Albie's stag, and searched for him.

Windley stood apart, blood streaking his clothes.

His jaw was granite-tight, shoulders squared beneath the gore-spattered leather.

Fingers curled and uncurled at his sides—not trembling, only hunting for something to fight that wasn't there.

The focus in his eyes had shattered, but the soldier's reflex still prowled beneath the shock.

Albie kept talking, yet Windley's stare tunneled straight through the older knight, as though the words never reached him.

I had to get him out—*now*.

"I'll take him, my knight," I rasped, voice raw from tears and dust.

Albie's bloodshot gaze snapped to me. "Queen Merrin?"

I didn't waver.

I pressed my palm to Windley's chest—heat and hammering heart beneath. "Wind. With me."

He moved on instinct. One hard arm cinched my waist; with a single, effortless heave he swung me across his stag's withers and vaulted up behind, muscle and discipline merging into one fluid motion. No questions, no falter—only the quiet authority of a man who decides in an instant and acts.

Together, we rode out of the slaughter.

At the woodcutter's cabin, Windley dismounted from his stag in one fluid drop, then extended a calloused hand.

I hesitated before lacing my fingers with his, matching the weight in his stare.

Inside, the single-room shack felt like a relic of another life. Dust hung in shafts of light. I found the bucket, hauled water from the well, and returned with a soaked cloth.

Windley sat on the cot—elbows braced on his knees, shoulders squared, blood drying along the lines of muscle. He didn't flinch when I pressed the cloth to his forearm; only the tight set of his jaw betrayed the strain.

He let me work. I washed away crimson and grit, the only sound our breathing and the drip of water into the basin. When my hands were finally clean, the dam burst—I folded to the floor beside the bed and let the weight crash down.

I wept—

For Windley,

For Beau,

For myself,

For every soul left cooling in the grass.

A moment later thick arms hooked beneath mine; Windley lifted me, effortless, and settled onto the cot with me anchored against his chest. His heartbeat thrummed steady under my ear, an iron drum beneath battered leather.

He spoke no consolation—he simply *was*, all heat and steadiness, letting my storm expend itself against him. Side by side, we breathed. Side by side, we grieved, until silence wrapped us in a rough-spun blanket.

Time drifted—the crackle of the distant wildlands, the dull thud of shovels somewhere under the stars.

At last he bent, voice gone to gravel. "You fit here, Merrin." His cheek rested at my temple, arms cinching with quiet certainty. "Stay close, my queen."

So I did.

We fused to each other while the hours smoldered, the fire guttered low, and Albie and Rafe moved through the darkness, laying the dead to rest.

20

THE BETRAYAL

This story would be better if Beau were the one telling it. Beautiful, regal, freckled Beau.

If Beau were narrating, you wouldn't have to face the painted field. Or the things that happened next.

But these moments matter, captive ones. Pain shapes who we become.

I woke to the heat of a fire. Someone had built one in the hut's small fireplace, and I'd been rolled close to it in a makeshift nest of blankets. My body ached from disuse.

I didn't know how much time had passed, but enough for Rafe and Albie to return, for Windley to sit upright on his own, his hair now shifted to peach. The three sat around the dwelling's only table, speaking in low voices, barrels and debris serving as makeshift chairs.

I pushed myself up from the throws, feeling like a creature emerging from hibernation, and cleared my throat. "Albie?"

The guards rose abruptly, but only Albie approached. The other two retreated deeper into the shadows.

"My Queen." Albie knelt beside me. "You're up sooner than expected. How do you feel?"

"Groggy." I rubbed my eyes. "How long was I asleep?"

A pause. A hesitation. "A few days."

"*Days?*" My stomach lurched violently. How was that possible? Cuddling with Windley felt like mere hours ago. "I never sleep for days."

"You were distraught," Albie said in a soothing undertone. "I...took liberties."

I stiffened. My gaze skipped past him, landing on guilty Rafe rubbing his chest, then Windley standing quietly, arms folded, eyes fixed stubbornly on the floor. He no longer looked hollowed out. Color had returned to his face, composure frustratingly restored.

Albie released a measured breath. "This may come as a shock, but your favorite knave has sorcery in his blood. His kind can force people into sleep. I ordered him to use it on you while we tended matters here."

A long, heavy silence filled the cabin.

Then realization crashed through me like a physical blow.

Windley had used his power on me.

Not just once—but repeatedly.

Without my consent.

My breath stalled painfully. Heat flared inside me, flames licking hungrily through my veins, raging into my bones. The violation of having my own time stolen—my own body forced into submission—burned deeper than I could've imagined.

Windley knew exactly how deeply he'd betrayed me. It radiated from the tense set of his jaw, the rigid lines of his shoulders, the deliberate avoidance of my stare.

I tried to catch his gaze anyway, desperate for something—

acknowledgment, remorse, anything—but the coward wouldn't meet my eyes.

My pulse pounded in my ears.

He knew—and yet he refused to look at me!

No. He didn't get to hide from me now.

Not after the hours we'd spent grieving together.

Not after using my vulnerability as a balm for his own wounds.

Not after all those clandestine encounters, feeding our monster, again and again.

I was worth more than that.

The room seemed to ignite around me, every breath fueling the fire.

"Have you lost your senses?" My voice cracked, hoarse from days of forced silence, and fury. "Beau is out there somewhere! We were so close—and you—you had me slumbering in some goddess-forsaken shack!"

Windley shifted uncomfortably but still wouldn't meet my gaze.

Albie attempted to soothe me, his voice infuriatingly calm. "I understand your frustration, My Queen. It wasn't an easy call to make, but it was best for you. You should never have seen..."

His words trailed off. The unspeakable truth of what we'd witnessed hung between us.

My fists clenched painfully. "You had no right!" My voice lashed through the cabin, lacerated and trembling. "None of you! Pray tell, what happened in the *days* while I was held captive in my own body?"

Windley visibly flinched, but remained silent. Rafe grimaced, hand still pressed against his chest. Albie bowed his head in somber reverence.

"We found Giant's Necropolis," he said, "but it isn't as easy to access as we'd hoped. The remaining cavalry are camped at the entrance, trying to craft a way inside."

The fire behind me snapped and anger surged, hot enough to scorch—until that single line snagged my fury mid-rise.

"Wait—the *rest* of the cavalry?" A spark of hope cut through the heat. "There are survivors?"

Albie nodded. "A dozen. They were out scouting during the attack. No one knows what butchered the others; there's no clear sign of the beast responsible."

He straightened, laying a cautious hand on my shoulder, as if half-expecting me to bite.

The caution was justified.

"There's one more thing, My Queen, but brace yourself." Albie took a deep, rusted breath. "We're sure Queen Beau is somewhere within. The scouts found her namesake ring. She seems to have left it behind intentionally."

Her namesake ring. Just as I had an emerald ring to prove my identity, Beau had a garnet one.

"Evidently, she tore off pieces of clothing as she traveled, leaving a trail. The ring was the last clue, just outside the Necropolis."

Clever Beau. Brilliant, resourceful Beau!

Of course, she'd done something like that.

And if she'd left a clue outside Giant's Necropolis, it meant she'd been alive when she entered it.

A weight lifted, and I pressed a hand to my heart. "That's excellent news, Albie! Why are we here? We must proceed to the front lines and assist the cavalry!"

Albie retracted his hand. A wise move. Because what he said next made me want to bite him for real.

"No, My Queen. I'm bringing you back to the Crag."

I laughed at him.

But Albie wasn't bluffing. "You said you came for the birds, yes?"

"I *came* for Beau."

His voice hardened. "There's a creature capable of wiping out an army here. This is no place for you. I won't allow it."

My nails bit into my palms. "Albie, if you think I'll turn tail and run home while Beau is in danger, then you don't know me at all." I turned furiously toward the two traitors behind him. "Are you hearing this?"

Neither moved.

Albie's brow creased sorrowfully. "No, My Queen. I'm afraid I do know you that well. I reckoned I'd have to take you by force."

He motioned behind him. "*Now*, lads!"

And they had the audacity to obey him.

"Windley? Rafe?" My voice dripped venom, sharp enough to pierce armor. "I command you to stop!"

Neither met my eyes.

"Windley, so help me—!"

I staggered back, but they were fast. Too fast.

In an instant, Rafe was behind me, locking my shoulders in an iron grip, as though I were a common thief to be subdued.

"I'm sorry, Your Majesty," he whispered roughly, regret fracturing his voice. "Know that I'll stay. I'll find her in your stead."

As if that made it any better. As if that made it acceptable!

I thrashed violently, kicking, writhing, but his hold was stronger than my wrath.

"Be careful of her," Rafe warned, casting a wary glance at Windley.

Albie furrowed his brow. "Of her?"

Yes, because unbeknownst to him, I held a secret weapon.

They who aided me before.

They who made me stronger than any magician, Spirite, or knight.

How kind of Rafe to remind me.

Seething, I let rage take hold, eyes slipping shut as echoes slithered forth.

"We will kill them all! Rip them asunder!"

"No!" That wasn't what I wanted. Surely there was something less...extreme? Something between willingly submit and rip asunder?

"mErrIN?"

But before I could rein them in, Windley spoke for the first time since my waking. His voice was dull, distant—and brought no comfort.

"Turn around, Sir Albie. You aren't going to like what you see."

What the hell did that mean?

I snapped my eyes open, finding Windley's magnetic presence closing in, firelight dancing shadows across his unreadable face.

At last, he looked at me.

He didn't even look sorry. He looked...impatient. Like my resistance inconvenienced him.

"Windley!" My voice broke, raw with betrayal. "Don't do this."

He said nothing.

Then, with predator's eyes cast aside, his hand slipped beneath my shirt.

I sucked in a sharp, horrified breath.

Windley's touch had never been hesitant. He was a thief of space, distance, focus—and I had always welcomed it.

Always before.

Not now.

His fingers splayed over my stomach. A sick heat spread

outward, waves of warmth radiating from where his palm flattened against me—shameless, invasive, and utterly wrong.

I twisted, fought desperately.

But Rafe held me fast, and Windley didn't let go.

I was queen, yet they stripped me of my power. And I despised them for it.

"I'll never forgive you if you do this!"

Windley sank slowly to his knees before me, eyes darkened by something inscrutable—regret, determination, emptiness? I no longer knew him well enough to say. With a cruel tenderness, he pressed his lips to my stomach, stealing my strength, my defiance, my choice. One arm coiled around my waist, steadying me as I thrashed, his hold unyielding. A pulse of numbness radiated outward, draining my will as he lingered, drinking me down in slow, deliberate sips.

This was nothing like our stolen kisses or playful grazes.

My heart thundered—but not with thrill.

With fury.

My veins writhed—but not with pleasure.

With rage.

My skin prickled—but not with anticipation.

With revulsion.

Slowly, inexorably, my strength drained from me. Shivers took hold, crawling insidiously through my bloodstream.

When Windley finally pulled away, lips slick with stolen life, his eyes glowed mesmerizing, predatory emerald green.

My body stilled.

Windley wasn't my confidant. He was a spider. And I'd flown straight into his web.

Everything between us—the precious trust, the whispered secrets, the simmering tension that had bloomed in shadows and silent understandings—all reduced to ash. Obliterated by the brutal truth of his betrayal.

Had I been merely a plaything to him? Another conquest to boast of, another challenge conquered, to see how close he could come to breaking a queen?

Inside, I screamed. I wanted to spit venom at him, at all of them—to claw and kick and send the wrath of a thousand dark hands crashing down upon them—

But it was too late. My body was no longer my own.

Windley had done this to me. For *days*, at Albie's command. Ignoring my wishes, dismissing me as weak. As a burden. Something to be managed.

My consciousness slipped, rage fading into helplessness.

The last sensation before darkness claimed me entirely was Windley's mouth pressing gently—far, far too gently—against my damp forehead, kissing me just as tenderly, as devotedly, as he ever had.

The softness of it hurt more than the betrayal itself.

A voice slipped through the void.

"Merr?"

...

...

...

Something was shaking me.

"Merrin?"

...

...

...

"You should be able to open your eyes. I didn't give you that much. Tch. *Glutton*."

I knew that voice. Just as I knew that mossy, homesick scent.

A forest?

I swam through the darkness, clawing toward the voice, toward the scent, toward waking. And when my lashes finally fluttered open—two dazzling emeralds stared back at me.

Relief, remorse, tenderness, guilt—emotions warred openly on his face.

Windley.

I forced myself upright, blinking against the clearing's eerie radiance. We were in a thin stretch of forest, settled on luminescent moss that glowed beneath me. Above, stars peeked through the treetops, winking like mischievous imps.

Windley lowered his hood, letting his peach-colored hair breathe in the cool night air. His cheeks were dirty, his hairline damp. He placed his hands on my shoulders, searching my face, worry deep in his brow.

"Are you okay?" His voice was ragged. "I told you I'd never harm you, but I'm a goddess-damned liar. Is there a better word than 'sorry'? 'Sorry' feels too weak. Tell me the word, and I'll say it, Your Majesty."

I stared at him, chest rising shallow. It was a struggle to breathe at all with his hypnotic eyes boring into me that way.

He noticed.

"...Oops." He covered his eyes with one hand for a moment. When he removed it, they'd dulled back to their usual black. "Better?"

I nodded, clearing my throat, shaking off the strange haze.

"What's going on, Windley? Why are we in the forest? Where are the others? And just how many days have I lost this time?!" I glanced around the moonlit clearing. No one else.

He shrugged lightly, offering a faint, uncertain smile, as if not sure how I would take the news. "Well, I abducted you. Sort of."

I blinked. "What?"

"Queen-napped?"

"I understand the word, Windley. I meant—*what*?"

"Riiiight." He exhaled, shifting uncomfortably. "I didn't agree with Sir Albie's command, so I went ahead and disregarded it."

I gaped. "You did what, now?"

He answered as if we were chatting over breakfast. "I argued with Rafe for days. Poor fellow's lovesick; he almost sided with me, but he couldn't risk losing his chance to rescue naughty Queen Beau. Sir Albie, meanwhile, has been circling you like a fretful hen, so I..."

Windley studied his palms, as if half-shocked by what they'd done.

"I'd never have forced the sleep if there'd been another way. Albie has the cavalry eating from his hand; I needed someplace to stash you before I could break ranks. Every hour you were under felt like theft, Merrin—I was hunting for a way to wake you sooner, not dragging my feet."

I stared. "So you rendered me unconscious in front of Albie just to spirit me off into the night?"

"That's the short of it."

"...And now you agree I should stay and help find Beau?"

"Oh, goddess, no. I think it's a terrible idea." He shrugged. "But I also think it's your call to make."

A cord snapped tight inside my chest. I went silent.

Windley owed me no oath, yet he'd wagered both rank and honor to defend my freedom of choice. He had out-played Albie for my sake. No other knight—certainly none sworn to another court—would have dared as much. After all, an army guarded a queen's obedience as fiercely as it guarded her life.

Same defiant rogue as ever.

A ripple of half-forgotten affection rolled in, swift as storm clouds over the horizon. I stepped into his surprised arms.

"I forgive you," I murmured—then added, just as quietly, "but I won't be forgetting."

He exhaled, a rough little laugh against my hair. "Fair. Forgetting would be far too generous."

I drew back, meeting his eyes. "So start earning my trust again, knave."

Something grateful and reckless sparked across his face. "Always was partial to impossible quests."

A flutter skipped across my pulse, but I only lifted a brow. "Excellent. First task, then: what's the plan now?"

Windley released a breath, stretching his arms behind his head like this was just another casual stroll through treachery. "I'll take you to the Necropolis so you can see for yourself what we're up against, but we'll have to travel through the wood on foot so they don't find us. Sir Albie will have my head."

That part was expected.

But—

"On foot?" I squinted. "You didn't carry me all the way here, did you?"

He wiped his brow dramatically. "Lucky you're a slight little thing."

Beau was slight. I was not.

Pandering, if I'd ever heard it.

"Windley! Why didn't you bring the stags? It would've been much faster!"

He scoffed. "Because yours is a defiant dimwit—he'd trumpet our position inside a mile. The others already ran a supply loop to the cavalry camp; they're bone-tired and I didn't fancy dragging them through another sprint. And once we reach the Necropolis, hooves won't help. You'll see." He lobbed a pack my way. "Food, fresh tunic—something that isn't glazed in gore. Wash up quick; we've got ground to cover." A crooked half-smile. "Think you're up to a night march?"

I slung the pack over one shoulder and gave him a flinty once-over.

"If I collapse, you get to carry me again."

"There's a creek past that glimmer." Windley gestured toward a silver seam between the trees. "Make it quick."

I turned toward it, but paused, noting the glowing footprints trailing behind me.

"What do we do about these?"

"Ugh. Can't you quit being so damn magical?" Windley muttered as I tried—and failed—to tiptoe clear of them.

I leveled him with a dry stare.

He only answered with a slanted, wry smirk. "After dark we'll hug the edges—thinner moss, dimmer prints. We'll manage."

I left him by the fire, making my way toward the creek, leaving a shimmering trail in my wake.

The water was crisp against my skin, soothing the residual heat of stolen sleep. I washed away the remnants of unconsciousness, dressed quickly in a fresh shirt and trousers, and twisted my hair into a knot atop my head.

Easiest for traveling.

Easiest for fighting.

Fighting what, though?

Even as I dressed, my thoughts dwelt on Windley's state of mind. His spirits were high, as if our escape had somehow washed away the horrors of recent days. But I knew better. The massacre was still there, lodged deep in my chest like a rusted dagger.

It had to still ache in him too. And if it did, he would never tell me.

"Windley?" I called gently as I stepped back into the clearing.

He didn't even look up.

"Yes, I'm fine. No, I don't want to talk about it. And yes, you can have a bite of my apple." He raised a half-eaten fruit, presenting it grandly.

"Generous of you to offer me the *core*," I countered wryly, stepping closer and resting a comforting hand on his shoulder. "But alright," I added quietly. "I'll respect your wishes. Just know if you ever change your mind..."

"I know." His hand covered mine, fingers curling slightly. "You're the one I'd turn to, anyway," he murmured, sincerity clear in his voice.

21
NECROPOLIS

Moving through the forest—just the two of us, free from judgment for the first time—was liberating. Perhaps a caged bird never truly understands captivity until the sky is finally hers. Like a woodland nymph, I hopped back and forth, dipping my feet into the thicker moss to watch my blooming footprints appear, then vanish into darkness.

My power made me feel invincible, confident I wouldn't be captured again. This time, I'd act decisively, and with Windley by my side, we'd be unstoppable. Echoes prowled restlessly at the edge of consciousness, eager, hungry. But I kept them at bay, whispering promises into the shadows:

"Soon," I told them. "We'll unleash our rage on whoever took Beau."

We traveled swiftly, purposefully skirting the massacre site. I knew we were close when Windley steered us deeper into the trees without explanation, eyes fixed stubbornly forward. Had it been me, I'd have wanted comfort. But Windley wasn't me. He had his own ways of coping.

"I have a question."

"If you're announcing it, it must be important," he quipped, flicking a sideways glance at me.

"Why haven't Rafe and Albie caught up yet? Stags move faster than people."

Windley pursed his lips. "Call it luck."

"Oh my goddess. Did you *seduce* them?"

"I did not!" he sputtered. "I...may have borrowed some energy while they slept. Not much—just enough to ensure a suitable head start."

"Using your powers of *seduction*?"

"The Queen of the Crag would do well to behave, or she might find herself without a guide," he drawled, though he wore a telling half-grin.

I planted a hand on my hip. "It is, after all, just straight ahead, isn't it?"

"Royals are so tiresome."

Good—we'd moved past the hardest moments.

"By the way, your hair is peach now," I pointed out. "Rather summery."

"Is it?" He tugged a pastel strand, eyeing it skeptically. "Don't get too attached. I expect you'll see it turn *every color* before we rescue your lost queen."

My lost queen? Odd phrasing.

"Nice callback," I said, brushing past the thought. "But the sunset wore it better."

Around the time the morning sun spilled gold across the plains, distant hoofbeats echoed from the west. A lone scarlet rider galloped near the tree line, pausing to jot notes onto parchment.

Windley crouched low in the grass. "Bartolomew," he said, watching.

So, he did know the cavalry members by name. Distraction over comfort seemed to be the right choice.

"Going to introduce me?" I asked.

"Nah, you wouldn't like him. He's too well-mannered."

At midday, we paused to rest and eat, determined to reach the cavalry campsite and the entrance to Giant's Necropolis by nightfall. As I'd done for days, I blew the royal whistle.

"I still find it disturbing that those birds track your blood or what have you," Windley remarked. "For years, I assumed they memorized castle routes."

"You should have Mother Poppy tell you the tale when we get back. She's got the perfect storytelling voice—especially around a fire."

"I won't concentrate with that buggy stare of hers." His eyes narrowed suddenly. "Why are you looking at me like that?"

Because I'd just remembered something crucial.

"With everything happening, I'd forgotten! The night you showed up at the Crag, I was preparing to leave for the Clearing. I'd been researching Beau's lost echoes, trying to help her. There was nothing useful in our archives, but Mother Poppy recalled an old fable. How did it go? Something like... Long ago, when the moon was different, and two crowns were lost—"

"You mean the broken crown?" Windley interrupted. "I know that one. My keeper's daughter told it to me as a child. It's a common bedtime story in the south."

"Your keeper's daughter? What's a keeper?"

He flushed slightly—rare, for Windley. "Forget it. Not important."

A keeper. Scars. His aversion to his past. An elixir that erased memories.

Windley wasn't one to offer deep revelations freely. For the longest time, that hadn't bothered me. But now, his withholding made my ribs ache. Why did I feel he owed it to me to let me in?

Because we'd grieved together? Because our monster had grown? Because I wanted him to trust me the way I trusted him?

I clutched a handful of his cloak. He glanced down abruptly, eyes startled by my sudden touch.

"Truly, I do hope someday you'll confide in me, Windley. It seems I'm hungry for it."

He studied my expression carefully. "Why, Majesty?"

I wasn't entirely sure, so I answered honestly. "Royals rarely have genuine friends," I admitted in earnest. "But I count you among mine. I'm a good keeper of secrets, aren't I?"

"Hmph." He flashed his teeth in mild frustration, then softened just a bit. "I know, Queen Merrin. Maybe someday."

A strange reaction. I didn't fully understand it yet—but I would before the day was done.

He cleared his throat. "You still want that bedtime story?" A rueful quirk of his lips followed. "I promise—no sorcery in the telling this time."

"Just the story, thanks."

With a long-suffering huff, Windley hitched one hip against a fallen log, planting his boot on a knot of roots like a bard about to command a tavern:

"*Long ago, beneath a moon that ruled both night and day, a heavenly crown fell and fractured upon the earth. One half sank to the sea, the other lost among the trees. A simple maiden found the forest half, yet only half its whispers reached her ears. Mistaking wisdom for warning, she commanded the burning of the wood. Heaven, in fury, reclaimed her crown. But years passed, and the sea returned the other half,*" *revealing her tragic error. With humility, she repented, and the heavens forgave her. Crown restored, she became the eternal guardian of the wood."*

He shrugged. "I suppose the moral is not to act on half-truths—or something similarly preachy."

See? Even the south's fables had morals.

Given his fractured memory, Windley recalled the story with surprising clarity.

"Mother Poppy's was slightly different," I said. "She focused more on the listening—how the crowns were lost when no one heard the forest's sorrow, and regained by those who finally understood its whispers. But there are definite similarities. You're not half bad at storytelling. Perhaps you'll make a decent archivist once your bones become too brittle to heft a hatchet."

He shot me a devilish leer. "That'll *never* happen."

We continued through the forest for hours without tiring. Windley had my stolen vitality, and I had the echoes—feeding strength into my muscles, easing my fatigue. There was a delicate balance between letting them close enough to invigorate me and keeping them at bay so they couldn't overwhelm my senses.

"Do you need to rest?" Windley asked periodically.

"Haven't you heard I'm *magical* now?"

"Haven't you heard I've *always* been magical?"

"So it's old news, then," I teased.

"Naturally."

Our monster thrived.

As evening approached, Windley stepped out of the trees briefly to gauge our bearings. "We're close," he said, returning. "There'll be scouts. We'll stick to the woods, but we should be ready to sneak. Hopefully, your glowing feet won't give us away."

"Perfect," I said, recalling midnight treks through the castle to snack on tartlets. "I excel at sneaking."

His eyes gleamed. "As do I."

From there, we crept carefully, keeping close to the cover of trees and bushes, the forest bathed in sinking golden light. Just as shadows began stretching wickedly across the forest floor, Windley caught my sleeve and pulled me behind cover, ears perking at something my human senses hadn't detected.

He leaned around me, his arm across my chest, holding me back as he searched ahead. A sudden urge arose—to blow on the tiny hairs at his neck, just to set him off-kilter—but I abstained.

A moment later, I heard them too: people, quietly talking as they moved nearby.

Windley nodded for me to look. Through the foliage, I saw two scarlet-clad cavalry members—a tall girl and a fair-haired man—gathering mushrooms into a basket. Windley studied them closely, then leaned in, his lips brushing my ear.

"They're lingering. Let's wait it out."

Fine by me. Windley was pressed warmly against me, holding me perfectly still, breathing softly near my neck.

"Damn it." He glanced at the sinking sun. "We don't have time for your fuckery, Phylo," he muttered. "He's had it bad for her for months, but he's a terrible flirt. They could be at it all night." He eyed my wrist thoughtfully. "Care to spare some of that magical vitality of yours? You seem to have it in abundance."

"What exactly are you planning to do?" I whispered.

He wiggled his fingers dramatically. "I'm going to *muuurder* them—Ow!" He rubbed his head where I'd flicked him. "What do you think I'm going to do?"

"Fine. I suppose I'll enable your questionable methods." I offered him my palm.

Holding my wrist like a gentleman, he lightly brushed the tip of his nose against it, slowly sliding upward toward my elbow, nuzzling. When he returned to my wrist, he placed an unhurried, savoring kiss there. "Turquoise should do the trick."

I swallowed, forcing composure as I watched his hair bleed from peach into snowy white. His eyes melted from black to stunning, swirling turquoise. They didn't ensnare my blood the way the emerald ones had, but they were mesmerizing all the same.

"Be right back," he whispered, then sauntered confidently toward the pair, hood drawn low.

"Who's that?" Phylo's voice floated back to me.

"Halt!" the girl commanded. "Oh—it's just you, Sir Windley. What are you doing here? Weren't you taking Sir Albie and Queen Merrin back to the Crag?"

The words jarred me. Windley was supposed to march us home?

I'd thought rescuing Beau—the very reason he'd stormed into my room—was his whole purpose. She was, after all, his queen.

If anyone, I'd expected Rafe to be sent back, not Windley.

"Ready?" Windley was already back, his turquoise eyes dimmed, hair still white, hand extended to me.

I glanced beyond him. Phylo and the tall girl were lost in each other's arms, oblivious.

"What did you do?" I asked suspiciously, taking his hand.

"Some say Spirite power feels like falling in love. I just gave them a little push—amplified what they already craved. Should buy us time. Come on."

"So you're basically a cupid?"

"A chubby baby in a loincloth?" His brow lifted. "You wound me."

We tugged up our hoods and continued stealthily through the woods until Windley pulled me down again behind cover.

"We're beside the cavalry's camp. When I say, move to that tree and wait." He straightened slightly, checking for the right moment. "Now."

I darted from our hiding spot to the indicated tree, cautiously peering around its trunk. Six scarlet-cloaked guards bustled around tents, and nearby, wind stags grazed on grass painted red by dying sunlight. The guards appeared to be constructing some sort of wooden vessel from the forest's timber.

My heart twisted painfully, knowing three dozen others should've stood alongside them.

Windley slipped beside me, settling his hands on my shoulders, his chin a gentle weight atop my head. "Again. That tree over there. Ready...now."

I darted toward the next tree, but when I peered beyond its shelter, my breath tangled in my throat at first sight of the fabled southern mountain.

Giant's Necropolis wasn't merely a hill of bones—it was a towering heap built from enormous skeletal remains, monstrous in their magnitude, rising from the center of a glass-smooth lake that mirrored the evening sky. Colossal ribs arched toward the heavens, femurs thicker than tree trunks stacked like ancient stones, and empty skulls gazed sightlessly across the waters, eerie guardians of a forbidden graveyard.

Albie's warning about the difficulty of reaching it now made perfect sense.

The cavalry was building a boat.

Windley joined me, releasing a tired, knowing breath at the

sight. His fingertips tightened, a subtle pressure against my shoulders.

"How are we supposed to get way out there?" I breathed.

"Haven't thought that far," he admitted quietly. "But we'll figure it out. Come—I scouted a cave down this way."

He guided me from tree to tree until we safely distanced ourselves from the cavalry's camp, stopping where the forest met the lake's rocky shoreline. The water stretched dauntingly wide before us, the bone mountain rising steeply, impossibly high, with no clear structure atop it to imprison a queen.

"Wasn't there supposed to be an extra-large giant collapsed on top?" I questioned.

Windley pointed into the distance. "The foot of it's over there. The cavalry circled the whole lake already. According to them, there's no other way across."

We stood in tense silence, staring at the dark, rippling water. Windley and I couldn't hope to build a similar boat alone.

"Spirites don't happen to have superhuman swimming abilities, do they?"

"Like...a merman?" he replied, fully deadpan.

"I'll take that as a no."

The cavalry had the right idea. A boat seemed our only option. But the troops from the Clearing weren't under my command, and Albie would never permit cooperation.

We were on our own.

My stomach clenched tightly as my gaze lifted once more to the imposing Necropolis, its skeletal remains gleaming ominously in fading twilight.

Was Beau truly somewhere within that monstrous tomb?

The southern mountain is huger than expected...

Huger than expected? Did that phrase hold meaning?

Before I could puzzle it out, a scathing voice sliced through the trees behind us:

"*Windley*, you selfish prick!"

I spun to see a familiar figure slumped atop his stag, dark waves of hair disheveled and damp with sweat.

Rafe's usually meticulous attire was dusty, wrinkled, and streaked with grime. His tunic was loosened as though he'd been clawing at it for breath. A trembling hand pressed against his chest, his face sickly gray—ashen beneath the moonlight.

"Oh, right," Windley said offhandedly. "I gave Rafe a considerably smaller dose than Sir Albie. Figured we could use his help."

Rafe's glare could have melted steel. "Bastard! I've been following your damn trail for hours. You've dug yourself into a pit so deep—and now they'll think *I'm* involved in whatever insubordination this is!"

A sight. Rafe was actually furious. His usual detached calm was utterly shattered—breathing uneven, hair plastered to his forehead.

But he wouldn't get the chance to keep fuming.

With a choked gasp, the magician convulsed violently, his body jerking as if struck. He scrabbled desperately at his chest, eyes wide in shock, before tumbling from his stag and hitting the ground hard, limbs twisted as the relentless frost finally overtook his body.

22

A FROZEN HEART

The air at the Necropolis was different. Thicker. Stiller. The usual nighttime hum of the wildlands had dulled, as though the land were holding its breath. Beyond the treeline, the black sea licked the shore, a shifting mass of obsidian under the moon's gaze. The wind carried the scent of salt and decay, biting cold against my skin.

I pulled my cloak tighter.

"This is worse than last time! His chest is practically frozen! Feel it, Windley."

Windley didn't look keen.

"*Feel* it."

At the forest's edge, where the shore kissed the land, I seized Windley's hand and pressed it against Rafe's frostbitten chest.

The teasing lilt faded from Windley's voice, replaced by quiet intensity. His brow furrowed as he traced the icy imprint with careful fingertips, palm pressing flat to absorb its chill. His gaze narrowed—probing, contemplative.

"Interesting," he breathed. "That isn't a disease at all."

I stilled. "It isn't?"

"No." He spread his fingers, sensing something deeper. "It resonates like a hex. A powerful one."

"A hex? Those are real?"

Windley's eyes flicked to mine, somber now. "Real, rare, ancient—and incurable by ordinary medicine." His fingers hovered just above Rafe's chest. "It takes magic to battle magic."

That explained why the symptoms matched no known queendom disease.

"Who would place a hex on Rafe?"

Just how many secret lives was my guardsman leading?!

Windley sized up the unconscious magician. "You'd have to ask him. But a hex is relentless—fed by its caster's own lifeblood. Whoever placed this on Rafe hates him deeply enough to sacrifice something irreplaceable."

Alarm threaded through my chest.

I knelt closer, patting Rafe's cheek. "Rafe? Can you hear me?"

A groan—but barely a response.

I pushed a dark curl from his forehead and pressed fingers to his skin. Temperate.

Far from ideal.

The surviving cavalry was just around the lake. Albie was surely awake and pursuing us. Beau was near yet impossibly far, separated by uncrossable water. And Rafe lay barely conscious, breaths shallow.

"Windley?"

He exhaled through his teeth. "I know. Do what you must. I'll keep lookout—as well as...keep watch."

I glanced at him. His double meaning was clear.

With a nod, I leaned over Rafe, slipping my hand beneath his laced-down tunic, carefully avoiding the sculpted planes of his abdomen. I was glad he was nearly unconscious. Perhaps it wouldn't feel as charged if he wasn't fully aware.

Before my palm touched his skin, I let the forest's clamor inch into my thoughts.

"MeRrin!"

The echoes rallied, vibrating with excitement at being unleashed again.

Yes, I kept returning to them.

With my hand pressed against Rafe's chest, I sank deep within myself, plunging fearlessly into that shadowed realm, feeling the echoes rush forth to meet me, eager to prove their merit.

Warmth pulsed outward like heat from a blazing fire.

Still, Rafe didn't move.

"Rafe?" I placed my other hand against him. "Can you hear me?"

Nothing.

"Rafe?"

Still nothing.

"RAFE!"

Not even a twitch. The longer it continued, the more frantic I became.

"Windley! Something's truly wrong—it isn't working!"

In a flash, Windley was behind me, breath warm against my ear.

"Why worry? Rafe said your magic surpasses even his clan's elders. You're a queen, ruling thousands, yes? You healed him before, yes?"

His chin rested atop my hair, hands gently brushing over my shoulders.

"I have all the faith in the realms your power can overcome this hex. Calm your soul, breathe, and try again, lion queen."

A familiar tingle trickled down my spine. I concentrated on

his warmth, his grounding touch, the unwavering belief in his voice. Instead of simply letting the echoes creep closer, I shut out the world—and fully embraced theirs.

"*MErrin!*"

"*MeRrIn.*"

"This one is deserving of merit," I told the darkness, and the darkness surged in response. "He holds a queen's heart and bravely protects the realm. Come as close as you can without harm."

Amplified whispers roared around me. My palms throbbed with otherworldly energy.

Rafe made a small noise, then another. His back arched, fingers clutching over mine.

"M-more," he croaked, releasing a cold puff from deep within his throat.

I rubbed warmth into his skin, recalling how he'd guided my hand to his neck before, seeking comfort like a chilled child.

His breaths deepened, and I cupped his stubbled cheek. "Rafe, you're warmer now. Is it working?"

His throat flexed. "Please...just a little more."

As I fed the echoes into him, Rafe pushed himself upright, one hand braced on the ground, the other gripping mine. His fingers tightened; his eyes found mine—amber, intent—and he inhaled in sync with me, jaw locked.

"The heat's stronger than usual. You feel...good, My Queen."

From behind, Windley made a strange noise.

See? This was exactly why he needed to be present! Rafe looked flushed and desperate, and those words weren't meant for me—they belonged to Beau. I was merely a proxy.

This time, Rafe knew what to expect, so there were no theatrics. He closed his eyes, suppressing himself, shuddering, and released a long, unsteady breath as the last of his frozen heart melted.

Then he freed me, took his head in his hands, voice frayed. "Goddess damn it." He glared past me at Windley. "Not one word from you. *Ever*."

Windley lifted a lazy shoulder. "I'm on your side, chap." He added under his breath, "Though I'd say that was indeed a 'pleasure' face..."

Rafe's head snapped up. "Apparently you aren't on my side, *chap*, because you kidnapped the queen, jeopardizing my station out here." He gestured toward the bone mountain. "How would you feel if it were *her* up there instead?"

It took me a moment to realize by *her*, Rafe meant me.

Was he insinuating our relationship mirrored theirs? Ridiculous. Rafe and Beau were lovers. Windley and I were mere flirts.

But beside me, Windley went still.

"Rafe," I blurted suddenly. "What exactly are you implying?"

Rafe stiffened, then quickly dropped to a knee before me. "Your Majesty. Though sworn to protect you, I'm also bound to Sir Albie. Had I defied him openly, I'd lose my station—and he'd have sent me back. I humbly seek forgiveness."

I sighed. "Rise, Rafe. I understand why you acted as you did, and I absolve you."

But ever Rafe-ish, he remained rigid.

I crouched, resting a hand on his shoulder. "Beau is fortunate to have someone who treasures her so deeply. Will you partner with us to rescue her?"

He clenched his fist. "Even after...?"

"Of course. Beau is like my sister. And you are her secret love. I'll take responsibility for any trouble you may incur—say I forced you into it."

"Caveat being you don't turn on us," Windley chimed in lightly. "I'd hate for us to become enemies, Rafe—especially now that we've grown so close."

Rafe arched a brow. "When did that happen?"

Windley ignored him. "But first, you owe us the truth about that hex. Magic this powerful usually involves love, revenge—or both."

Rafe rose to his feet. "What are you talking about?"

"Your ailment," I said. "Have you done anything to warrant the ire of someone powerful?"

Rafe's fingers brushed his collar. "I don't..." Truly confused.

Windley waved dismissively. "Think on past exploits—anyone particularly nutty or notably witchy."

Still gripping his shirt, Rafe turned toward the bone rubble across the water, where his damsel awaited. "What's your plan to cross the lake?"

Windley cleared his throat. "I hoped you wouldn't ask just yet."

Rafe gave him a dead-eyed stare. "So really, you have no plan."

Windley sniffed. "If you want to be pessimistic—"

I stepped between them. "Let's find cover first. Take us to your cave. With Rafe's magic, my echoes, and Windley's...abilities, there must be a way."

"Sex power," Rafe muttered, adjusting his disheveled attire.

Windley scoffed. "It's not—" He exhaled tersely, pinching the bridge of his nose. "For the last time, Rafe, I'm not an incubus. Those things aren't even real."

"And what exactly makes you not one?" I asked, perhaps too quickly. "For...curiosity's sake."

"The lack of wings and horns is a solid clue." Windley motioned impatiently for us to follow. "Come on. The cave's this way."

We had barely taken two steps when nearby underbrush exploded in a sudden flurry. Another widowbird shot upward, wings beating frantically as it wobbled into the sky.

My heart leapt—Beau had sent another message! Did she somehow know we were close?

But the bird faltered midair, circling unsteadily back toward us, landing in a graceless tumble at our feet.

"Oh, poor dear," I gasped, already crouching. My fingers skimmed gently along the bird's trembling feathers.

"Dear?" Windley echoed dryly, standing at a careful distance, distrustful of the creatures as ever.

Rafe crouched beside me, studying the bird intently. "It's injured. These feathers look newly grown—probably won't fly properly until they're fully back." Carefully turning the bird's leg, his expression darkened. "The message is gone." He woefully revealed the frayed remains of a string.

Windley edged cautiously closer. "That explains the delay," he noted. "It'll recover, at least. But whatever took its feathers also took Queen Beau's message."

Disappointment lashed in my chest. What vital news had been lost with those feathers? But determination quickly took over. "At least we know we're on the right track," I said resolutely. "Beau is close. She's counting on us."

Windley's gaze softened, suspicion fading beneath understanding, and Rafe clenched his jaw before offering a firm nod.

Without another word, we hurried on.

23

THE MAGICIAN'S FOLLY

Night settled over the Necropolis as we made base near the lakeside cave Windley had scouted. Giant skeletal remains loomed like nightmares, their shadows twisting over black waters. The sheer magnitude made my skin prick. What other horrors from Mother Poppy's stories awaited to prove themselves real?

While Windley and I racked our brains for ways to reach the mountain, Rafe stood at the shore, sword in hand, murmuring an incantation under his breath. Windley had theorized that perhaps Rafe's frosty moon magic could build a bridge across, but Rafe had never produced ice like that outside battle. Now, he was at the water's edge, slashing at the lake and attempting to freeze a path forward.

None of it was working, though the creativity was commendable.

Through the trees came the heightened sounds of cavalry returning to camp for a meal. They were closer than I'd realized. My nerves clocked it. Time was slipping away.

I turned back to the Necropolis, a dull homesickness

forming in my chest. Was Beau truly in there? I saw no obvious signs of captivity, no visible stronghold among the remains— just bones and the eerie, glistening lake surrounding them.

Wouldn't you love to see the southern mountain someday?

Yet everything pointed here. Beau had left a trail—sent confirmation via widowbird.

The southern mountain is huger than expected.

Something about that phrasing...

Huger.

Beside me, Windley shifted with impatience, casting a side-long glance before clearing his throat. "Not to push, Majesty, but have you considered consulting your...friends?"

A phantom pressure tightened at the base of my skull.

The darkness was always there—a constant reminder of untapped power. I'd drawn from it multiple times, each moment blurring the line between desperation and control. Yet the last time I'd tarried too long, something else had found me.

That hand. That voice.

Unfortunately, fear was a luxury we could no longer afford.

I had no illusions that the echoes were safe allies. They hungered, threatened, tempted—and this entity, whatever it was, had power beyond even them. I'd been naïve before, recoiling at the first touch of darkness. Now, I refused to be blindsided again. If it held power—dangerous or not—I would confront it, understand it, and claim it as my own.

Steeling myself, I tipped my head once more toward that shadowed realm, bracing for the inevitable grip around my throat.

"MeRRin!"

The darkness slid over me, airy yet dense, cool and wispy like the thickest fog. I opened myself to it—and to my own feelings about our current predicament.

The thought of Beau being wrenched from her bed.

The thought of her trapped in a cold, damp place.

The thought of her fallen cavalry, desperately trying to reach her.

The thought of an unknown enemy deserving of punishment.

"They had *no right* to take her," I pressed into the darkness.

It surged in response, thick with excitement, writhing, ravenous. A tide of voices slipped through my senses—eager hands clawing forward.

"Yes," the mass whispered, coiling. *"But first, you must find a way across the lake."*

"The mountain is huger than expected," I told it.

And then I waited.

A pause stretched in the void. Then, like ink seeping into water, a shape bled forward from the abyss. Not shadow, not quite being—something in between.

It came fast.

The hand was around my throat before I could react.

A perfect recreation of the force that had seized me before —fingers woven of smoke and rot, yet solid enough to command flesh. My pulse pounded, body tensed, but I did not lurch back. This time, I wouldn't let go. This time, it would give me answers.

The grip held firm, urging panic to rise, but still I did not yield. I forced my breaths composed—until, gradually, the pressure loosened. Fingers dragged beneath my jaw instead, tilting my chin upward—not a threat, but an evaluation.

A sound not quite laughter rippled through the dark. *"Your fear of me wanes, Merrin. Good. You're learning. Fear is the barrier between you and what you were meant to be. It's the shackle keeping you small."*

I didn't like the way it said *meant to be*.

I narrowed my eyes into the void. "If you weren't here to kill me, a gentler greeting might've helped."

"*Oh, I don't wish to kill you.*" The fingers brushed my throat one last time, withdrawing like a whisper fading into an unfinished sentence. "*The bloodlust writhes in you now, Merrin. It's branded to your soul. You're not prey. You're the storm that will unmake the world.*"

A cold prickle laced my veins. Not fear, but *resentment.* "You mean to *use* me?"

The response came soft and delighted, slipping into my ears like a lover's secret.

"*It has already begun.*"

I clenched my fists. "If by unmake you mean *ruin*, know now that I don't exist to destroy—I exist to protect. That's my will—not yours."

The shape shifted, weaving around me without definite form—just the impression of something vast, untethered, and waiting.

Then—

"*You can only resist for so long. Your true self is already coming to light, and soon, you'll be the one to unmake things.*"

Wrong.

But was it?

I had drawn from the echoes. Wielded their power, felt the raw rightness of their hunger. The echoes had spared my allies, but they'd killed for me. And I'd let them. Commanded them. Wanted it.

I swallowed hard. "Why do you want me to *unmake* the world?"

"*Because it must be done. And because, deep down, it's what you want too.*"

The words reverberated through my bones. I was losing my grip. None of this mattered. Soon, we would have Beau back, and I wouldn't worry about this cryptic force. This power would no longer be mine to bear.

I lifted my chin. "If you have nothing to help retrieve Beau, then I'm done listening."

The darkness stirred.

"*meRrIN!*"

"*MErriN!*"

And then, just as I forced myself upward—

The darkness tightened like a noose.

"*The mountain is huger than expected...*" A whisper, slick and thin, slithered against my ear. "*Where lies the base?*"

My breath left in a sharp gasp—but no sound existed in this void—as behind closed eyes, the abyss twisted, the world flipped—and I plummeted, unmoored, through a dark world.

The night sky spiraled out of control, stars streaking past like smears of light. Below, the black lake surged upward, swallowing the sky whole, as if the world itself had inverted.

And then—impact.

Ice-cold water slammed into me, crushing, suffocating. I wasn't just falling into the lake—I was pulled into endless blackness. Shapes danced around me. The Necropolis loomed, but wrong. Its skeletal silhouette stretched in the abyss, edges wavering through disturbed glass.

No. Not a reflection.

An illusion shattered.

The mountain wasn't rising from the water. It was sinking *into* it. The base wasn't above—it was *below*.

And there, at the bottom, cradled within a hollowed-out, metallic cage, swaying like a lost relic—

Beau.

In this illusion, her body hung weightless, hair unfurling in slow, silken waves. Her eyes were closed, hands floating at her sides. Her crown glinted faintly.

She wasn't moving.

A shrill ringing pierced my ears.

No—no, no, no—

The vision wavered, collapsing in on itself. Yet the feeling remained, tugging at me like a tether.

The mountain is huger than expected.

She was here. Beneath the surface.

I gasped back to reality, breath heaving, body convulsing as I lurched upright. "She's under the water!" I cried, choking on air.

The moment the words left me, Rafe froze.

And then he ran.

"Rafe, wait!" I screamed.

But it was too late.

With a whispered incantation, a sliver of ice bloomed beneath his feet. A narrow, fragile bridge shot across the lake, barely wide enough to hold him.

"Rafe! That doesn't look safe, mate!" Windley warned. "Where the hell are you going?"

But Rafe didn't stop. His breath came frantic, steps sure, his focus locked on the water ahead like a man possessed.

At the same time—

"What's this?" Windley's gaze caught something at our feet in the weeds. He crouched, plucking a small, rolled scrap of parchment tangled in the grass. His face paled as he unrolled it.

I pray you get this in time! I didn't know before! Her goal is Timber. Don't let Timber anywhere near the southern mountain! Especially not at night!

Windley's head snapped up. "Shit! RAFE, GET OUT OF THERE NOW!"

But again, it was too late.

The moment Rafe reached midway across the water—the lake erupted.

A massive skeletal fist burst from the depths and snatched him mid-stride.

Rafe barely had time to react before it yanked him under.

The bridge of ice cracked, splintered—then shattered.

"RAFE!" I shrieked, lurching toward the water.

Windley caught me hard, arms locking around my waist as I thrashed. "Don't!" he growled. "You'll be next!"

I fought against him, breath coming in ugly sobs. "No, no, no—"

The lake stilled.

Ripples faded.

The surface was empty.

There was no sign of Rafe.

A sickening kink clenched deep in my stomach.

Windley's breath faltered, his grip loosening, voice edged with disbelief. "A living giant...? Mate, what have you done?"

Rafe was gone. But my body refused to accept it. "No," I denied it. "The oracle's power—if it could heal him, it can bring him back! I just have to—"

I twisted toward the lake, summoning the echoes so fiercely my fingertips burned, my nails turned black. Darkness swirled, closing in, curling greedily around me.

The lake did not answer.

But something did.

A low, resonant hum vibrated through the air—deep and ancient.

I stiffened.

Windley's grip returned, this time at my elbow, his breath

tight with anticipation at my ear, as from the heart of the Necropolis came a bone-shattering groan—an avalanche of shifting debris, thunderous echoes swallowing the night. As if something enormous had exhaled beneath the lake.

Windley pulled me closer, one hatchet raised, fangs flashing silver in the moonlight.

And then we just stood and watched it.

At the base of the Necropolis, the largest skeleton began to stir. Bones rattled and realigned beneath streams of moonlight, becoming whole again, knitting together with threads of starlight into a towering giant: ethereal, immense, and utterly terrifying.

Above, the moon began a slow, impossible descent.

My stomach plunged as its glow touched the crown of the skeleton's skull, for what followed defied every truth I knew.

The moon did not halt.

It sank into the creature—fusing, warping—until no celestial body remained in the sky.

Until the moon *became* the creature itself.

Silver.

Not decayed. Not grotesque. Light flowed across its form, filling empty spaces, sinew and flesh weaving from pure starlight. Cascading luminous hair, spun from the night sky itself, spilled down the giant's back, radiating an ethereal glow.

It rose, a living monolith taller than any castle keep, its face crowned with a celestial orb where the moon once hung.

Windley whispered a curse, voice hoarse with awe. "Sweet stars...it's waking."

Eyes snapped open—two swirling pools of astral light, ageless and piercing in the dark. A pulse of power radiated outward, the lake shuddering beneath its weight.

Slowly, deliberately, the giant lowered its gargantuan gaze toward the waters below.

And then—

The lake heaved. Something shifted beneath the surface. At first, it seemed only waves, a churning swell of water and foam. Then I saw it clearly.

The giant's lost hand rose from the abyss, shimmering as it fused seamlessly into place. Gleaming in starlight, enormous fingers unfurled like petals, carefully revealing what lay within—

A drenched, motionless figure.

Rafe.

My chest cinched tight, breath crystallizing like frost in my lungs.

Windley went rigid beside me.

Rafe lay utterly still, bathed in moonlight, cradled in the palm of a giant.

24
THOSE WORDS

"Rafe!" A strangled cry ripped from my throat.

The giantess lifted him from the depths like a prized catch, his body limp in her grasp.

I lunged toward the water, but Windley yanked me back, every muscle in him taut. "Wait—*wait*, look."

Within the giant's fingers, there was a twitch. A stir of breath. A spark of life.

"He's alive!" I gasped—then quickly clamped a hand over my mouth, remembering the cavalry in the not-so-distant dark.

Not that it mattered. The towering lunar colossus had already captured their attention—distant shouts and the clang of steel betrayed their movement.

Rafe's chest rose and fell in shallow, stuttering gulps.

Then suddenly—

He began to struggle.

Sensing resistance, the giantess's fingers curled slightly— not tightening, merely holding. Her head tipped gently, observing Rafe as though studying a petulant child squirming in her grasp.

Meanwhile, Rafe kicked against her, boots scraping, hands shoving—a fight that only made her grip firm. But not firm enough. With a final wrench, Rafe forced himself through the gap in her argent fingers, plunging into the murky shallows below.

He disappeared beneath the surface.

Again, I lunged forward, but Windley swiftly caught me by the waist, pulling me back against him. Both of us stood frozen at the water's edge, breaths held, eyes on the waves.

Until Rafe broke through, dragging himself toward shore in slow, unsteady strokes.

"Oh, thank goddess." I doubled over.

Windley, too, exhaled with relief, attention flitting between the giantess and Rafe's struggle, his hand still steadying my back. *"Come on, mate. Move it."*

Until finally, Rafe clawed his way onto the sand, gasping and collapsing onto all fours.

"Good to see you alive, chap. Not the wisest stunt, but I'll give it points for flair."

That was all the reassurance I needed.

I dashed toward the half-drowned magician, leaving Windley behind. "Rafe!"

But before I could reach him, Rafe whipped around, eyes wild. "Stay back, Your Majesty!"

I skidded to a halt.

Shakily, he staggered upright—soaking wet, body heaving from exertion. Cold mist curled from his skin, frost slicking his frame. His gaze climbed higher, drawn inexorably to the towering figure looming over us.

A single name escaped him, riding on a breath of awe: "Luna?"

"You *know* her?" hissed Windley.

Rafe's wide eyes reflected the ethereal glow shining down

upon us. Sword raised defensively, he took wavering steps backward to where Windley had reclaimed me. When he spoke again, his voice was threadbare with disbelief.

"The moon goddess—I've seen paintings. My clan has drawn power from her for generations, but I never knew she could take form. I never imagined she'd step into our world."

A goddess. A *goddess* had taken Beau?

My earlier vision flashed vividly through my mind—the lost queen beneath the lake. Had that been real? Or was all of this some elaborate trap?

Windley edged closer, voice lowering to a wary hush. "Well, mate, *moon goddess* or not, she's looking right at you."

He wasn't wrong. Unease rippled through my chest as the giantess fixed her full, moonlit attention on bewildered Rafe.

"At last," she spoke, and a sudden gust of wind whipped through the clearing, forcing us back a collective step.

Her words were something beyond language—a celestial chime slipping into the cracks of the mind like an ancient song.

I pressed in closer to Windley, whispering, "Can you feel that?"

Windley's fingers flexed around his hatchet. "I feel something." His voice lowered further. "But I don't think it's meant for us."

Luna's expression was unreadable, devoid of malice yet steeped in something weighty. "Conjurer of mine," she intoned at Rafe, voice ringing through the night. "At last, you come to pay your debt."

Windley stiffened. "A *debt*, mate?"

Rafe flinched, breath quickening. "To Luna? I owe nothing but fealty. Goddess, then queen, then allkind."

As was the way of many.

Yet whether he acknowledged it or not, a debt existed, and everything had been building toward this moment.

The frosted handprint.

The face in the moon.

The frozen heart.

The signs had been there—we simply hadn't understood them until now. This journey was always about a haunted young magician and the pretty, freckled queen who had stolen his heart. Windley and I were merely side characters, swept up in the unraveling of their story.

Rafe stepped backward, searching desperately for solid footing—but Luna saw his retreat for exactly what it was.

"Do you intend to evade me again, Rafael?" she murmured, silver lashes lowering. "A shame. I'd hoped you would come willingly this time."

"Rafe?" I questioned. "Who's Rafael?"

"Doesn't matter. We need to move. *Now.*" Windley's words were a warning at my ear. A slight pull, as if to steer me away— but he faltered, because he saw it too.

Behind Luna, the lake was changing.

Not water.

Silver.

The surface roiled, a shimmering tide rising—and within it, I saw them.

Figures. Dozens. Then hundreds. Gleaming, hovering, lunar soldiers awaiting command, their forms shifting between liquid and light.

"Fuck."

That was Windley.

Luna shook her sparkling hair, and two shooting stars burst free. But they didn't fall. They became missiles, streaking toward Rafe like arrows loosed from a spectral bow, turning into little beings the moment they hit the ground.

Rafe rolled away from them, and they followed, their move-ments too fluid to be human. They shifted between form and mercury, like quicksilver assassins. Was it really these creatures who'd torn through Beau's cavalry and slaughtered three dozen trained soldiers in a heartbeat? Something this beautiful responsible for such brutality?

A spike of nausea surged, disbelief warring with dread.

This time, Rafe was their target.

And the command was seemingly given. The silver wave broke, and from its depths, a scouting party surged forward.

Realizing it, Rafe met Windley's eyes in a look of silent camaraderie—then bolted, drawing the creatures away. His sword lashed out in a flurry, but his blade barely impacted. The gleaming figures rippled, reshaping around the metal like water reforming in a stream.

Windley cursed under his breath, attention flicking between Rafe's desperate struggle and me—calculating his next move—before snapping into action.

"Into the cave with you, Your Highness—*now*."

"Your *Highness*? You never call me that."

The entrance yawned wide behind us, a dark void carved into the jagged hillside. His hand closed around my arm, steering me back.

I resisted, frustration binding my chest. "Windley, I'm not—"

He spun to face me, eyes fierce with intensity. "Merrin, listen to me. Whatever happens, they can't know who you are. She clearly sees us as no threat. If the goddess realizes what you're capable of... Go. Now. While we figure out how to best these things."

He didn't wait to see if I obeyed. Turning on heel, he launched himself toward the fight, hatchets flashing as he hurled himself at the nearest creature. His strikes were razor-precise, relentless—but the silver beings twisted out of reach, shifting and reforming like liquid steel.

Windley's growl deepened into a feral snarl, his attacks turning wilder.

Rafe panted, backpedaling as he fought, lungs working in short, erratic bursts.

"Rafe!" I called, stepping forward—while annoyed Windley clashed in an effort to keep them off the beleaguered magician. "Is your full name Rafael? That isn't what it says on your papers."

His head jerked toward me, incredulous, even as he swung his sword in another desperate arc. "My full name is *Rafe*. I do know it, though—Rafael was the name of my clan's progenitor. But he's been dead a century!"

I suspected centuries were nothing to a goddess.

Then perhaps this was mere mistaken identity.

Windley had chosen his fight. Rafe had chosen his.

And I—I was not defenseless.

The darkness stirred at the edges of my mind, offering its power freely. I could call upon it—let it consume, burn the night clean, *unmake*.

But no.

I was not a weapon waiting to be brandished.

I was a queen, and queens wielded more than brute strength.

Words held power too.

Straightening, I stepped forward and lifted my voice into the night. "Goddess Luna!"

Windley's head whipped toward me. "Are you out of your mind? Knock it off!"

"Goddess Luna!" I flung my arms high. "I think there's been a mistak—umph!"

Windley's grip locked around me like iron, his warning rasping low at my nape. "Don't draw attention to yourself, *reckless maiden of the wood*! I thought I made myself clear! If she

THOSE WORDS • 241

finds out you're the Nemophilist, she'll see you as a threat and exterminate you!"

I fought against him, pulse hammering as he dragged me toward the cave. "I have to try, Windley! She has Beau! That's why we're here—isn't it? To save *your* queen? You need to stop worrying about me and focus on her!"

With a guttural snarl, Windley spun to face me. Moonlight outlined his pointed ears, accentuated the dirt smudged across his cheeks, and illuminated wild strands of hair that fell across his face. "Argh! Stop saying that, Merrin!"

"Saying what?"

"That Beau is my queen!"

I froze, breath catching in my throat. "But she is your—"

"No!" Suddenly, his hands grasped my shoulders, his dark eyes blazing into mine. "*You* are my queen!"

A sensation akin to missing a step on solid ground rushed through me.

Something between us had just shifted, irrevocably, and it was a thing we could never take back.

Desperation shadowed his every feature. "It's you. The one who holds my devotion...it's *obviously* you. How can you not see that?"

"No, Windley," I whispered, voice barely audible above the distant tumult. "You...you're oathbound to Queen Beau."

His expression darkened. "She's my queen only by *chance*."

The words splintered, jagged with years of pent-up anguish.

He closed the space between us. "Think back to the night Beau vanished—why do you suppose *I* was the one who rode for you? I knew the loss would shatter you. I deserted my post, galloped through the dark, because even while I swore to hunt for her, every thought was of you. I couldn't stand the idea of anyone else breaking that news. And when you insisted on coming along...I agreed, because it was my only chance to stay beside you."

A hush settled, thick as sap. The truth locked around my ribs. How long had he carried all this right under my nose?

It shouldn't have hurt—but it did. Heat licked the back of my neck, tension gathering.

"Windley, don't—" I shook my head. "Beau is your queen. It feels...wrong when you say things like that."

He raked a hand through hair now paling to brittle, smoke-tinged blue; something inside him fissured.

One pacing step, and my spine hit the cave wall with a muffled thud.

His palm smacked the stone beside my head. "Tell me, Your Majesty—what frightens you more: that my first loyalty is already yours, or that I've spent years petitioning Albie for a transfer he keeps burying just to serve at your side? I never wanted rank or glory. I've only ever wanted you."

And I knew exactly why it rattled me: admitting it meant facing—

"I'm in love with you, darling," he said, the confession dragged raw from his chest. "Maddeningly so. Tell me you know that."

Beyond the cave, blades clashed against spectral forms. The cavalry had arrived—their battle cries punctuated the night, hooves pounded, moon-forged warriors shrieked in combat.

Yet the din receded, muted and distant, as if the world had slowed for just the two of us.

The night blurred.

"Say that again," I breathed.

Windley's eyes softened, tenderness breaking through years of careful restraint. "I fell in love with you a long time ago." His voice weakened slightly, as though he'd held those words too close, for far too long. "And I ache for you endlessly, knowing I can never have you."

He was so close now, I could feel the warmth of his breath. His thumb brushed across my cheek, committing the touch to memory, already mourning its loss. "Please...let me have you. Even if it's just this once."

I didn't stop him.

Instead, I welcomed him—eager, thoughtless.

Because Windley—reckless, dashing, beautiful Windley— was kissing me openly.

Surely.

Deeply.

As if he'd memorized me in his dreams and was finally savoring me in reality.

And me?

I was savoring him right back.

In Windley's arms, I felt wanted. Others had admired me, desired me even—but never like this. Never with a longing powerful enough to fracture my logic and set my heart ablaze. His kiss was a revelation, intense and consuming, the world fading until all that remained was the warmth of his mouth, the desperation of his touch, and a truth I could no longer deny.

A kiss of endings. A kiss of beginnings. My first kiss, yes. People rarely made advances on queens.

Only Windley—bold, foolish, wonderful Windley—would dare.

When he pulled away, his eyes held cautious hope, as though he'd caught something wild and waited to see if it would bolt. He searched my gaze for any flicker of understanding—afraid I would shatter his heart, half-expecting that I would.

"I just needed you to know," he said, voice low but steady, "in case I never get another chance."

I pulled a shaky breath between us, chest tightening as a tear slid down my cheek.

"Is this your power, making me feel this way?" I asked, pitch no louder than rustling leaves.

A spark of his usual devilry flashed, then softened into a patient smile. "No. That's just us—the current between us." His thumb skimmed my knuckles, tone holding the same quiet certainty. "And if you feel it...then it's your choice what we do with it."

His hand settled at my back, guiding me close again. His lips grazed my cheek; the next words brushed the shell of my ear. "I want you, and I would give up everything to have you. So...think about that and let me know, lion queen."

Then his demeanor shifted abruptly, the mischievous, commanding Windley I knew snapping back into place.

"Now, for fuck's sake, Merr, don't taunt the goddess."

I caught his arm as he stepped away. "You know I have to, Wind. It's Beau."

His smile was resigned. "I know."

And then he was gone—back into the chaos—leaving me pressed against cold stone, fingers brushing my lips as I tasted him.

I had known it all along.

Yet I had ignored it, pushed it away, because acknowledging it meant confronting feelings I wasn't ready for. Choices that could change everything.

But now wasn't the time.

Breathe. Settle. Focus.

Outside, the battle raged, Luna's light blazing.

Windley had left me reeling.

But I had work to do.

The necropolis was a mess. Luna's silver warriors had multiplied, an army of spectral forms nearly overwhelming the guards. Cavalrymen desperately battled to shield Rafe, silver figures shrieking frustration as he continued slipping from their grasp.

High above, Luna watched impassively as arrows sailed harmlessly past her ethereal feet.

No. That wasn't the fight.

I shoved away from the stone, stepping forward, echoes pulsing and swelling in my chest—borrowed power surging, stolen from Beau for this moment.

My voice cleaved through the night, strong and sure, echoing across the battlefield:

"The person you seek is not with us!"

The words rippled outward, pausing the maelstrom for a fleeting heartbeat—as though the ground suddenly locked beneath our feet.

Then—

"My Queen!"

Albie's voice split the air, cutting through me like a snapped bowstring, harsh and direct. Across the battlefield, he charged forward atop his exhausted stag, battle-worn, sweat glistening at his temple, eyes aflame with determination. His sword, Faylebane, glinted beneath the watchful gaze of the moon goddess as he slashed at one of Luna's spectral warriors, who twisted swiftly away from the blade's path.

The sight of him hooked painfully into my chest, snagging on something vital.

Dear Albie.

My guardian. My protector. My knight.

Guilt surged cold through me as his calloused fingers grasped mine, already trying to pull me onto his mount.

"I'm sorry, Albie. I did it for Beau."

His grip tightened, his voice urgent. "None of that matters now, My Queen. Mount up—I'm taking you out of here."

"No, Albie." I planted my feet against his pull. "I'm staying to fight."

His expression darkened, chin lifting defiantly. His voice cracked like thunder. "Absolutely not, Merrin!"

Never did he use my name alone—raw proof of just how greatly my actions had wounded him. His gaze aged instantly with worry, fear, disappointment, anger—all painted painfully across the familiar lines of his face.

I hated myself for putting them there.

"Forgive me, Albie," I whispered fiercely, my voice strained with emotion. "But for once, trust that your queen knows her own heart and strength." My free hand covered his, fingers squeezing lightly. "*Please*, trust that you raised me to have clear judgment."

His jaw clenched, fury barely restrained beneath his skin.

"I know you love Queen Beau," he answered, tone hard, "but your actions are selfish. Not befitting a queen. Think of your people!"

"I am thinking of them," I replied unwaveringly. "And Beau's people too. Let me go, Albie. I'm not afraid."

But I knew he never would.

I pressed his palm gently, lovingly.

"I love you, my knight."

And tore away—

Racing toward the shore, toward the lake, toward the blazing glow of the goddess.

"My Queen!" His voice broke, stripped of formality and decorum, desperation laid bare. "I won't let you do this!"

Albie's anguished shouts chased after me, but I didn't look back. My fingers plunged into the lake's shallows, sand humming beneath my palms, the echoes roaring to life inside me.

"Great Luna!" My voice rang out, clear as a bell, steady and strong. "I am Merrin, Queen of the Crag and friend to Beau, whom you've taken. Rafael serves under my protection."

A readying breath.

"I come to negotiate—respectfully and humbly—for Queen Beau's safe return!"

At last—

I had Luna's attention.

The lake shuddered beneath me. Massive bones shifted and tumbled into the water, waves rippling outward. Above, Luna's towering celestial form stirred.

A voice, smooth as moonlight, curled delicately into the night:

"Another royal?"

Luna bent toward me, her enormous celestial eyes alight with interest, almost playful. The ground quaked again, bones crashing and slipping into the lake. Waves surged to the shore, knocking me off balance.

I fell forward, palms sinking into wet sand.

And then—

I was scooped upward, Luna's massive hand wrapping around me—impossibly yielding, impossibly cold—lifting me effortlessly from the ground as though I weighed nothing at all.

Her glacial breath brushed coolly against my skin.

"What are you doing way out here, little one?"

A pause.

Then, her massive eyes narrowed with celestial curiosity, and slowly, irresistibly, a smile like moonlight parted her lips. "Ah," she breathed, voice like starlight piercing the darkness. "It is you who has claimed the Nemophile's Crown."

25

THE NEMOPHILE'S CROWN

The goddess lifted me high above the battlefield, the lake, the mountain of bones.

She might've intended a gentle ride, but at her scale, the abrupt ascent left my limbs weightless and my stomach wrenched.

Below, voices shouted—Windley, Rafe, Albie.

They grew fainter.

Then—silence.

Luna raised me before her face, where a cave-sized mouth parted, revealing a tongue vast enough to swallow me in one take. Her skin, shimmering with frost-kissed moondust, radiated winter's chill. Beside her massive fingers, I was a mere tree frog—one tensed muscle away from being crushed.

"Yes." Her voice swept over me like frozen wind. "The Crown suits you well. Perhaps now, its long-awaited purpose shall come to pass."

The Crown.

I understood now—by Nemophile's Crown, she meant the echoes.

Then...was Windley's bedtime story true? Had a figurative crown truly fallen from the heavens, granting its wearer the power to hear the wood?

If so, that wood now clamored at my ears, urging destruction. Was that the "purpose" she spoke of? I dearly hoped not—and I intended to find out. But first, I needed to secure Beau's release and Rafe's survival.

Luna seemed oddly familiar with mortal intricacies—at least judging by her speech. Perhaps she could be reasoned with.

I knelt in her palm, mirroring the subjects who knelt before my throne. "Goddess Luna, thank you for receiving me. But I fear there's been a mistake. The magician down there is not who you seek."

"I felt his feet upon my soil," she declared, words ringing with absolute certainty. "Rafael is there."

"No," I corrected with diplomatic care. "He is one of my royal guards—a magician of the north known only as *Rafe*. As his queen, I appeal on his behalf."

Luna tilted her head, flecks of starlight cascading from moonlit lashes. Her otherworldly words rolled through my mind. "It matters not what name he wears now. In another life, he was bound to me. I granted him great power—power that carried through each iteration of himself. But our pact has been broken. He carries a debt unpaid. Now he has come to face it."

Poor Rafe. What terrible luck! It wasn't even this version of him who'd earned the goddess's wrath—it was one of his past selves. One who'd struck a bargain he didn't even know he'd broken.

"What did Rafael promise you in exchange for your power?" I asked, hoping for some way out.

Luna's expression turned distant, wistful, almost romantic. "The only thing a conjurer may truly give: his heart. He swore it to me—but another holds it now, and I cannot reclaim it until it is released."

I stiffened. "You mean Beau? The royal beneath the water —is she...alive?"

Luna inclined her head, more fragments of stardust drifting free.

Relief poured quietly through me.

"But Rafael breached our agreement," she explained softly. "He was permitted mortal partners only to continue his line— never to give them his heart. Until this iteration, he obeyed."

And suddenly, I understood.

My hand pressed against my chest as if holding something fragile in place.

Rafe was in danger because he'd dared to love Beau.

And far below, he fought, unaware of what he truly battled. Unaware it wasn't only Beau's freedom he was clawing for; it was the claim to his own heart.

"But humans don't retain memories of past lives!" I argued. "How can this iteration uphold a promise he doesn't even remember?"

Luna's sigh moved through the air like the diaphanous rustle of silk. "His heart should have remembered, even if his mind did not. I warned him of the consequences should he ever give it to another. Yet he swore his heart was cold—impervious to mortal warmth." She shook out her hair, silver strands cascading over her shoulder. "I felt his heart warming, so I preserved it. Each time he called upon my power, I encased it anew." Her attention drifted toward the battlefield. "Yet it seems he has found the one capable of thawing it."

My pulse quickened.

Leave it to Beau to woo an impossible love.

Rafe's frozen heart. It wasn't a disease. It was a warning—a constant reminder that he'd broken the rules.

But love, as I was coming to understand, answered to no rules at all.

"That's why you took Beau? To lure him here?" I asked. "Why not take Rafe himself?"

"I did not intend to take the other royal." Luna's voice held a hint of regret. "My moonbeams followed his scent, but her heart was stained with his. And so, they brought her to me instead."

Moonbeams—the spectral warriors she'd named.

I stared.

It had all been a mistake.

A horrible mistake.

Beau and her queendom had suffered this affront...because the moon had failed to tell the difference?

I swallowed my frustration. "If you didn't mean to take her, then why seize her echoes?"

Luna's luminescent gaze flickered, puzzlement clouding her ethereal features. "That was not my doing. The mortal queen set aside the Crown on her own."

I froze. "Beau?" That couldn't be right. I'd seen her devastation at the fortress when she lost the echoes. "That doesn't sound like her. She took her role as the Scarlet Wood's oracle seriously—she was honored by it."

Luna tipped her head, ribbons of light shifting across her pale form. "I do not believe it was her intention. The moment she became a conjurer, her body rejected the Crown. No bearer of such power may wear it."

I tried to follow. "A conjurer—like Rafe? But Beau isn't a magician."

Then the goddess, stitched together from bone and moonlight, spoke words that stole the breath from my lungs—filling in one great missing piece of this puzzle:

"Maybe not, but the child she carries is. Their blood is bound; thus, she can no longer wear the Crown."

Beau was with child.

And Rafe was the unborn child's father.

A scandal, certainly—but that paled beside the rush of relief, terror, and awe that surged through me. My thoughts flashed to Beau's mention of losing the echoes—one sentence she'd never finished.

Tonight. Just after...

Just after she and Rafe had conceived a child, apparently.

I could scarcely breathe. Beau's future—our future— suddenly took on a starkly different shape. A queen carrying a common knight's child...

"You must release her!" I pleaded, voice shaking as I clutched desperately at the goddess's frost-rimed skin. "Please —you cannot keep a queen with child imprisoned!"

Luna's voice remained light, untouched by the turmoil below. "It is not my wish either." She regarded me evenly. "The moment she releases her hold on Rafael's heart, I will set her free."

But how was Beau meant to do that? How could one simply release their hold on another's heart? And for that matter, why should love require permission from an outsider to exist?

"Forgive me, Goddess—does that mean he will no longer love her?"

Luna answered far too softly for so brutal a truth. "Just so. Without a heart, love cannot live."

Ice scalded my throat. Beau would keep loving Rafe, but he would be changed, unable to love her back.

That wasn't devotion; it was a sentence. The agony of loving someone who couldn't, wouldn't, or shouldn't return it was anything but merciful.

I ache for you endlessly, knowing I can never have you.

Windley's confession knifed into the thought. He already carried that same sentence every day.

The double unfairness hit like a mace, ripping open a truth I'd been trying to sew shut.

With renewed urgency, I pressed determined fingers to my neck, voice abraded. "Goddess Luna, is there anything that can undo Rafael's debt?"

She studied me, then drew me closer, as if seeing me anew. "I may have said no before a heart like yours walked into my dominion."

Had I known we were stepping into a *dominion*, I might have trodden more softly.

Luna's glimmering eyes held a knowing look. "Are you willing to offer your heart in exchange?" Her tone was coy, as if the answer had already been written in the stars. "Although... you would have to retrieve it first—from the one who has stolen it."

A symphony of cords plucked in my chest.

Even the moon knew what I refused to say.

I steadied myself. "My heart? You mean I'd lose the ability to love entirely?" My voice tightened. "That's no choice at all—it's cruelty."

Unfazed, Luna's amusement shimmered in the air. "I have all the time, little one, if you need a moment to consider."

I needed more than a moment.

Turning away, I searched the vault of sky—stars winking like whispered secrets—while far below Beau's guards still battled for Rafe's heart.

We had crossed leagues of wilderness, endured grief, betrayal, and revelations that rattled the soul, all to arrive at a single, brutal equation:

An ultimatum.

A sacrifice.

Something precious for something precious.

I was born to serve my people, sworn to protect them.

But was I truly willing to surrender my own heart so Rafe might keep his?

Ah, Queen Merrin. Is this you hinting you'd like to know my secrets?

I would never harm you, Merrin. Never.

Stay close, my queen.

Calm your soul, breathe, and try again, lion queen.

I want you, and I would give up everything to have you...

No. I wouldn't sacrifice that.

I wasn't a martyr, or a saint.

I was a warrior—and warriors do *not* trade their hearts lightly.

"There is no other way?" I asked, still facing away.

"I was promised a heart," Luna replied, "and a heart I shall take."

So be it.

I closed my eyes and flung myself into the only force I trusted to stand against a goddess.

"*MeRRin.*"

A thousand bodiless fingers brushed me, wending along my skin—testing, teasing, waiting. I dove fearlessly into the void, past grasping whispers, deeper into darkness than ever before.

"Are you there?" I whispered to the presence beyond all others.

From the abyss—below the echoes, below a thousand restless voices—something vast stirred and answered:

"*I am. Will you learn my name?*"

"What choice remains?"

"*Know this: once spoken, you will stand revealed. There is no turning back.*"

Power pressed in—not gravity, but something larger than realms or crowns. I should have expected it; every step into darkness has a price.

"Then give me everything," I said, voice steady. "Enough to defy a goddess."

A low, fathomless laugh threaded through my mind, tugging at the seams of my resolve.

"Very well," it whispered. *"Then learn my name."*

The air trembled. Something ancient unspooled beneath my skin, snaring itself in the marrow of my bones.

A word. It bled onto my tongue, burning—ancient, dangerous, irrevocable. I held it in.

When I turned back to Luna, I was no longer a liege pleading for mercy.

I was a queen preparing for war.

"Goddess Luna, I do not wish to make you my enemy! But if you offer me no other way—I will take Beau by force! This is my final warning."

The goddess watched me as a mother might observe a child wielding a dull blade. "It will only prolong the inevitable, little royal. I will come for my conjurer again."

"Then I will remove your means to materialize in this world," I vowed, as shadows began to writhe around me.

Luna sighed, luminous eyes shifting. "It is your prerogative to try."

But I was already moving.

The echoes surged like a silent crescendo, twisting through the air like unseen hands.

With a burst of wind at my back, I hurled myself from her palm—swallowed by the yawning expanse of her open mouth—and spoke the name the abyss had given me in secret:

"EXITIUM."

A mountain-shattering blast erupted from within the moon

goddess's throat, surging outward like a thousand blades scattered free. Silver fissures spiderwebbed across her celestial form, fracturing violently. Her entire being shattered, exploding into shards of starlight that rocketed toward the heavens. The bones beneath her collapsed with a thunderous roar, crumbling into the lake below.

And I fell.

Fell through a storm of lunar dust.

Fell through the disintegrating Necropolis.

Fell deeper, cutting through the wreckage as I plunged into the mountain's heart.

Where a body floated, freed from the goddess's breath.

Beau.

Beautiful, regal, freckled Beau.

At last, I had found our lost queen.

Relief surged through my veins, so potent it stole my breath as I clutched her limp, drifting form against my chest. *Hold on, Beau. I've got you now.*

Darkness found its way around us, filling our lungs in place of water, lifting us toward the surface. My body shook— not just from invoking the darkness's name, but from sheer, overwhelming shock. This time, though, the shock was welcome.

We broke the surface.

The world had changed.

The mountain was gone, replaced by jagged shards of bone encircling the lake like a skeletal crown. Above, Luna had returned to her celestial form, her sorrowful gaze watching from the heavens.

I dragged Beau onto the shore, collapsing to my knees beside her, hair dripping, clothes clinging with lake water. We were filthy, drenched, shivering—but none of it mattered.

Her eyelashes fluttered gently, and when her doe-soft eyes

met mine, warmth flooded my chest. Tears spilled free before I could speak.

"Merrin?" she asked, her voice no stronger than spun sugar. "Am I dreaming?"

A breath unwound from my soul, like a century-old chain snapping loose. I laughed.

"Dearest Beau," I whispered, words quivering with relief. "Were you waiting long?"

26

EXITIUM

I helped Beau stand, and together we limped along the far shore, now ringed by skeletal fragments.

Beau clung to my shoulders, her face pressed into my neck. "Oh my goddess, you came for me. You! You actually came yourself! What were you thinking?"

I tightened my hold around her waist. "Not just me. Rafe, Windley, and Albie, too."

She lifted her face from my shoulder, gazing toward the distance, where a wall of bones separated us from the others. "The guards are here?" Her voice was quiet, thick with soft, not-so-secret yearning.

"Yes, *naughty*. Your *lover* is here." I arched a brow. "And you have *so* much explaining to do. I know everything—or at least as much as Rafe would share."

Which, come to think of it, wasn't much.

Beau stiffened, moisture glistening at the corners of her lovely, tired eyes. "Oh, Merrin, forgive me! I wanted to tell you so many times, but I didn't want to hurt you. It's just so...unconscionable. Rafe is sworn to you and your court."

And to a goddess, as it turned out.

"Don't worry about that," I said. "I just want you to be happy. Your love won't have many allies, but I'll be one."

She sniffled, delicate and uncharacteristically unsure. "Really?"

"Of course, Beau. Besides...Windley and I might have a thing happening, too."

Her eyes twinkled despite exhaustion. A slow smile crept onto her face. "Truly?" A breath of laughter escaped her. "Well, that only took a decade. He must be glowing."

"Did everyone know but me?!"

She giggled, airy and bright.

I groaned. "Goddess damn. He can be far hotter than you'd ever imagine. Beau, what kind of queens are we?"

She shook her head, taking in the irony of what we'd done— the impossible roads we'd chosen. "Only time will tell," she said softly.

I sighed. "I'm going to need advice. Of the two of us, you're far more experienced."

A faint smile ghosted her lips. "It's easier than you'd think."

"What is?"

"All of it." Her fingers brushed against the damp fabric of her sleeping gown. "And also...more painful." She glanced over her shoulder at the lake, its surface eerily still. "By the way, how did you blow up the mountain and retrieve me? Explosive powder? You must have needed quite a lot."

I exhaled slowly. "Not explosive powder exactly..." It was too much to go over. "I'll have to give you the short of it."

I recounted how I'd found the echoes—or how they'd found me—and how I'd become a conduit for their power.

Beau's response wasn't what I expected.

Her face fell. "Oh no." Her grip tightened urgently on my arm. "Merrin, I'm so sorry."

A strange chill prickled through me. "For what?"

She swallowed hard, her expression stricken. "I wondered which royal they would attach to. I wouldn't wish that burden on anyone."

Burden.

The word lodged, wedging itself between my ribs like a splinter.

"What do you mean, burden?"

Beau's wide, grave eyes held mine. "There are things about the oracle's power only my family knows—and for good reason. If others knew the truth, they would fear the bearer." She steadied herself. "Merrin, I know there's much to discuss, but if the echoes reside in you, you must hear this first—without anyone else listening."

I stilled, loosening my hold around her waist. "Beau." My voice came out thin. "You're scaring me."

Beautiful Beau took my shoulders, fingers tightening with fierce intensity. "You *should* be scared. I'm scared for you." Her throat bobbed, grip unrelenting. "The echoes can't cause calamity alone. The oracle's true duty isn't to subdue them—it's to *bear* them, so no one else must."

She hesitated.

"The truth is the echoes can't exist freely; they need a host. And my family ensures they attach to the next born of our lineage. We train our entire lives to resist their pull. When I whisper my intentions into the forest, I'm not doing so to silence the echoes—I'm doing so to silence myself."

Her admission was like a brand, searing itself into my new reality.

"That's why I was desperate to find them! Why I feared who might discover them. I should be glad it was you. But even you need to be careful, Merrin. They are dangerous."

It was like a weight strapped to my ankle, plunging me

beneath an unforgiving sea. I stepped back, untangling from her grasp, staring down at my hands—the hands that had wielded shadows as weapons, swallowed a goddess like nothing.

Had I been wrong to give in to them?

But each time, I'd had no choice!

Beau reached for me. "I'll take them back if we find a way. I have methods for calming my spirit. This isn't something you want to live with."

A dull ache spread beneath my collarbone. "I'm afraid that's impossible," I said ruefully. "At least for another nine months or so."

Her startled expression said she didn't know yet.

And I didn't get a chance to tell her, because the others found us, emerging through the bone wall, riding the stretch of lake.

While the remaining cavalry swarmed, Albie at their front, two figures hung back from the rest. Two who couldn't show their emotions openly.

As Beau's cavalry knelt in reverence around her, she clutched her heart and gazed past them—beyond the armor, beyond expectations—to where Rafe stood, waiting at the tree line. Only once truly alone would he go to her, gather his queen into his arms, and allow himself to acknowledge the things they hid from the world.

And there was another like him.

Lingering at the outskirts.

Stag-less. Waiting.

His expression unreadable, eyes shadowed.

Yes. It was a difficult path we'd chosen.

As if in testament, Albie was there suddenly, overwhelming me. "My Queen! Are you injured?"

"I'm fine, my knight. Better now that I see you unharmed."

He lowered his voice so others wouldn't hear. "It almost looked like that spell came from...you. But *that can't be right, can it?*"

A warning.

I met his stare head on. "Don't be silly, Albie. That was the goddess's doing. She said Beau, as oracle, is essential to balance. I petitioned her—she opened the way for me." I let the lie settle, deliberate: "And that is the story you'll command Beau's guards to repeat, yes?"

After all, a queen who kept nature peaceful was a treasure. A queen who could bend it was a threat.

Albie dropped to one knee. "As you wish, My Queen."

I sank into the damp earth beside him, wrapping my arms around his burly frame, whispering, "We found her, Albie."

"You found her, My Queen. I was wrong to confine you. You have more strength than I knew." His voice was colored with emotion. "Aye, I'm ashamed of what I did. I promised your mother I wouldn't let harm befall you, but you aren't a child anymore, and a knight has no right to defy a queen."

Were there more lines etched into his face now than when we'd first set out? Had each new crease been carved by the joys and trials we'd weathered, by every moment that shaped us along the way?

"You know you're more than just a knight to me, Albie."

He smiled—a gentle, fatherly smile—and tucked my hair behind my ear. "And you're not just a queen to me, my dear." Then, as he had so many times when I was a child, he pressed a fond kiss to my forehead, his mustache tickling against my skin.

For a moment, warmth spread through my chest.

But warmth had a way of slipping away.

As I pulled back, my gaze drifted again to the devilish guard standing off in the distance. Albie followed my line of sight and released a long, familiar sigh. "I wish you wouldn't," he murmured.

"I can't help it." The words came softly, a confession neither of us truly needed spoken aloud. "It's been there a long time, and it won't listen to reason."

Our monster.

Silence settled between us, restless as the night air.

"The kin of the Cacti's a good lad, you know. You'd like him. Handsome boy. Good bloodline."

"Maybe." But it wasn't about that. It had never been about that. "But this is something I need to do. The real reason you ignored all those transfer appeals you never thought to mention."

Albie stiffened just the slightest fraction, but his expression didn't waver. "Diversion on holiday is one thing. Within your own throne room is another."

A lump rose in my throat. "I won't command you not to follow me, Albie—but I ask that you don't."

His gaze held mine, heavy with quiet sorrow. And then I saw it—the silent surrender. The understanding that I could never be tamed. That I had never been.

A weary breath left him, gentler now. He didn't stop me. Didn't ask me to reconsider. Instead, his hand brushed mine as I passed—a final tether, delicate as a whisper, before letting go.

I moved past him into the wreckage. The battlefield was still settling, the air thick with dust and magic.

Wind.

There he stood—the disheveled silhouette of a knight who had earned his name. Battered, his face cut, his clothing torn. When he saw me coming, he moved with soundless precision around the other side of a piece of splintering bone, out of sight from the others.

This conversation was not something Beau's cavalry should see.

I followed, weaving through the debris and skirting jagged shards—only to be seized.

Windley's arms wrapped around me, his face buried in my wild hair. He smelled of amber and evergreen, edged by something darker—like smoke that hangs in the air after lightning scorches the woods.

"I thought you were gone," he rasped, clutching tighter. "I thought the giant crushed you. When you survived it, I thought you blew yourself up. When you survived that, I thought you drowned."

His fingers flexed against my back, his breath unsteady against my skin.

And beneath it all, I felt the rapid pace of his heart.

"It was one thing when that rebellious soul of yours was locked up in a castle," Windley continued. "But out here...it's too much. To feel for you is torture, lion queen."

I wasn't sure how to do it. I wasn't sure how to tell him.

So, for once, I just...

"Windley."

I leaned into him, my fingers gripping the torn fabric of his shirt, my face pressing into the solid warmth of him—feeling the rise and fall of each breath, the unsteady terrain of muscle and bone beneath.

"Outright killing me would be faster," he murmured, his chin brushing my hair for just a moment before he rested back.

"How would you like me to do it?" I played along.

"Spear me through the middle," he said. "That should be quick enough."

"I haven't a spear," I argued.

"Then use a pointed stick."

I tilted my head. "And waste a perfectly good stick?"

A hint of a smirk flitted across his lips as he finally let me go.

Even like this—beat up, drained, in torment—he was impossible to look away from. He was...too good to look at.

The space between us thickened—old, familiar, crackling almost magnetically like embers in the cold.

I traced the edge of his hair, once white, now deepened to an iridescent storm-blue, streaked with something untamed.

He caught my wrist. "Don't toy with me, queenie."

But I wanted to toy with him, tease him, hold him, torture him, keep him. I wanted to touch him, kiss him, tackle him, lie with him—let him drain the strength from my veins. I wanted to hide away with him in the forest fortress, slip through shadowed halls, and never emerge again.

I took his face in my hands, my thumbs brushing over the cuts along his cheekbones. "I'm sorry, Windley."

His expression grayed, tension bracketing his mouth.

"You're another queen's guard and one of my best friends, and that's why..."

Something sharp fractured behind his eyes—like glass cracking beneath a careful touch.

"...it took me so long to realize."

For a moment, I wasn't sure he'd even heard me.

Then, slowly, his features softened—not in relief, but disbelief.

"Realize?" he echoed quietly.

A tremor fluttered through my words. "I think I'm desperately—irrevocably—in love with you too," I breathed. "Is it meant to feel as though a single touch could anchor my entire soul? As though I'd rather never return to the queendoms than lose this?"

Windley's eyes widened; for one suspended heartbeat he simply stared.

"That sounds...accurate," he managed, swallowing like a man relearning how.

I didn't give him time to think. My arms looped around his neck and I pulled him into a kiss. His mouth claimed mine—hungry, possessive—each stolen second treated like a lifetime's ration. I pressed against him, heart thrumming as heat rose between us.

He guided us down, folding both of us into a crouch behind a jagged shard of bone. His hands roamed—confident, reverent—sending shivers rippling through my limbs. When his lips traced a searing path along my neck, I arched into him, sensation sparking over my skin.

"It feels good," I whispered, tilting my head to grant him access.

His answering smile brushed my throat, voice rough with restraint. "That's the problem, queenie. Now that I've tasted you, I won't want to stop."

A delicious thrill coiled in my belly.

"Then don't," I breathed, pulse hammering.

His mouth trailed slowly up my jaw—achingly slow, as if we truly had all the time in the realms. Teeth caught my earlobe, teasing, firm. "Does this make us secret lovers now, too?" he murmured, dark amusement curling through each word.

Exhilaration and terror tangled inside me.

"I'm not sure what it makes us," I admitted, gaze fixed on his lips, "but I fully intend to kiss you again. At least once more."

His wicked mouth curved, promising ruin. "You've made a terrible mistake indulging me, Your Majesty."

A defiant spark flared in my chest. "Would it be worse if I said I knew exactly what I was doing?"

Knuckles grazed my throat, lifting my chin until our mouths hovered a breath apart—

And then he stilled.

Voices—hoofbeats—closing fast on the other side of the bone wall.

In a heartbeat the spell shattered, battle-sharp reality crashing over us.

"They're coming," I hissed. "We have to stop—someone will see."

Windley's breath left him in a frustrated growl, yet he hauled me upright in one fluid motion. We steadied each other, still light-headed from the sudden snap-back. His hands lingered on mine, lips parted—caught between smoldering want and the need to hide it.

"Mask on," he muttered. "Back to the performance."

I swallowed the last of the heat, tugged my cloak straight, and schooled my face for court-perfect calm. "Goddess help us," I muttered—then paused, wincing inwardly. "Perhaps not *that* goddess."

But as I turned, a hand caught my shoulder, quietly insistent.

"Wait."

That single word dropped into my chest like a stone.

Windley's tone was grave, careful, just like when he'd told me Beau had vanished. "There's something else you should know. It won't make you happy, but I want to be the one to tell you."

I searched his expression. "Wind?"

His gaze grayed, caution and care heavy in his eyes. "Battles aren't won without casualties, Merrin. You did what you had to do, and you should suffer no regret."

"Why would I?" I asked. Beau was safe. We were reunited. We'd freed our monster—

Windley squeezed my shoulder. "Remember the guard mapping the land near the woodcutter's hut—Bartolomew?"

The polite, well-mannered one. A knot cinched in my throat.

"He didn't make it. The blast from the Necropolis... He could've been anywhere, Merr. Fate chose him, not you."

A breath caught—and that meant—

Luna's face hung high above, a single silver eye in the dark, watching as I clung to Windley's cloak, sobbing for the soul I'd sacrificed to save my dearest friend.

"He died because of me," I whispered. "What have I done?"

Windley drew me closer, letting the slow, solid drumbeat of his heart steady mine.

"Bartolomew wasn't a bystander. He rode into that valley knowing the stakes. Your call saved two queens, saved Rafe, and stopped Luna before she froze half the north. Hard math, but true."

Tears burned hot. "It still feels wrong."

He waited until I met his gaze. "We'll carry him home with honor. Then we keep moving—that's how his sacrifice matters. Bartolomew would have traded his life for Beau's freedom, for the thousands who need the Scarlet Wood alive. One life shielding countless others. Remember that when the whispers start muttering otherwise."

The knot in my chest loosened by a thread. He folded me into his arms, and the silence settled—heavy, but bearable.

We would learn later that Luna hadn't massacred Beau's cavalry at all.

Something far, far worse had.

27
UNTIL NEXT TIME

The night after retrieving Beau, we made camp deep in the Emerald Wood, the chill of approaching autumn heavy in the air. Everything seemed lighter—as though the burden of what we'd endured had finally eased.

I stroked Ruckus's silky fur, amused as Beau, now dressed in one of my riding outfits, tugged uncomfortably at the seams of her trousers.

"I look like a boy," she muttered.

"Yes, but a cute one," I teased.

She huffed, adjusting the waistband. "I feel...indecent."

"You'll get used to it," I promised, nudging her gently. "Britches let you ride faster. Just imagine the footraces we'll have in the Scarlet Wood."

Beau shot me a dry look, pulling at the fabric again. "Sometimes I swear you were born into the wrong body, Merrin."

I'd always believed bodies were wonderfully versatile.

Despite everything—the horrors she'd survived, the loved ones she'd lost—Beau held herself together admirably. She'd grieved in solitude, then alongside me. Now she stood strong for those who remained, a true queen. Yet beneath it all, I knew her pain hid.

She gazed up through the canopy, blinking away moisture that had glistened in her eyes all day. "The moon will turn gold soon," she murmured softly. "We won't return in time for the Lunar Festival."

I looped my arm through hers. "Then next year's shall be twice as grand to make up for it."

But as I followed her gaze skyward, my insides gave an uncomfortable squirm.

I doubted I'd ever look at the moon the same way again. I'd made an enemy of the goddess trapped within, and only time would tell whether I'd truly broken the hex upon Rafe's heart.

For now, at least, he seemed well. But I noticed things now I'd been blind to before—the subtle lift at the corner of his mouth when Beau spoke, the fleeting touches of his hand as he passed by her.

Perhaps someone had to know love themselves to recognize it in others.

Speaking of—

A finger trailed down my arm.

"Thinking of ways to misbehave, Your Majesty?"

I turned—to find Windley, his come-hither smirk far, far too obvious for this setting—and I quickly checked around to make sure none of Beau's other guards saw.

Rafe was discreet.

Windley? Not so much.

Had his actions always been this obvious? Had they gotten worse? Or had I truly been that oblivious?

Maybe our monster was simply more unruly than theirs.

I could hardly wait to return home—to escape these watchful eyes. Drinks on the veranda. Stargazing in the belvedere. Secret walks through the wood...

But if I was honest, little else about going back appealed to me.

Things felt simpler out here.

A wandering soul was a free one.

I toyed with my mother's necklace, wondering if she had ever felt that same draw—if she'd hidden a quiet yearning behind her regal composure.

Around us, the night grew merry, with the cavalry elated at having recovered their lost queen. Albie stayed nearby, watching me closely, openly disapproving of the way Windley's hand brushed my back whenever he thought no one else was looking. The betrayal in the woodcutter's cabin felt like a distant memory now. I knew my wrinkled knight had acted out of love, however misguided. And to be fair, I hadn't exactly told him I suddenly possessed insurmountable power.

Ever my protector, he fed the cavalry my fabricated tale: the moon goddess had rescued Beau from an unknown captor.

And that story—the lie of it, the legend—would be recorded forever in the royal archives of both our queendoms.

For now, my secret was safe. I would carry the echoes for Beau until she was ready to take them back. Bartolomew's sacrifice had proven their destructive potential. And Windley—

Windley was proof of mine. Proof of what my own reckless heart could unleash.

Beau was the responsible choice for such power.

The fire crackled, its glow illuminating the weary faces of those who had survived. Albie sat nearby, nursing a tin cup of liquor, watching over me through a drunken haze. Beau curled beside me, her fingers carefully threading through my tangled hair, coaxing out the knots.

A feather drifted into my lap—pure white, almost luminous in the fire-glow.

"Another one!" Beau breathed, eyes widening. "That

makes four tonight. Where in the Emerald Wood would a bird this pale even come from?"

I twirled the quill between my fingers. "Maybe a widowbird's down feather?"

She shot me a look. "Widowbirds are black as pitch, Merrin."

Undeterred, she raked gently through the rest of my hair, as if the phantom dove itself might be nesting there.

I chuckled and flipped the feather into the flames, watching it curl to ash.

Yes.

For a fleeting moment, all was right with the world.

But only for a moment.

The cavalry was drunk.

Albie was drunk.

My head rested comfortably in Beau's lap, Rafe and Windley observing us from across the fire. The warmth from the flames felt like a gentle warning, quietly urging me to remain where I was—to not retire for the night.

I didn't listen.

"Lion queen?"

A naughty voice was at my ear.

I opened my eyes to darkness. "Windley? What are you doing here? This is the queens' tent."

Beside me, Beau purred quietly in her sleep, curled like a kitten.

"Was Albie right?" I accused. "Are you a bounder?"

He snorted. "If I were, you'd be my first target."

I sat up, rubbing sleep from my eyes. "Are you all right? You look...strained."

He exhaled a thin stream of air, pinching the bridge of his nose. "Sorry, I didn't think you'd be asleep yet. I have a strange headache, and I feel the urge to take a walk."

I frowned. "A headache?"

"I've been getting them the past few days, but tonight's especially brutal. I'll clear my head—find a stream, perhaps." He rolled his shoulders with a grimace. "I would've told Phylo or another guard, but most are dead-drunk. Don't let them leave without me. I'll be back by morning."

I kicked off my blanket. "I'll come."

Windley shook his head. "No, you should rest. You've just defied the heavens, haven't you? That had to have taken a lot out of you."

"I've already got my cloak." I grabbed said cloak and seized his shirt collar. "Besides, I've been waiting to get you alone."

His dark eyes glinted in the shadows. "Oh? And what exactly do you plan to do with me? Can't wait to find out. Truth be told, I might've come here hoping you'd follow."

In the dead of night, we slipped past the dying fire—fingers entwined, footsteps glowing faintly behind us.

His palm was warm.

His knuckles strong.

Desire crept up my neck at the realization we were truly alone—away from camp, away from watchful eyes.

Windley kept glancing at me, as though afraid I might vanish with the sunrise. I wanted him to look at me that way forever.

We wandered through the trees, chatting easily, gloriously at peace, until nearly an hour had passed.

That was when Windley made a sudden, pained noise and pressed a hand to his temple.

I stopped abruptly. "Windley?"

His blackstone ring glinted as he rubbed his forehead. "I'm fine," he said, voice tight. "Walking really does help, but it's determined to disrupt our night. Shame—I finally have you alone, and I'm impaired."

I cleared my throat lightly, concern edging into my voice. "I wonder what's causing it. You said it's been happening for days?"

He gave a low hum. "Mm. But never like this. Before it was dull—tonight, it's sharper."

Instinctively, I scanned the darkened woods for something helpful. "Over there," I said, pointing toward a patch of tangled underbrush. "Moth rose—it's good for aches. If we find some vera, I can brew a remedy."

I tugged his hand, but he resisted. "Not that way."

I paused, blinking. "Not that way?"

He hesitated, pressing harder against his brow, wincing.

Unease goose-bumped my skin. "Windley? What's happening?"

"I don't know. It feels like something's battering against a locked door inside my head." His brow furrowed deeper. "But walking this direction eases it somehow."

My pulse quickened. A headache relieved only by traveling a specific direction? That wasn't natural.

I planted my feet. "Something's wrong," I urged, tugging him swiftly. "Let's turn back." The woods pressed closer, shadows thickening around us, heavy and suffocating.

Windley faltered beside me. "...Shit." His grip tightened painfully around my hand as his gaze darted through the encroaching darkness. "I didn't realize we'd strayed so far."

We'd barely pivoted to head back before I saw it—

A mound of tangled forest growth, shaped too precisely like a human silhouette.

My fingers dug into Windley's palm, nails biting his skin.

"What is it?" He whipped around. "What do you see?"

Before I could answer, the mound straightened—

And stepped forward.

Windley's hatchets were instantly in hand. "Stay where you are," he snarled, voice edged with threat. "Unless you want to lose a limb."

A figure draped in a long, hooded cloak.

My breath caught, my mind racing to identify who else could possibly be this far out in the wilderness.

The figure didn't stop.

Windley stepped in front of me, arm braced across my waist.

A lone figure emerged between the pines and began to clap —slow, deliberate—each echo rolling through the trees.

"Well, well..." crooned the stranger—velvet voice gliding from honeyed baritone to lilting alto. "The instant your little tricks sparked in the Emerald Wood, we felt the pulse clear down south."

"Halt!" Windley barked. "Name yourself—state your purpose in this wood."

The clapping stopped. Moonlight caught a flash of teeth.

"Eight years gone, and the prodigal still bites." A soft chuckle. "And look—you've collared something potent for a pet. Clever boy, Windalloy."

Windley drew a sharp breath; his fingers tightened on the hilt at his hip.

Windalloy. It couldn't be coincidence. *Eight years*—that was exactly how long Windley had been with us.

And by "collared pet," they meant...

Windley didn't respond. His entire body went rigid, breath

carefully controlled—but his knuckles whitened dangerously around his hatchets. "Who are you?" he demanded.

"Come now." The figure tilted their head, amused. "The effects of that crude elixir must be fading, now that you've stepped foot on southern soil. Surely you remember your *master*."

Windley visibly flinched as the figure lowered their hood, revealing a strikingly handsome face—pale skin, elegant features.

But the eyes chilled me most: gleaming, intoxicating lavender.

A Spirite.

Windley staggered, a sharp cry tearing from his throat. "Argh! No...I—"

Panic flared through me. I clung to him, preparing to summon the echoes. Whoever this was, I wore the Nemophile's Crown—I could end this now!

Darkness surged at my fingertips—

"*MErrIN?*"

"*Merrrrin.*"

But when it had passed, Windley merely jerked upright, his breath steadying. And calmly—too calmly—he remarked,

"Oh. I forgot about all that."

He turned, just enough for his lips to brush my ear—a breath-light caress, pulse-quick beneath its restraint.

"Run, lion queen. Back to camp. And don't look back. Ever."

The force of his command cut through every instinct I had —to stay, to fight—because I recognized, in the pleading timbre of his voice and the anguish searing his eyes...

He wasn't asking.

I'd barely made it a few lighted steps when three more

hooded figures erupted from the trees. Rough hands seized my arms, dragging me back into suffocating darkness.

As shadows swallowed me, my last image was Windley—unmoving, resigned—facing his forgotten history as if awaiting judgment.

It seemed Windley's dark past had finally caught up to us.

Well, captive ones, perhaps we've lingered here long enough. Rest now, if you can—there's much more to come.

Until next time, with all my love,
Merrin